Forestedge

Forestedge

A Fin de Siècle Romance

Thomas Stinner

Zebra Rock

Forestedge: A Fin de Siècle Romance

Publsihed by

Zebra Rock

© 2023 Thomas Stinner

To contact the author, or for typeset and design inquiries,
please write to: zebrarock.creative@protonmail.com

Published by Zebra Rock

Edited & Cover Art by Thomas Stinner

Typeset in Crimson and Libre Caslon

ISBN: 978-0-6456400-0-7 (eBook)
ISBN: 978-0-6456400-1-4 (Print on Demand)

First Edition, December 2022

"He was the second son of the Clarence family. Everybody knew about him and his bad character: a man as devious as he was handsome, that brought grief to his unfortunate father."

Lothario. Misfit. Villain. Arthur Clarence Jr, the offspring of a wealthy Cumberland copper mining family, returns to his ancestral home to find everything having changed. The promiscuous Madhist War veteran grapples with his position in his family due to the untimely death of his older brother, the physical alterations in his aging father and his foster sister, Evangeline. Having loved her like a genuine sister, she has grown up to become the perfect lady. Shocked that his affections have turned from love to lust, will Arthur find closure and belonging on his quest to overcome his sensual impulses, or will he live up to his scandalous reputation?

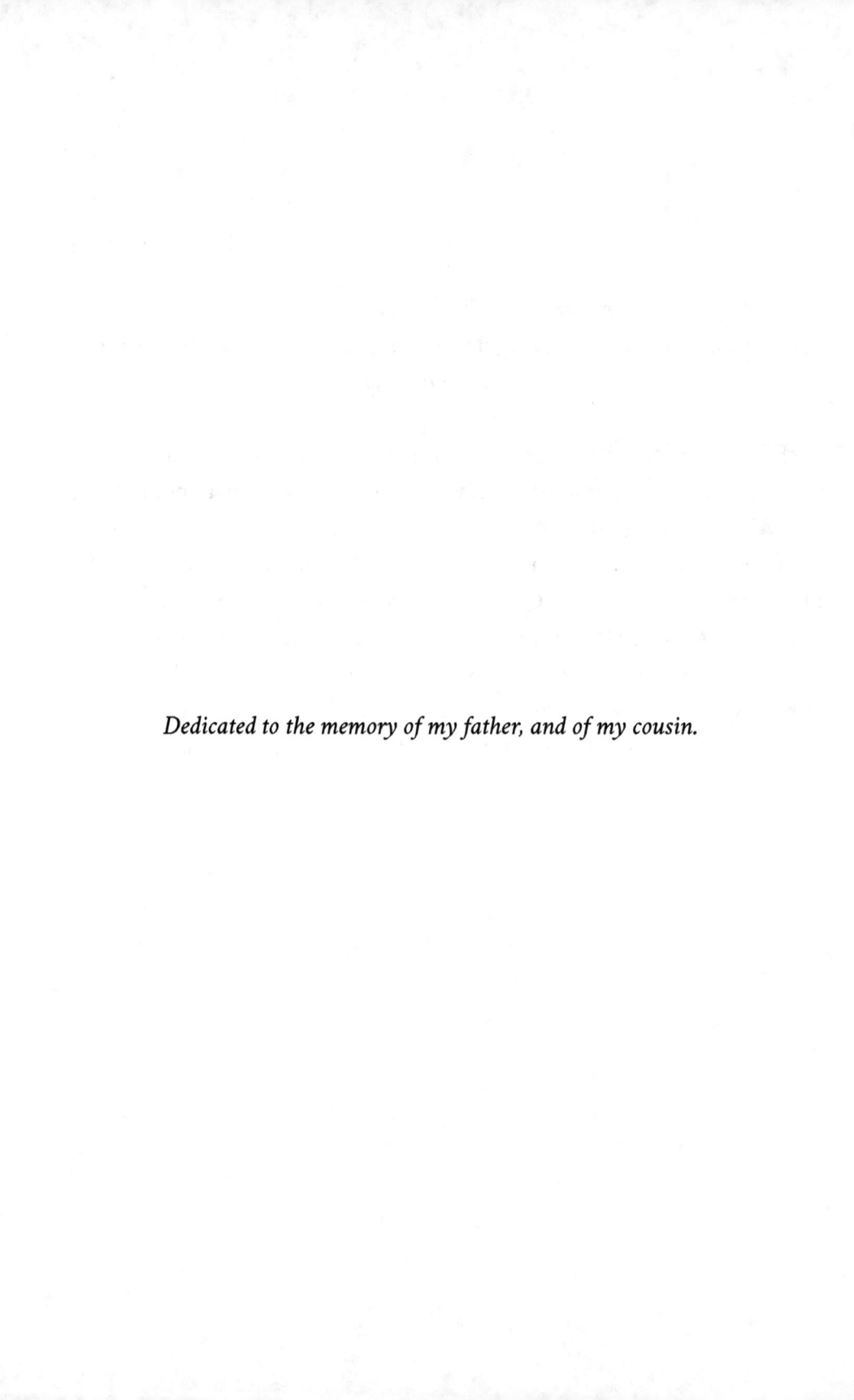

Dedicated to the memory of my father, and of my cousin.

Acknowledgements

First and foremost, I would like to thank my dear friends *Aubrey* and *Emily* without whom I would not have found the confidence to push forward with this project. Both of them have given their time to sincerely read the novel, and to provide me with input towards the improvement of the manuscript.

I would also like to acknowledge the artists of *www.pexels.com*; the providers of fonts for the *Open Font License (OFL)*; and the programmers and testers (and other staff) of *Scribus* and *GIMP*. Open and free resources provide an opportunity for self-publishing within a non-professional's budget.

Finally, I would like to thank you, *the reader*, for taking this novel into hand (in whichever incarnation) and giving it a read. I am hopeful that you will enjoy reading it as much as I did writing it.

PROLOGUE
The Wolf residing at Forestedge

U pon hearing that I would come to Forestedge Manor she showed it to me: a wolf she called him and handed me the article from the *Gazette*. Truly, I'm surprised that my sister held on to it for so many years. She must have a strong fixation on young Mr Clarence." Mused the shrill voice.

"Oh, do tell what did it say?" demanded another, a hoarse voice.

"My sister refused to let me read it properly, but apparently it was about him dishonouring a young lady." A peevish laughter followed by an awestruck "Oh my!"

"Maybe I should have nicked it after all? You are curious, are you not Miss Hollings?" the shrill voice inquired, taunting Evangeline.

"I am not," she replied flustered, yet maintaining a certain calmness, "and I am not interested in reading tabloids like the *Gazette* either."

"Of course, circulars like those would not suit your sensitivities." Warbled the hoarse voice.

I was unsure if she was flattering or mocking her. Edging slightly closer to the windowpanes of the winter garden doors, I peeked in.

"You should introduce him to us!" the two girls on either of Evangeline's side exclaimed excitedly. They were both dressed in their finest visiting toilettes and had their hair fashionably arranged up in buns. Their attempts to look mature created the opposite effect. It was as though I was seeing children in fancy dresses mimicking adults.

Evangeline, too, was wearing a stuffy reception dress. Contrarily, and true to herself, her hair was arranged half-down with a ribbon tied into it.

"I am ... I don't think he would appreciate my bothering him. He is quite the reserved person and does not socialise beyond necessity." Evangeline answered. I could clearly see her cheeks become tinted in a faint red. She furthermore insisted, "It has not been long since he returned either. He does need his rest."

"Oh, Miss Hollings. It's endearing how flustered you become over your foster brother." The lank girl to her right laughed. Sarcastically.

"And why shouldn't she? I saw him in passing. Young Mr Clarence is in fact so tall, dark, and handsome ... my heart skipped a beat. Does he have a velvety voice, I wonder?" the plump-faced girl on Evangeline's left asked with girlish pathos. Impatiently she stared into the face of the tea party host to receive an answer.

"He—" Evangeline reluctantly uttered while fidgeting with the saucer.

However, before she could find proper words to reply, the right side interjected, "Tall, dark, and handsome indeed, Miss Everett. I chanced a glance, too. Do say, Miss Hollings is his character more *akin to Heathcliff* or *Mr Rochester?*"

Were girls their age even interested in those types of antiquated romance novels? Evangeline eyed them in puzzlement as their eager faces beamed with mischief. They were evidently making fun of her. She took a sip of the fragrant tea, and as she removed the cup from her lips replied shyly, "I never thought of Arthur that way."

"Arthur. How lovingly she says it." Miss Fawcett scoffed, looking over to Miss Everett.

"Of course, she would not think of him like that, Miss Fawcett. You know Miss Hollings." The round-faced girl remarked.

"Indeed, the pure Miss Hollings does not pay attention to the opposite sex, not even if she has a prime specimen roaming the halls," The lanky Miss Fawcett agreed, "A paragon of virtue! No, do not think that I do not appreciate your sweetness. It's admirable how you have lived like a recluse for two years. After all, we were only ever able to catch glimpses of you on Sundays at mass … and yet, you seem to have caught the attention of many a man. I am not insinuating that you are tempting them consciously. However, please stay as sweet and oblivious!"

"Oh, yes. Even my slothful brother became eager to never miss out on mass." Miss Everett chimed in. And they both clucked like silly hens.

Their attitude greatly irritated me. This must have been the first tea party Evangeline had the chance to host and those snout bands had nothing better to do than to mock and ridicule her. The countryside truly was a dreary place to only offer two insolent brats like them as her peers. Thus, I decided to enter. Evangeline's ears were red as she became aware of my presence.

"Pardon my intrusion …" I began, and after a brief customary introduction and niceties I stated my business: "I was wondering if you would have liked to join me out, Evey," I lied, as I did not really harbour any genuine intention of taking her anywhere, "but seeing that you are still entertaining your guests I will go by myself." And then shot either of them an impatient glance.

In truth, I had become curious upon hearing from old Francis that Evangeline was entertaining female guests in the winter garden. In the whole month that I had been at the estate, there was a constant stream of correspondence but not once had anyone called upon her. I was slightly disappointed to see them then. Those obnoxious pests did not seem like they were her friends, and I pondered on how the topic had come to an article about me just as I stood at the doors.

"Oh, truly? I— It's such a shame, I would have loved to join you for a walk." She replied with a timid but lovely smile. She may have wondered the same thing, feeling anxious about the thought that I was likely to have overheard their conversation.

I remained for a few moments, looking at the trio. Having both girls sitting on each side of the round table created an image of the delicate Evangeline being the centrepiece. A radiant rose adorned with shrubs, highlighting her beauty: her perfect posture and refined air, her delicate frame contrasted by the awkward ones of her peers, the golden blonde hair warmly glistening in the sun, as its rays flooded through the many windowpanes of the winter garden. Finally, the serene blue eyes looking at me inquisitively as I lingered on.

"Well, then." I said bluntly, and without further ado I exited the room.

Having not even fully shut the doors behind me, I could hear the shrubs whisper under their breath, 'Oh my,' and 'Evey, he calls her.' They giggled stupidly.

"What awful guests she has." I muttered to myself while making my way back to the reading room. But they were not as awful as her foster brother, for as I beheld the beautiful Evangeline, I could only think of one thing: I wanted to defile her. Her very existence irked me.

1
Vision

I was different, more complicated, my mother used to tell me. My very birth had been a burden to her, confining her to bed for several months. However, my older brother Harold was the perfect first-born son. An easy birth. A person naturally gifted. His character gentle, respectful and patient. He was never spiteful, and in fact a splendid big brother. He knew when to be stern and when to be understanding. Like every other person around him, I could not help but love my brother. For every positive quality he possessed, I exhibited the opposite. There was a certain inevitability in me turning out to be the bad apple. Especially when Evangeline was taken into the family. Her father was a colonial official in India. She was only six years old when her parents both suddenly died of typhoid fever. Having no remaining close relatives whatsoever, my parents decided to take her in. Mother was a girlhood friend — in fact the best girlhood friend of Mrs Hollings — as they both visited the same ladies' boarding school. Therefore, she regarded it as more than a duty, rather as a calling to take the poor orphan in as ward. Before joining the estate, Evangeline had never spent one day on English soil and it must have been strange for her to come alone to live at a cold, remote place so very different from the vibrant and warm subcontinent. The first time we met was over the summer holiday when I was twelve. Harold and I returned to the manor soiled from foot to crown. As it was our habit, we had been spending time in the forest surrounding the estate. She, having arrived earlier than expected, was already seated in the drawing room when we entered. Her legs hopelessly dangling down as she sat in the big armchair: fine features and big crystal blue eyes, a pink ribbon fastened atop the waves of golden hair, a white summer dress. Evangeline was the perfect semblance of a bisque doll, the most delicate I'd ever seen. After Mother had introduced me as her new brother, she beamed at me with uninhibited innocence. I fancied the idea of being an older brother as well, I thought it a chance to prove myself useful and responsible to my family. And seeing her just strengthened my resolve. The young girl had an otherworldly atmosphere around her. I instantly took a liking to this child as the feelings to protect and dote on her took roots within my heart. Evangeline too, seemed to have quickly grown fond of me and started following me around after a few days. We would play and read together. When she was frightened, she would hide behind me, if there was something that impressed or excited her, she would show it to me first, if there was something on her mind, she would consult me. In the seven years before I went away, I did everything for her that a loving older brother could, and the greatest reward for me was her happy smile. It filled me with a strong sense of pride to be admired by such a sweet and pretty child. Our relationship remained that affectionate until I returned from my military service.

Mother, as well, was very pleased to have gained such a lovely daughter. Maybe at times, she saw the semblance of her departed friend in her. The young girl's kind disposition and charming nature swiftly made her the centre of attention. The sun around which our family started to gravitate. With her addition to the Forestedge estate I became the troublesome middle child. Her person matched that of my family more than mine. I did not hate her for that. I had never hated her for diminishing my own presence, it was not her fault that I was unmanageable for the others. However, with the passing of Harold and Mother, the balance of our home was destroyed. My return from action was just to further upset it, and among the many changes that had occurred, I had found her transformation into the sanctified angel of the estate the most bothersome.

"I was told that you will be visiting the Garden Mansion of Irvine junior this afternoon, boy?" Father inquired as he had finished his breakfast.

"Yes, during my absence he wed Miss Childs and I did not have the chance to congratulate them yet, sir." I briskly answered, as I was in the action of getting up from my seat. I did not wish to hold any conversation on my schedule and felt irritated that he was informed about it by a servant.

"It looks to be a pleasant spring day. The first in a while. You should take Evey along, she did not have any opportunity to leave the estate." Father firmly suggested with a jovial smile on his face. I looked over to her, and she flinched as our eyes met. Flustered, Evangeline avoided my gaze.

"Uncle Arthur, I really do not wish to impose myself on Arthur … and I am worried about you, too. You were so unwell yesterday."

Father immediately rejected her protest, "Nonsense, you mustn't be cooped up in these halls. You have been in here much too long. A young girl like you needs the sun. Besides, there are more than enough people and Doctor Armitage, in the manor to aid me, if I should come to require help."

"But—"

"Enough objections. You agree, don't you, boy? Evey should enjoy the nice weather and different company." Father said, his expectant eyes fixed onto me.

"Yes, sir." I answered monotonously, hiding my annoyance.

"Then that is settled."

And so, it was.

"I am sorry that you are unable to ride out to your friends, now that I have joined. Even though it would be such a quick and nice ride." Evangeline said, hardly audible over the rattle of the double brougham.

"Don't concern yourself with it. You are not to blame." I replied dispassionately.

The truth was that even a short distance to the Garden Mansion might have increased the pain caused by the injury on my left flank. I hadn't yet gotten used to riding for long stretches. As she was observing the scenery of the countryside from the window, she asked, "Who are we meeting today?"

"You are asking me only now?" I retorted annoyed.

I was not keen on taking her along, as she would be very mismatched with the crowd I called 'my friends.'

"I … apologies. I merely want to greet them properly." She answered almost whispering.

She may have been aware of them in some capacity as each of them came to the manor at least once before. However, how was she supposed to remember people that never interacted with her directly? I went out of my way to give her an explanation on who they were, of course only mentioning the essential and omitting the negative. Mr James Irvine was the son of the merchant who owned a big store in Carlisle. Irvine Senior had frequented our house, as Mother loved to shop and to furnish the manor with the Irvines ever since I was young. Therefore, James as oldest son, would always be dragged along. We played together as we were of the same age, yet honestly, I always disliked his docile character. He was a shrinking violet. Eventually we wound up at the same boarding school. Mrs Celia Irvine, born to Baron Childs, was the youngest daughter of then impoverished nobility. Whenever I saw her, she would relentlessly chase after me in search for entertainment. The three of us were frequenting the same social events. Thus, we became what one would consider 'childhood friends.' The other two guests that we would meet at the Garden Mansion were Frederick Thornton esq., barrister and a fellow boarding school mate of James' and I, and his respective lady friend (for a lack of another word) Miss Jennifer White. The last guest, of whom I knew nothing about

I looked at Evangeline intently while explaining, and again was reminded of how much she had grown. Her face was modestly turned to the side, while her posture was elegant and refined. Under her shoulder cape, she wore a shirtwaist suit with a pleated skirt, adorned with delicate lace trimmings at the bodice and collar. Accompanying this outfit, she put on a simple boater, similar to mine, however with a veil. It seemed rather impractical regarding her hair arrangement. The ends of the long blonde hair gathered on the seat around her hips. Both had become fuller with the passing of adolescence. In the past, we would have taken a smaller carriage in which we would have sat next to each other with her leaning into me, sometimes holding my hand because she was much younger. We would have lively chatted about everything. Perhaps then she would have inquired more about my friends, wondered what would be served to high tea, or have made trivial remarks about the landscape. But at present, I wanted none of it: not her intimacy, not her affection, not even her opinion. There was a wall between us, and it was good that it was there.

We arrived at the Garden Mansion, a former vicarage of moderate size with paddocks and a barn, the Lakeland Fells were prominent in the distance. Close by the mansion was a small lake, just at the edge of its confines. To my surprise Celia was personally there to greet us as we dismounted the carriage. As was her habit from childhood when she met new people, Evangeline went to stand behind me.

"Oh my, Arthur-Dearest," Celia exclaimed, holding out her hand for me to kiss it, "You were bringing company? I did not know."

I gave her the desired greeting.

"Congratulations on becoming Mrs Irvine, Celia. Before you drift into wild speculations: this is Miss Evangeline Hollings, my foster sister. You may remember her?"

Evangeline introduced herself again with courtesy.

"Oh yes, now that you mention it, I remember a pallid … ah, no, a ghostly figure fluttering behind you whenever there was a gathering at Forestedge. So, it was you!" Celia laughed; her lips curled up to a smile but coldness emanating from her venomous green eyes.

She looked quite stately and honest in a watering-place dress that was buttoned up to the neck. The light colour contrasted the unruly black curls, which were tied up and fastened with an ornate comb. This modest show did not suit her person at all. Matching her pace, we quickly went out to the patio on the backside, where the rest of the party was already seated. Sitting to the left was Thornton. He had hardly changed in the five years in which I was away, except for the fact that he had more pronounced widow peaks. His smile was still sly and of the quality that could make ladies mistaken it for genuine infatuation. Not due to similar looks but due to similar success with the fairer sex we were often compared, the major difference being that I never put up any pretence in regard to my intentions. The face clean shaven, the light blonde hair groomed back, and a suit of the latest fashion: he looked trustworthy if one did not know his character. Next to him sat Miss Jennifer White and as expected of Thornton, she was a beauty worthy of being printed on postcards. She had the extroverted charm of a performer. And finally, there was the host: weak-chinned James, who presently sported a moustache that was lighter than his ginger hair. Possibly he had it to make his still boyish face look more mature.

After giving everyone our formal greeting and introduction, we were seated for high tea. In contrast to my adolescence, I had become less vain about my appearance, simply having clad myself in any proper old boating suit at my disposal for the outing. This of course drew the attention of my friends, who made sarcastic remarks about my choices, all in view of my return from Africa.

"Clarence, were you robbed off your trunk on the passage back? I could swear that I've seen that suit five years ago." Thornton said with a deprecating smile.

"You should have let me know that you were short on proper clothing! If you had, I could have sent someone over to fit you out." James joined in, half-joking and half-serious.

"Oh, pay them no mind Arthur-Dearest. You look as dapper in that suit as you did back then. Even better now, I must say." Celia complimented me with a delighted snicker.

Unsurprisingly to me, there then was an onset of questions and snide remarks.

"I still can't believe the vanishing act you pulled, Arthur. To do volunteer service just like that! It's truly something only you would cook up in your brain." James exclaimed.

"Indeed, you were about to enter *Sandhurst* anyway. All of us thought that you had *illegitimate reason* to quickly escape the country." Thornton laughed.

"Very true, there were numerous speculations, but no one ever came forward with anything." James added.

Then him, Thornton and Celia laughed in unison, whereas Evangeline and Miss Jennifer silently drank their teas with puzzled expressions.

"But what does it matter? The service surely made you even more virile and handsome, Arthur-Dearest. You are a sight for sore eyes." The lady of the house said flirtatiously.

James, not hearing or minding this remark, instead turned the topic to my latest exploits.

"It is good to have you back after you barely survived Sudan. That must have been harrowing. You still look quite ill at ease. Even though, you do have a faint tan left on you." He noted.

"I was mortified when I heard what severe wounds you received; I hope your body did not suffer too much." Celia joined in, studying me from top to toe with lascivious eyes.

I explained that I was still recovering, and that I did not want to further discuss the matter. At least they had the decency to respect my wishes and the subject shifted towards my tag-along.

"You should have sent someone over to inform us that you'd bring Miss Hollings, I feel quite elated to have someone new at our place. I would have prepared something more special." James said with sincerity.

"Oh, Dear, you know how Arthur loves surprises and fails to adhere to standard etiquette." Celia blathered, while resting her chin on her hand. Keenly she stared at Evangeline, who in turn averted her gaze and looked over to me.

"Indeed. Clarence, you should have let us know." Thornton chimed in and also turned towards her, "I doubt that you remember me, I came to visit at Forestedge Manor one summer. You were but a small child. You have grown into quite the lovely lady if I dare say so."

He had benevolent smile on his face, that completely belied his intentions. Thornton was a gambler that always liked to bet on getting more exquisite things than he already had. Especially regarding women. There was an indecent flicker in his eyes, that I knew just too well. Miss Jennifer seemed to easily catch onto it, too. And before I could rebuff him, she diverted the topic yet again. This time towards Evangeline's sense of fashion.

"I think the way in which your hair is arranged looks quite lovely, Miss Hollings. It's very … youthful … uhm … innocent."

What she tried to insinuate was that Evangeline did not have the allure of a mature woman, as she was still wearing her hair half-down with a ribbon fastened into it. She did look slightly childish, and it made her appear younger than her actual age. Evangeline plainly noted that she was uncomfortable with her hair all the way up. She was not an avid follower of the trends, was her excuse. But I knew, as I looked at her, she must have yearned to return to her former self. The full mourning period for my brother and another year for my mother had confined her for over two years in the tight and dreary costume. I was certain that she must have been happy to return to a lighter look.

"Innocent?" exclaimed Celia, "Oh, with Miss Hollings' beauty I find this arrangement quite salacious. Afterall, a lady must only have her hair down in certain settings. How can you be so at ease with such a promiscuous brother around?" she added with a puckish grin.

James, Thornton, and she laughed heartily while Miss Jennifer put on a quizzical smile, not understanding what they could be alluding to. Evangeline on the other hand shot me a glance and then cast her eyes down. Her ears turned red.

"Speaking of promiscuous," Miss Jennifer began, "have you read the *Gazette*? There was a major scandal concerning the heiress of the Benham house!"

"Oh yes, I read that. Benham … hm … that name rings a bell." Celia mused and looked at me.

"Benham?" James joined in, also looking at me.

Finally, it was Thornton that exclaimed, "Of course, Benham! The third daughter's name was Mimi … no, Mary …" he was thinking aloud.

"You are totally off, Mr Thornton. It's Florence." Celia said coldly and took a sip from her cup.

"Yes, exactly, Florence. I remember her! She was quite fetching. That daft las— ," and he stopped himself as Evangeline looked at him with curiosity, "that delicate lady, she was one of Clarence's flames. Am I mistaken?" he had a childish smirk on his face while asking me this.

"I don't remember her." I answered bluntly. I honestly did not.

"Tut, aren't you a cold one?" Celia chided me, her smile became more devious, "to forget the name of a lover that threatened to kill herself."

At this Miss Jennifer gasped in awe and looked at me as though I was a festering wound.

"I thought she actually went and did herself in." James mused, fondling his moustache.

"Oh, she tried to, but it was a rather pathetic attempt. I think she only went far enough to get Clarence's attention," Thornton explained, "it did not seem to work, though."

And the three of them laughed maliciously while the two ladies were very uncomfortable. I simply sat in silence, wondering how in the past I was able to carelessly laugh with those three about such sordid affairs.

The plan for the afternoon was to take a boat onto the lake, at the foot of the Garden Mansion. I did not feel up to it as I worried that the pain of my injury would increase by rowing. Evangeline, however, looked eager to see the view of the lake and I agreed to us joining in. We went over to the boats that were laid out on the lake's edge by the servants. There was one oar missing. It appeared odd that the boats were so far off from the boat shed which was out of view, but Celia insisted that it was a nicer ride from the allocated spot.

"Seeing that we have our able-bodied friend Lance Corporal Clarence with us, I suggest he go and fetch us a new oar. I'm not keen on carrying it all the way." Thornton said leisurely and glanced at Evangeline.

"We can call a servant to fetch one. Afterall, Arthur is still recovering." James suggested, faint undertones of anxiety in his voice.

Celia went to stroke her husband's arm, an awkwardly distant show of affection for her.

"Oh, but it will take even longer to go to the house and tell someone. Who knows if the weather will not change in between? Come now, Arthur-Dearest, you don't mind, do you? I will show you where the boat shed is located, and we will be back in a jiffy!" she said.

I could feel her plotting something as James nodded helplessly. However, without any protest I went off with her. The shed was further away than expected, behind a slope that let the group we left behind vanish from sight.

"Are you not worried leaving your sister behind with Mr Thornton?" Celia asked mockingly, the emphasise on the word 'sister'.

"I am not really worried, seeing that Miss White and James are around. I am more concerned about your distasteful remarks. You mustn't say such unsavoury things around Evey." I answered, chastising her.

"Oh, Arthur-Dearest! You never were one to care about conventions. But here you are caring about your Evey's ... your foster sister's delicate mind. That's very sweet. Very responsible." She gloated.

"Some ladies are delicate and sensible ... unlike you." I retorted, growing annoyed with her.

"You have become quite the rigid man in the Army, haven't you? I don't really mind, *as long as the right parts of you will become stiff.*" She laughed.

It appeared to me that marriage had not changed Celia: she was still a well-endowed beauty with a despicable character. As we reached the shed and entered, Celia continued, "You do not seem to enjoy her company, however."

I did not entertain her with an answer.

"Or is it the type of enjoyment you would want from her company not available to you?"

Her mouth was still rotten as ever. Angrily, I slammed my fist against the wall.

"Watch what you are saying!"

Celia closed in on me, a seductive fire in her eyes.

"Oh," she moaned, "I like it when you are angry! I really missed that."

She started to stroke my face, moving up to caress my hair.

"It's so much shorter than before, but it suits you. It looks a bit lighter too. Wasn't it a dark brown before."

I turned my face away from her, as she continued to fondle it.

"Must have been the African sun …"

"Say did you miss me, if only for a little?" she asked with an ominous sweetness.

"I did not think of you even once." I answered without hesitation.

"Hm," she mused, and finally gloated again, "All your thoughts must have been with the *ingénue* back yonder."

Furious, I turned to look at her, but before I could say a word we kissed, and she caressed me elsewhere. I was not inclined to resist her, therefore I turned her around. Pulling up a heap of fabric revealed her bare bottom between the split drawers. I slipped my fingers in between her thighs. She must have been dripping with excitement the moment I left the carriage.

Leaning in over her shoulder, I tugged her hair and whispered into her ear, "You are still the same old bitch in heat."

Taking my insult as a compliment, her reply mingled with heavy breathing, "Hush, Arthur and hurry up!"

Then, I mounted her like a stud would a mare, with raw animalistic passion. Equally stupid as loveless. It was laughable how easy to please she was, and I wondered to myself how James must be failing her. She must have arranged this whole encounter. Once I finished, I buttoned up again and suggested we hurry back.

"They may wonder where we have been so long."

"Oh, shush," she huffed, "What do you mean by long?" Celia laughed, and covered herself again with her skirt.

"I never understood what James sees in you … Why did he even bother marrying the likes of you?"

"For one, he's just such a loving man: he loves me and *all* my faults; and for the other, you would not ask for my hand." She answered, adjusting her hair ornament.

"Because you are not a woman one should wed." I retorted.

We returned with me carrying the missing oar over my shoulder. However, Evangeline was not to be seen with the group.

"She seemed slightly uncomfortable around us." Miss Jennifer said, casting an evil look on Thornton.

"I sent her straight after you." James further explained.

Maybe he was not as gullible as I thought him to be. Yet, if she had gone after us just shortly after we departed, we should have at least seen her on our way back. Celia grinned maliciously. Announcing that I would look for her, I threw the oar down and turned on my heel. One could not miss the boat shed. We did not see her because she did not want to be seen. Did she reach the shed and peek in, observing silently? With swift steps I reached my destination, and she was sitting just at the side, concealed by the shade. It was easy to overlook her, however she could see anyone that left or approached clearly. She flinched as I called out to her. Out of breath I asked her if she was all right. Her hands were resting on her knees as she sat in the grass, the skirt spread out all over and dirty. She did not look up to meet my eyes and tugged nervously at the veil of her hat.

"I … I—" she stammered and then abruptly paused.

With a pensive look on her face she finally answered, "My ankle … it hurts," and pointed down.

"Did you fall?" I asked, deciding to play along.

"Yes …" she mumbled, "I tripped and fell."

Wherever did she plan to run to for her to end up behind the boat shed? I knelt and sightly lifted the hem of her skirt to reveal her boots.

"Which one?"

"The … the right one!" was her hurried answer.

From the corner of my eye, I could see that her face was flushed. She flinched again as I gently squeezed the ankle, her whole leg started to tremble.

"From your reaction I can infer that it can't be too bad. Anyway, do you want me to carry you on my back?" I inquired, an urge to tease her had overcome me.

"No. I can walk. Your arm will be enough." She answered, and still would not dare to look at me. I stood up first and reached my hand out to her. She meekly took it, and she held onto me as we slowly walked back in silence. After apologising to the party that we were unable to go for a boat ride with them due to Evangeline's apparent injury, I let them know that we would find our way back to the carriage ourselves.

"Such a caring gentleman and brother. I am very jealous of you, Miss Hollings." Celia trilled sarcastically.

I knew that she would not pass on this opportunity. We wished them a good afternoon and went away. On our way home Evangeline fell asleep in the carriage, or at least she pretended to.

Once we had returned to Forestedge, it was young Francis the valet and son of our head butler that greeted us. After the tiering party of hyenas at the Garden Mansion, I felt annoyed at having to see his face as well. He immediately noticed something wrong with the young miss. I explained what happened as Evangeline still was acting very reclusive, maybe due to pain?

"And just when you went to meet sir's friends. Miss Evangeline, would you like me to lead you in seeing that Master Arthur is still in weakened state." He offered, glaring at me as if I was to be held personally accountable.

Along with the other servants that had been working for our house a considerable time, he would barely mask the antipathy he held towards me. It was mutual, but I was too distracted by the day's events too entertain his provocation.

Evangeline asked young Francis not to notify the doctor yet nor Father, as she was uncertain whether she wouldn't be better by the next day. She strongly objected and did not want to stir up an unnecessary commotion. The pain had subsided already, she insisted.

Eventually, the afternoon and evening passed by without major events. Father inquired about our visit over supper, and we really had nothing to report other than that we left early, while omitting the reason for it. Her calm countenance never changed during her deliberation, which made me wonder if she truly had seen anything. Or had I scared her that much with my attitude that she would become nervous when she was left alone with me?

As always, I was the last person awake, lounging in the smoking room and indulging in drink, nobody attending to me. I stared at the painting on the wall which Father must have had moved in there, as he barely frequented the place anymore. The family portrait was painted by one of the finest artists of the north. An eternal reminder of better times that had faded: strapping and upright, Father was fair-haired with hazel eyes, his whiskers, and moustache similar in appearance to the late Prince Consort. To Father's right it was Harold, the soft edges of adolescence already gone, almost a fully grown man. Harold looked very much like Father, sans the facial hair. Seated in front of him, with just as much regal poise as the Queen herself, was Mother. Her auburn hair was like the hues of Scottish autumn foliage, and the eyes a matted blue like its skies. To the right, there I was: I had her eyes, but my hair was of a muddy dark-brown colour. At fourteen I was not that far away from my final growth spurt, but had yet to surpass both, Father and Harold in height. I wondered if I was then more manageable lacking those inches. Finally, next to Mother was small Evangeline. The face of the matriarch was beaming with pride at such a wholesome family. Seeing the painting every evening for more than a month, I had been pondering on the many changes: Mother and Harold were dead, Father a shadow of his former self, my youthful enthusiasm and carefreeness had vanished, and Evangeline was a grown woman. Truthfully, none of these people remained in this manor. Instead, they all had turned into spectres staring down on me from their square confinement, stuck within a frozen world.

Having been with my regiment abroad, it was shocking to see how things had changed so much in my absence. Thinking of her under different skies, Evangeline still was an innocent, unknowing child. I could not believe that she was of marriageable age, and yet she had proven to hold secrets as well as any adult. I was sure that she did see Celia and I in the boat shed. There was no way that she would not have, and the thought made me restless. I hated it. That she saw that debauched side of me. Our relationship had become distant since my return, this on my own accord, but to worsen it was unacceptable for me. While it never bothered me much what others really thought about me, I never wanted her to consider me *a villain*. Thus, I got up to see if it was not yet too late to mend things with her. Walking up the main landing, my heavy footsteps echoed in the hallway of the east wing that led to the bedchambers. I was at a loss to what it was that I wanted to tell her. For a few moments I silently waited in front of her chamber. I was not an eloquent person and trusted that taking action first would lead to some sort of solution. Soft moans escaped through the cracks of the door. Wondering if her ankle did in fact cause her pain, I wanted to gently knock. However, not having been properly closed the door fell ajar at the lightest touch. Looking in I immediately halted my actions as she came into view.

A sensual chiaroscuro scene presented itself to me: with her back facing the door, Evangeline sat on the edge of the bed. Hunched over, she gently rocked back and forth. Her slender shoulders plunged forward, moving continuously. Strands of her hair had come loose from her braid and fell over her back, gently swaying while the contours of her body were outlined by the moonlight. Her exited breathing was growing evermore erratic and culminated in an exulted sigh. Before she could come back to her senses, I carefully closed the door and quietly walked away. I went on to my own bedchamber next to hers. That night, while I thought of her, sleep would not find me at all.

2
The Faerie Queene

The next day, I avoided Evangeline more than usual. It looked like her ankle was not bothering her anymore as she walked to her seat at the table perfectly fine. While we did indulge Father at breakfast, neither of us ever addressed the other. Only when exiting the manor towards the patio on the backside, I saw in passing that she had sat down to read something while enjoying the warming rays of the sun. What else she did over the morning, I did not know. I went for my walk over the estate and into the woods, still unable to sit on a horse for a long time. The pain in my flank had increased. I was not certain if it was due to carrying the oar or my encounter with Celia.

I returned earlier than usual, as it was a particular rainy April afternoon. Having dozed off on the sofa in the reading room I was startled by a sudden thud. Evangeline stood in the centre of the circular carpet that adorned the seating area. A thick volume dropped by her, had fallen right next to my hand which was dangling down the edge. She must have been surprised at finding me there, too confounded to do anything than stand and stare at me. Still drowsy I sat up and took the volume from the floor. Turning it around in my hand I remembered the weight, and a feeling of irritation bubbled up within me as I smelt the musty scent of the browned leaves. It was Spenser's *Faerie Queene*, and it was the copy I was forced to study in the past.

"Here you go."

I held it out to Evangeline who would not move an inch.

"Are you going to take it or not?" I insisted, annoyed.

She swiftly snatched it from my hand and went to sit in the armchair opposite of me, leafing through to the place where she had stopped at.

"Are you fine with me staying here or should I go?" I asked.

It was the first time that we were all alone. Not even a single servant in sight. Whether for this reason or another, there was a strong tension overlying the leisure of the reading room.

"You may stay." She answered curtly without looking up.

Still not fully awake I remained seated to observe her.

"Do you really enjoy reading something so tedious?" I inquired, as while I knew she liked poetry, I could not fathom how anyone would enjoy that one voluntarily.

"It's a lovely poem," she insisted, and looking up to me added, "It has wonderful themes." Then she went on about the allegories of virtue and goodness. I knew that she was a bright child, therefore I wondered if she was trying to insinuate something. Deciding to humour her, I enquired as to where exactly she had stopped reading.

"Book III: Arthur, Guyon and Britomart part ways." She replied, her cheeks becoming lightly tinted.

"Oh, are you suddenly feeling shy for saying my name out loud?" I teased her, laughing.

"To be honest, I was contemplating on how you and Arthur of the round table do have nothing in common but the name."

The tone of her answer was surprisingly sarcastic, and I was taken aback.

"Aren't we both cavaliers and magnificent knights?" I countered, irritated.

With a loud thump she closed the volume and stared squarely back at me to say, "The knight resists sexual temptation." She rose from the armchair, and then added, "It is funny because Mrs Irvine is nothing like Caelia either."

I was in awe, and perturbed. She had never behaved that way towards me. From when she had joined the family, she had never once sneered at me. *Not her.* I could not let her leave like that, therefore I quickly stood up and grabbed her by the wrist.

"You did see us!" I exclaimed, tense. Embarrassment and anger mingled as I beheld her consternated expression.

"And if I did?" she countered defiantly, repulsion written all over her face.

I did not answer as fury grew within. I hated this rejective attitude she then showed towards me.

"You did not say anything."

"Was I supposed to? It was an unsightly thing!"

"Unsightly ..."

Hardly composing myself I attempted to ridicule her instead, "So I am not a virtuous person. What of it? Do you fancy yourself Lady Britomart? You are no paragon of virtue either. I clearly saw your solitary vice."

What kind of expression was I making? In the heat of the argument, I really could not tell. Her countenance made a sudden change from tense and anxious to soft and almost ... eager. The crystal eyes then looked up to me as I was still holding her firmly by the tender wrist.

"You ... watched ... ?" a strong determination that contrasted her usual timid demeanour emerged, "So ... you were watching ... " she confirmed.

"And you did not stop even though you noticed? You are one shameless brat."

It appeared to me that our roles had reversed. My hands started to tremble with disgust and anxiety. With excitement. She did not answer and simply continued to stare at me awaiting further chastising, or something else? The unexpected lack of fear and defence aggravated me. I grabbed her by the shoulders as a strong urge to seize her overcame me. Surprised, she dropped the volume onto the ground again.

"You ... are you not omitting crucial steps? Or, — Don't tell me you have done this with a man before?"

I leant over to leer at her. I saw the absurdity in the question myself.

After all, in the past two and a half years she had been incessantly sacrificing herself for the sake of our family. Left alone to take a burden onto her own. And yet, thinking that there was the tiniest chance of my accusation being true unsettled me.

"I have yet to kiss one." She answered daringly.

"Did it make you curious? Would you like to try?" I taunted her, not knowing what I was doing anymore. She provoked my ire as my foster sister, and simultaneously thrilled me as a woman. Desperately I waited for the slightest squirm or wriggle so that I may let her loose. Let her escape. She was perfectly still, looking up at me. Every inhale of hers drew me closer.

She lifted her chin and asked, "And if I wanted to?"

Then, before I knew, I pressed my lips onto hers. I wanted to scare her, I kept telling myself. This was simply to frighten her and placate what men could do to someone with such low defences. Yet, I could not help but satiate myself in the moment Evangeline's surrender. Instead of pushing me away, she gently placed her hands onto my chest. Their warmth seared through the fabric of my clothing. The sensation of her soft lips made visceral voices whisper in my ear, demanding I do more. Pushing my tongue through to meet hers in a deep kiss, I then knew that she never had kissed before. Her muscle twitched in confusion at my intrusion. When she struggled to find her breath, she firmly gripped onto my waistcoat, and I wondered how a discussion about *The Faerie Queene* could have gotten so out of hand. Opening my eyelids slightly to have a look at her, our eyes met. She then firmly bit me in the lip. Surprised I broke away and touched my mouth, watery blood escaping from a small cut. Not looking back, she stormed out of the room, while only an afterimage of the flurry of golden hair remained. *The Faerie Queene* was listlessly left on the floor.

Changing my habitat, I remained in the smoking room for the rest of the afternoon and even passed supper on. It was unlike me to run away from an issue, but this time I could not face Evangeline without having properly thought the matter over. Afterall, tackling it head on is what had gotten me in the situation of the afternoon.

Unexpectedly, Father appeared at the door closely followed by young Francis. He inquired if he may join me. Curious at this rare request I did not see a reason to reject him. As he laboriously bent down on his cane, Father was helped by the valet with taking his seat in the armchair next to the chaise longue. He coughed loudly, and I hurried to extinguish the cigarette that I was smoking. Then he instructed Francis to wait outside, as he wished to discuss a private matter.

"How is your recovery progressing, boy? Good, I suppose?"

I doubted the sincere interest of this inquiry as he had failed to ask me so far. Yet, I answered courteously, "Better by the day, sir. Thank you for the concern."

"Did Doctor Armitage say anything about when you will be able to return to your regiment?"

"He did not make any estimate and suggested I take my time recovering." Was my curt reply.

In fact, our house physician had told me that the broken bones were all as strong as before, but that the severe wound on my left side was still somewhat precarious. The constant discomfort was caused by how it had healed badly, and the possibilities of miniscule particles of dirt still being lodged in my body was unverified. It was hard to tell. Furthermore, there were still a gloom and disquiet overhanging my spirits. Therefore, he could only advise me to rest properly, as it would eventually become a matter of pain management rather than healing. But this information I chose to keep to myself.

A silence that pertained our meetings enshrined the room. Subconsciously, my eyes wandered to the family portrait opposite of me. To then see him seated in the armchair felt odd. Hunched and crumpled, leaning on the walking cane with his bony hands, the flaxen hair turned to ash and all the virility faded away. It was not the father I used to respect, even though I had failed to show him that respect many times. I never feared him, but I held him in awe. I returned to a house of strangers, and I as well must have been strange to them.

Glancing around the room, an object on the gueridon table caught his attention. It was the volume of *The Faerie Queene* which I had taken along.

"Oh, it is a surprise to see you reading this." He noted, wearing his usual jovial smile.

"Evey left it in the reading room. She was the one reading it." I stated bluntly.

After I had moved to the current room, I aimlessly leafed through the volume. Eyes closed; Father nodded in jaggy forward motions.

"I see, so you *do* talk to each other. The two of you used to be on such good terms but now she appears to be fearful of you. And you act quite reserved yourself. Did something happen?" he inquired.

I denied and suggested that she may have been careful around me due to my injury.

"As you may have noticed, I was hoping for the two of you to be on amicable terms. After all, we are the only family she has left. Unlike you, I am not in a state to support her." He said solemnly, eyes still closed.

"In what capacity, sir?" I asked, surprised at this statement. She was every part of this estate other than in name.

Father opened his tired eyes to look at the family portrait.

"Poor Evey, to have suffered so many tragedies in such a young life. She was deprived of a happy future. The past years should have been filled with enjoyment and instead she was cooped up in these halls, obliged to wear the mourning dress for such a long time. There was neither the right time nor mood for her coming out to society. Now that you are here, she has the chance to live a little … before …" at this Father paused and his face wrinkled as though he was in pain, he continued, "before she will marry and leave the house."

"Marry? Even though she did not have her coming out? Are there suitors?" I blurted out, unable to mask my surprise.

"Oh, yes indeed. Thompson's son has taken quite a liking to her. She is a lovely and accomplished child after all, and she has proven to be quite capable in managing a household too, despite her age. However, before she takes on the responsibilities of an own household and family, she should experience a bit of carefree enjoyment. Go with her to social events, the theatre, the opera … any place enjoyable. After all, it is your responsibility as her brother to look out for her," and then scoffing he continued, "Well, boy, you would know when shady characters start to hover around her. Her innocence is her charm but also her weakness. Ward of the people that would exploit her." By these words he implied that my reputation preceded me.

I exerted all my strength to not grimace at this imploring speech. After all, Father was unable to see what had happened this afternoon, even though it happened under this very roof. I could feel my stomach turn.

"I understand, sir. I will do my utmost for her." I finally replied, earnestly.

After he had left, I drank in solitude. I simply wanted to forget the events of the afternoon and Father's pleading. I drifted into a light sleep on the chaise but was awoken by the single chime of the longcase clock. The embers in the fireplace had long died out, yet a dim gleaming penetrated my eyelids. A paraffin lamp was placed on the gueridon table next to the armchair which was a few hours before occupied by my father. Evangeline was seated in it, the braided hair dishevelled. She must have slept very uncomfortably on it. The blanket that covered her lower body fell to the floor when she raised her hands to rub her eyes.

"What are you doing here?" I asked, instinctively kneeling to pick up the blanket.

"I came to continue reading my book." She answered with a languid yawn.

For a moment I remained in the kneeling position as I still felt a lingering effect of the liquor. Then I looked up at her, the features obscured from the low angle, the light of the lamp drawing the dainty shape of her body through the nightgown. I threw the thick blanket over her lap and fell back onto the chaise longue. I could not think of a reason why she would want to talk to me alone in the dead of the night after what had passed in the reading room.

"You've been sleeping in the smoking room quite often these days. It is not good for your health." She chided me.

I did not answer.

Then she continued, "I have been waiting to hear your footsteps to see when you'd pass my room, for retiring to yours. But you hardly do. Francis told me that you suffer from insomnia. Would it not be better to try and sleep in your bed then?"

"I'm not fond of the beds in this house, they are too soft." I answered passively.

"How funny." she mused.

Evangeline was surprisingly chatty. Save for the afternoon at the Irvines, this was the first time that we held something akin to a conversation. She picked up the tumbler next to the lamp and traced the rim with her slender fingers, before holding it close to her fine nose, inhaling the residues of the spirits.

"You mustn't drink so much either." She chastised me.

"Evey, you can take this attitude with Father but not with me. If this is your lecture done, then return to your room." I said, harshly.

Seemingly reverting to her usual demeanour, she looked away and rose, but instead of leaving she suddenly sat next to me. With my mind still hazy I pondered if I was dreaming.

"I could read some passages from *The Faerie Queene* to you." She suggested with modest laughter.

"Oh, please! I pass."

"Do you remember that lullaby I used to hum? The one I used to hum to you too … my Ayah sang it to me when I could not sleep because the heat and the ominous sounds would excite my fancy. Would it help you to hear it now?" she offered, the dim light illuminating a gentle smile.

"I will pass on this, too," I told her annoyed, it was *her* proximity that excited my fancy, "Now leave me alone. You are a nuisance."

The smile faded and turned into a sombre expression.

"A nuisance? What exactly is it that I did do to upset you? Ever since you've returned you've been distant almost hateful towards me," and then, calm and collected, followed the question I had anticipated, "Why did you kiss me?"

"I merely wanted to frighten you." I answered disparagingly. My mouth felt dry as I told her the same lie, I had repeated to myself all afternoon.

She turned to look at me and whispered, "It did not feel frightening at all."

The pureness in her eyes belied the meaning of her words. Feeling encouraged by them and the liquor in my blood, I took her hand and pinned her to the long side of the méridienne. The slender shape shifted around beneath my weight, not to escape but to settle into a more comfortable position. Then I gave her a gentle kiss.

"Evey …" I uttered, as I carefully brushed aside the loose strands of hair above her brow.

"I can stay until you fall asleep." She offered with a shy smile.

"When did you become so coy?"

However, I did not wait to hear her answer. The lingering earthy taste of whiskey in my mouth was accentuated by her sweetness. Hesitantly, but surely, I could feel her tender tongue seeking out mine, clumsily imitating my actions from the afternoon. We were tangled in a knot that was repeatedly loosened and tied up again. Releasing her, she let out a sigh that was as beckoning as a siren's call, eagerly leading me towards a fatal course. I traced the fine structure of her cheekbones, first with my fingers and then with my lips. The collar of her nightdress was unbuttoned. Thus, I followed the soft trail from her neck to her exposed clavicle. A feeble tugging at my hair let me stop.

"Only ... only kissing!" she pleaded.

My forehead touched her face, which was hot with the fast-rushing blood. Immediately, I sobered up and rose from the chaise longue, turning away from her.

"You'd better go to bed now, Evey." I demanded, not looking at her.

There was a moment of silence, then followed by the rustling of her nightgown as she rose from her seat, and the low tinkling of the illuminated lamp as she grabbed it. A dejected sigh echoed in the semi-darkness. She faintly bid me a good night.

"Sleep well." She said.

And with her, the light vanished. No, she was not Lady Britomart but the elusive Faerie Queene herself: the end of my wicked ambition.

3
Enigma

The maxim 'from rags to rags in three generations' fit the current state of the Clarence household just too well. My grandfather, George Harold Clarence, was of very minor noble heritage. His father was landed gentry and had nothing to show for it but the traces of blue blood coursing through his veins; eventually, he died during the Napoleonic Wars. Young George was left an orphan that had to fend for himself until one day a distant bachelor uncle decided to take him in as ward. Thus, young George found himself part of the household of northern peerage in Cumberland. The uncle that treated him more like a valet than an heir bestowed everything upon him after his death, everything except for his title: a handsome but decrepit Georgian Manor erected as his testament to the world, a severely mismanaged bobbin mill and a meagre pension that was too little to live on but too much to die with. George was an ingenious but also ruthless person and by unknown means he managed to procure large shares of the local copper mines, resulting in Clarence becoming a household name in the Lake District. At the peak of mining in the area and the birth of his youngest child he had fully refurbished the massive manor, and contrary to his nature, became a charitable man that would support all those associated with him and his business.

This greatly impressed my father, his eldest son, who would imprint the expression noblesse oblige onto his heart. Well-educated, kind-hearted, and just as ingenious he would take on the legacy of Grandfather George, and even surpass it. He would live a life that was lacking want, offering comfort to all around him. But at the height of happiness a series of grievous events would make the House of Clarence a house of misfortune.

It all began with three deaths of disproportionate importance. The first death was the passing of my older brother Harold's favourite horse. Like me, he enjoyed horse riding and would entertain this activity every day. Harold then acquired an Anglo-Arabian mare as replacement. Not having had her for long he went on a ride one fateful morning. Upon returning to the estate she went into a frenzy, the reason remained unknown. Harold, unable to rein her in, was thrown off and hit the ground at a fatal angle — instantly dead. That was the second death. The witnesses to this accident were Father, from his study window; old Francis, the groom, and Evangeline, who awaited him on the patio. After that day she would not ride a horse again. My mild-mannered father to whom my brother was the greatest treasure he could ever call his own, flew into an unprecedented rage. The mare was executed by him with his hunting rifle while Harold's corpse had not even been moved from the lawn. That was the third death.

His passing put an end to the comfortable and complacent life of the inhabitants of Forestedge. He was the first born; his whole life he was groomed to receive it all: the manor, the business, the wealth, and Evangeline. In fact, the prize of her hand was something that my mother had arranged with her deceased friend in their maidenhood, long before any of us were born. It was for this reason for which she was never fully adopted into the Clarence family and remained Miss Hollings.

The loss of her beloved first born created a void in Mother that would swallow with it all the happiness she could feel. A void that could not be filled, especially not by me. After years of having created trouble for my mild-mannered and gentle parents, I had become a misfit that was in an act of desperation supposed to be sent off to Sandhurst. However, without following the intended path my parents had chosen for me I entered the service on my own accord. I did settle well into the military life. After I joined the 21st Lancers, then Hussars, and was posted in India, I calmed down considerably. I had not the slightest notion about how to run a business nor had I the desire to know how. There was no expectation for me to take Harold's place.

For Mother, who had already suffered through several losses of born and unborn children, losing him was the cruellest of all hurts. Within only half a year her health and sanity withered away. She would not eat; she would not sleep; and be seized by endless fits of sobbing and screaming. The only person that could offer her the slightest comfort was Evangeline. Having only been fifteen going on sixteen, she took upon herself the burden of caring for her and taking on the household matters. With the intense strain that Mother put on her, the servants could not help but start to view the young lady as saint. She always kept her composure and tirelessly did everything to please Mother, all the while managing what had to be done … neglecting herself. But all the efforts could not piece together the shattered heart and ultimately Mother joined Harold, more than one year after his passing.

Father who after my brother's death grew despondent towards the female members of the family, focused all his energies into diversifying business. It hadn't been too long since mining in the area declined, yet he wanted to maintain our wealth. A failed venture coupled with the death of his true love caused him illness. He would suffer from a fever that altered his physical being irrevocably. Again, Evangeline descended as the angel that would care for the sick. Business was taken care of by Thompson, Father's closest associate until he recovered enough to take part in it again.

All these events transpired while I was with my regiment. Evangeline herself frequently wrote me, the habit of corresponding with each other was established when I was still in boarding school. I may have been the only person she admitted her woes to: the exceedingly shaky handwriting and tear stained paper bore witnesses to them. A future without Harold and the responsibility of an adult at her age, I could feel her desolation and wanted nothing more than to console her in person. Eventually, the misfortune extended its reaches out from the estate and towards me as well. On 2 September 1898, my regiment that had never seen battle before went into a full-scale charge. At the *Battle of Omdurman*, we were sent out to reconnoitre and clear the way. Unbeknown to us, along with the 400 men in plain sight, another thousands were concealed in the desert. The ground fell away as we charged revealing to us 3000 dervishes, grossly outnumbering us lancers. I was wounded and barely saved by my comrades. One injury was especially severe hurling me into an agonizing cycle of recovery and infection that would keep me at the threshold of death. After several months, I finally became well enough to voyage back in order to recuperate at our manor.

It was Evangeline who greeted me in the driveway, tears in her eyes. She flung herself at me, the arms tightly around my neck, and I was hit with the revelation of how she was changed: no longer did she resemble the little sister whose picture I carried in my pocket watch. It was the portrait of a doe-eyed thirteen-year-old that had yet to see the cruelty of the world. During my ordeal I venerated it like an icon, hoping every day to become better so that I may support her. In that moment of reunion, the long blonde hair flowed sensually, I could feel the softness of her bosom pressing firmly onto my chest, my arms wrapped around the slender waist that was no longer straight but curved, and I beheld the suggestive rose-tinted lips that called out my name. She had become a lady, graceful and refined. Lascivious. The familial love that I held for her, the love that was my bedrock in my times of pain and despair, eroded like sand revealing to me a sinister ocean of carnal desire. I loathed her for having grown up, erasing the existence of the pure child which I loved. I hated her for having become attractive – attractive to me. Yet more than her, I loathed myself and my shortcomings. The failure to treat her as I used to. The fact that she had become an adult was hard for me to accept, but then I was exploiting it. The stress of all those tragedies piled onto her, it must have created want for warmth and affection. Considering the promiscuous returnee who I was, maybe she was hoping that I would have fulfilled her longing? Even just once. I could only conclude that this was why she did not push me away. That physical gratification was the only reprieve from the gloomy cage that was Forestedge. At least it always was for me.

I awoke to the rhythmic prattle of raindrops on the windowpanes of the smoking room. The faint rays of the early sun dyed the misty morning in an ominous light, creating an otherworldly plain, and making me question the reality of the night's events. However, as I rose the blanket Evangeline had left in the evening fell off me. I could yet smell the beguiling scent that was clinging to the fleece. All of it truly transpired.

It was very early, a time at which I would usually not have been awake. Exiting the room, I almost ran into one of the servants as she rushed by. It was one of those that had been employed after I went away, so I did not pay attention to her person; not knowing her name nor her face. However, by her plain shirtwaist and skirt I could tell that she was Evangeline's lady's maid. Lanky, with a long, freckled face and thick hair that made it look as though her bun would burst any second, she seemed only slightly older than myself.

"Pardon, sir, and good morning." She said hurriedly, bowing to me.

"You, what's your name?" I asked, still tired.

"It's Eilers, sir." She said without any noticeable accent. Her name was strange.

"Is Evangeline awake, yet?" I inquired, as I hoped to seek her out before we would need to be seated together again at breakfast.

"Of course, sir. She is in the music room, same as every morning at this hour, sir." She answered courteously.

Thanking her, I headed off.

The soft sound of the piano filled the corridor of the ground level as I walked through it. Carefully, I opened the door. The tall windows were decorated with golden brocaded curtains. The light that flooded through the glass panes created a certain warmth, as it was reflected by the pale-yellow walls. A similar crème and gold brocaded fabric was used to upholster the group of armchairs and sofa in the seating area in the centre of the room. It was set on an oriental carpet. Near the piano there was a small table that held a vase with a bouquet of fresh freesias, tulips, and sweet peas. It must have been changed frequently, if she was to be there each morning. Aside of some ornate plastering on the ceiling, there were almost no other types of decoration in the room. The centre of attention was drawn towards a pastoral landscape painting over the fireplace, flanked by two pagan brass figurines, a faun, and a nymph, on the mantel. The only object that weighed down the light and airy atmosphere of the room was the dark grand piano. Evangeline was playing with her eyes closed, and as to not disturb her I went over to a nearby armchair to observe her. Her body gently swayed as she played an allegretto, which grew continuously into a more nostalgic and dramatic melody. Then she suddenly stopped.

"I dislike this section." She finally said, twisting her upper body around to look at me.

"You have become quite virtuous." I remarked.

"But only when it comes to Chopin's *Nocturnes*, I played them for hours to no end at Aunt Grace's request." She continued, turning back to the keyboard.

Her fingers were aimlessly jingling another tune.

"Yes, I remember you writing about that in a letter," I replied pensively, "Don't you feel tired of hearing them yourself?" Surely, it must have made her sad.

"No, I don't really mind. It has become a habit. Would you like me to play piece for you?"

"You know that I am not particularly cultured in any sense. I have no suggestions."

"Then I'll play one that I like," Evangeline said, commencing with

44

playing a new tune gentle enough to let me hear her say, "It often made me think of you."

The melody this time was less melancholic, it started gently and would gracefully leap upwards, repetitions flowing into each other, finally rising dramatically to end on a gentle accord. Unsure when or if I had heard it before, it still stirred a feeling of nostalgia within me.

"Forgive me, Evey." I said, after she concluded.

Not leaving the piano bench, she turned her full body around to face me.

"Whatever for?" she asked.

"You know exactly what for."

"Was that something you feel sorry for?" she inquired with an enigmatic expression on her face that I could not decipher.

For a few moments, I searched for the right words to say.

"Listen, Evey, I am being sincere when I apologise. I know, it must have been an insult to you. I should not have done those things, I was frustrated ... angry and ... I had too much to drink, too. Unfortunately, that what you saw and experienced is the way I really am like. I don't have temperance around beautiful women. I never had any. Therefore, you should be mindful of the fact that you can't act nonchalantly like a small child around me, because you aren't one anymore."

She briefly cast down her eyes at this explanation. It sounded very flippant to myself.

I continued, "You had a hard time — I appreciate that — and I am not sure whether it is because you are now at a rebellious age, if you felt like testing me because I have not been paying attention to you, or if—," I had to pause, "or if it is because you miss Harold dearly. I am sure you want attention, but that is not the right way to seek it nor am I the right person to receive it from. Not in this way. You are my sister, even if it is not by blood. And you are a lady. You should think about your conduct and reputation." It felt embarrassing and hypocritical to lecture her like that. It was contrary to my own actions and that of other ladies I knew at her age, and especially contrary to my real thoughts and desires, even in that moment.

Evangeline simply blinked at me, still a sphinx-like expression.

After a short silence she said, "Yes … you are right. We are like siblings, aren't we? I am sorry as well; I was carried away."

And then remembering Father's words I hurriedly insisted, "I know that you have suitors, don't do anything like that with them either."

The thought of it made my insides turn.

"I would never!" she answered flushed, almost angry. Then she muttered, "I wonder if you are even aware of all the inconsistencies?"

"Pardon?" I asked, not knowing what she meant.

"You are right. Let's forget what happened in the past two days and carry on like before." She said, turning around again to close the lid on the keyboard.

"Yes, and I will try to be mindful of you too. Father asked me to take you out more often in the future. Therefore, it is inevitable for us to be alone on some occasions."

"I see." She plainly answered, rising from the bench without looking at me. Without even turning around. Then she walked towards the door and said, "It is almost time for breakfast. You should change as well, Arthur." and exited.

In the afternoon we were requested to come together to Father's study. I was feeling nervous, thinking that maybe someone did see or hear us after all. I met Evangeline at his study door, she too seemed slightly anxious, and cast me a look of confusion.

Old Francis announced our coming and as we entered, Father sitting at his desk bid us sit in the chairs opposite of him, as jovial as ever. We both sat down at the same time.

"What is with the glum faces, children?" he inquired.

"It's nothing, sir." I replied instantly.

"Uncle Arthur, it is unusual for you to call us into your study together. Is there something amiss?" was Evangeline's unrestrained question.

"Nothing of that sort," he laughed, and then added, "The two of you are always so tense together. I have talked with Arthur about this matter already."

"Oh, yes, he has vaguely informed me." She said and glanced over to me.

Then Father went on to tell her the same things he had told me the previous night, and he further announced to us that there should be a private dinner soon, for which he wanted to invite the Thompsons.

"Thompson, do you mean senior or junior?" I interjected, remembering that he mentioned junior as a suitor for Evangeline.

"Junior, that is. Senior is on a business trip to the continent. This is the reason I have called both of you to come. Evey, I know that Thompson junior has been sending you letters as of recent, and that you have been in frequent contact with his sister Miss Violet Thompson. Thompson father and son were a great help during my illness; therefore, I was wanting to invite them over for a dinner. I have talked this matter over with Thompson senior and seeing that Arthur is at an age at which one should settle, it would not hurt to introduce Miss Thompson to him as well."

"Pardon, sir?" I blurted out.

Evangeline did say nothing, but her expression was also clearly that of surprise.

"I am not in the reserves yet, only recuperating. As we talked before, sir, I will return to my regiment as soon as my health allows for it. And even then, I am not considering marriage at all."

"I know very well that you prefer to stay a bachelor, the Lord knows for how long. However, the way in which you consort with the fairer sex is not good for your reputation if you ever want to start a family of your own with a decent woman. It would do you better to calm down. While I am not implying that you should court Miss Thompson straight away, boy, there would be no harm for the two of you to become acquainted. She is of a good house, and I am sure Thompson senior would ensure that both of you are looked after. It would do you well to find a spouse to support you with your meagre wages as Lance Corporal." He said dismissively.

In the past I would have instantly flown into a rage, but as the tension was putting both my brittle father and Evangeline on edge, I chose to stay silent.

"As for Evey, you would feel more comfortable with having her here along with her brother, wouldn't you?" he asked subsequently turning to her.

After presenting us with these propositions, he continued to explain to us that since they came all the way from Edinburgh, we should accommodate them for a few days, and prepare some activities. The dinner idea had suddenly expanded to a three-day visit. All the while, I was wondering whatever happened to his speech about allowing Evangeline some time of enjoyment, for he was then evidently pushing her in the direction of Thompson junior and burdening her with responsibilities of the lady of the house again. It irritated me more than the fact that he was trying to set me up with a lady. Evangeline simply nodded and agreed, promising to fulfil her duties, and we both were sent out of the study again.

Afterwards, the two of us went to the reading room to discuss the matter. As the day before, I placed myself on the sofa while she sat down in the armchair.

"Whatever is Father thinking?" I wondered irritated.

"This has been a point of discussion more than once; I was honestly surprised about the request that he formulated towards you. After all I could go to those places if I took Eilers along as chaperone." Evangeline mused pensively.

"Why do you reckon he asked that of me then?"

"He wants to control you. He may suppose that if you spend time with me, you will not be out fooling around. In addition, I think that with regard to his health, he feels rushed to see both of us set." She said.

There was a perceptive answer I would not have thought of, probably as I already was thinking licentious things whilst I sat alone with Evangeline. Remembering the previous day as well, she became conscious of herself. She started to fidget with her hands, labouring to not look at me. We discussed what it was that was expected of us and what we should even do with the Thompsons.

"And you? How do you feel about this?" I asked finally.

"I think that Violet will not be to your liking." She answered plainly, ignoring any other possible implication my question held.

"Why is that?" I inquired, curious as to what she considered 'not to my liking'.

"It is hard for me to explain. You will see for yourself when you meet her." She responded, and to my surprise smiled at me exuding the same enigmatic airs she had around her in the morning. We left the reading room with each of us pursuing our own activities for the rest of the day, not being in another's company beyond supper.

The following day, it was curious to see that she had changed the way she wore her hair. In order to appear more mature, I supposed. From a generous gap between the collar of her day dress it was all tied up, with an intricate *chignon* — exposing a thin fragment of flesh, the tender and alluring nape of the neck.

4
'Ave ye heard the Crack?

The weeks passed with Evangeline being busy preparing for the guests. As opposed to what I had initially expected, she was far more mature than I thought her to be. In the time we spent apart our encounters had become water under the bridge. With passing time, I even became able to ride out again in the morning. Yet only for short durations as the stress on my body was making it still too painful. A day before the arrival of the guests, I went to my bi-weekly check-up at Doctor Armitage's quarters in the west wing, where all guest apartments were located.

"It's a shame, young Clarence, such a ghastly scar. I can only trust that they did their best, but I'm certain that this is not the best it could have been." The doctor said, whilst I was putting my shirt back on, "However, there really is nothing more that can be done about it now."

"I'm happy enough to have survived in that claggy hospital in Halfa, there were others not that fortunate." I said.

Thinking back to the situation in Sudan, I was truly blessed to have returned home, but it was even more of a blessing for us to have come out as victors. With that in mind, my wounds did not seem that bad as they were not in vain, and I added, "For honour and duty's sake, this is nothing."

Doctor Armitage threw me a bemused look and then chuckled.

"Pardon, young Clarence, I don't mean ill by it. It is just… who would have thought that those words would ever come from you? You truly have changed." He said with a benevolent grin.

As I looked at his gaunt bespectacled face, with the rough, craggy lines being softened by blue eyes that sparkled with amusement, I could feel my own become hot with embarrassment. It was true that none of those words had meant anything to me before and having me of all people utter them must have undoubtedly seemed alien to the doctor. However, he used to be in the Army himself, so he must have been sincere.

Doctor Alasdair Armitage had been the village surgeo for near to thirty years, and only recently retired. Despite his age, he was still sturdy and energetic. With the crown of his head bold, only the hair on the sides framing his face, the bony long fingers — as bony as the rest of his frame — he reminded me of a library-dwelling scholar, rather than a seasoned physician that was used to being called for all over the place. Leaving his practice to one of his younger colleagues, the old bachelor was invited to become the live-in physician at Forestedge. With Father having taken ill, and remaining weak ever since, a permanently present physician was helpful to Evangeline. The doctor was trusted by our family, not only because he helped during my complicated birth, but also with those of the unfortunate siblings of mine that did either not see the light of the day or died in infancy. Other than that, he was always called upon when there were injuries — of which there were many — to be treated, when family members, or even servants had taken ill. Having thus spent a lot of time at Forestedge, becoming part of the household only seemed natural.

"The service changed me, that is a certainty." I concurred, looking him square in the eyes.

My gaze must have somehow intimidated him, for he nervously adjusted his spectacles. With an insecure clearing of his throat, he apologised, "It was not meant as an attack young Clarence. I must say to some extent, I do wish that you'd return to your carefree ways again. However, in moderation."

"You probably are the only one, Doctor," I replied, smiling wryly. "If that is all … I will head out now."

"Just a moment young Clarence, it is not for your body alone that we meet up, but also for your mind. You are still afflicted by that perpetual gloom, it seems. I was told that you sleep in the smoking room and drink there in solitude. It's not advisable, and I recommend you stop that habit."

"Who told you this?" I asked, offended.

"Miss Hollings did, of course." He replied, with a surprised expression.

"She did ... did she—. When did you talk to her?"

"Occasionally, Miss Hollings comes to talk to me. As you may know, her spirits too had been low for a long time due to all the emotionally distressing events of the past years. It is amazing how a young lady such as herself was able to keep up such a strong front and care for your ill father, even though her inward world looked quite different. I was worried about her mental state several times. However ... " he said, while alternately stroking each cheek of his clean shaven face as a form of meditative movement.

"However?"

"Let me say this: ever since you have returned, she appears much better. Maybe, young Clarence, you should spend more time with her like you used to? Then you as well could improve."

Better because of me? We hardly interacted with each other and the last thing we did together ... I'd rather not have thought about it, nor the advice of the doctor to 'spend more time.' It would be averse to my emotional recovery.

"She is the industrious lady of the house now, Doctor. I would not want to disturb her with her duties." I said, rising from the sofa and going over to the door to exit.

"Well, it is a mere suggestion. While it is good for you to do exercise, you mustn't be alone all the time. It will not improve your state of mind." He castigated me with a stern look.

Standing motionless, I did not answer to his comment only looking at him disdainfully.

"Young Clarence, if you refuse even this method maybe I should prepare laudanum for you after all. It will not only help with the pain but with your mood, too."

"This again … Doctor, I told you that I even resisted the morphine as much as I could when in the hospital." I rebuffed him.

During the months in the ward, I saw how some of the convalescent soldiers had become desperately addicted to opiates over the course of their recovery, and it was a disturbing sight. Not only that memory appalled me, I too, had once gone along to an opium den and tried the drug: some people might have found relief in the tranquillity it provided them, but I felt panicked and trapped.

"If I want comfort, I'll find it with a woman. That will lift not only my spirits, but hers too." was my vulgar quip to distract the doctor from providing any other 'good advice.'

"I see that old habits die hard." He chuckled.

After that final remark, I bid him a good morning.

When I walked down the hallway, I could hear cheerful chatter escape from one of the apartments. The maids were taking their time cleaning the chambers for our guests. Concealing the noise of my footsteps, I came to stand close to the frame of the fully opened door, for I could have sworn that I heard my name being dropped in their conversation … and I was right. Again, I was the topic of gossip. I quickly peeked in to have a look at the servants. Because they were changing the linen of the bed, I was only able to see them from the back with a fleeting glimpse of their profiles. Two maids, one stout and quite young, the other one exceedingly plain and somewhat older. The younger one appeared to be from the area as she was strenuously hiding an accent, while her elder had a more refined speech.

"I did see Master Arthur up close on the landing. It was my first time!" the younger one said.

"Isn't he dashingly handsome?"

"My word! Truly smart!" the young one exclaimed, then pondered, "Although, he never smiles. Josie told me he had the most charming smile."

"Has he? I did not work here either when he was younger. He seems rather dark and gloomy … and they say his character is awful." The older one mused.

Then they both sighed.

"What a waste of fine-looking gentleman. The black sheep of the Clarences. I didn't know Mister Harold for that long, but he was such a wonderful and warm person. Andrew always talks of him admiringly and has been telling me how young Master Arthur was nothing but trouble to his brother. Mister Harold was always chasing after him and had to own up to his mistakes, too … Poor Mister Harold, may he rest in peace. To be so different from each other even though they were brothers." The maid with seniority deliberated.

"Andrew must know, he has been working here for so long. But to openly hate Master Arthur?"

"Oh, Andrew simply hates young Master Arthur, for several reasons. One of them is that he supposedly broke his arm when he was only a page boy in this house."

"He did? How horrible."

It was a story I did not think much about, but young Francis never seemed to have let go off. When I was eight and he ten, I was in the gardens having a lesson with my Aunt Gwen. She was teaching me about the plants and birds that could be found outside. Having forgot the pencils, she went back into the mansion to retrieve them for drawing purposes. Without supervision and bored, I tried to scale a ladder over the high hedges. However, the crooked construct leant to the side, and I tumbled down falling squarely into the dirt below. Young Francis, who as a newly employed page boy then helped the gardener with an odd job, saw and laughed. Surely, it was not meant maliciously. Only as malicious as a child's spontaneous laughter would have been. However, I lost my temper and lunged at him. We were caught up in a scuffle rolling around in the garden bed, while the adult servant was helplessly watching on. And then, me, unaware to our surroundings threw young Francis on his back, and in that action his arm hit the ladder that was still lying in the grass. Reappearing suddenly, my aunt pulled me away, stopping me from injuring young Francis even worse. This was one of the instances to which Doctor Armitage was called. It was a clean break, but it must have been very painful for the young page. Of course, my parents were mortified by this violent outburst of mine. They apologised to old Francis, who exhibited more understanding than either of them. I was punished with a caning — a common routine that made me none the wiser — and the whole thing was taken care of by Father paying for all medical expenses and giving both Francis' an adequate recompense.

"However, he never talks about it. Surely his father does not allow it, because as the head of all servants he needs to protect his masters' honour. I only heard it from Josie, too." The elder one explained.

It was impressive to hear that old Francis was keeping his own son in check. He was a commendable example of a loyal servant, even though it was for Father's sake and not for me that he was doing it.

"It's not the only reason Andrew dislikes him so. The young master and the miss were really close in the past, even though it does not look like it now."

"They were?" the local maid exclaimed, astonished.

"Aside of the stories told, one can tell by all the photographs in the manor. In them, she's always close to him and not Mister Harold," the other one said, and added, "Like true siblings. She cherishes him, it seems. I was there with the other servants that greeted Master Arthur upon his arrival. She flung herself at him so passionately, and I saw how Andrew's face darkened. It's pure jealousy."

"Jealousy, indeed! He adores the ground on which the miss treads ... He was so happy to be promoted to valet, personally aiding, and following the master. Only because it meant being able to ogle Miss Evangeline all day."

They let out spiteful cackles, while I took this information in, reminding myself to keep an eye on young Francis whenever he was around Evangeline.

"She is a wonderful lady. Taking up so many responsibilities at her age ... to think we are the same age! Such an angel, to take care of her family so well, even though they aren't related by blood." The younger maid proclaimed admiringly.

"It shows that pedigree is everything. Well but maybe not with regard to Master Arthur ..." the older maid sighed.

"They say that he needs rest, having fought valiantly in Sudan ... but really, all he does is ride out, wander around the premises or lounge in one of the rooms. Isn't he a loiter-sack? He should be helping the master." The young maid said derisively.

"Yes, he has been nothing but a bother to the master. Everyone says that," The older maid agreed, and with her penchant for going into detail continued, "to take him back after he disgraced the family and ran away. In many ways he is such a kind and good master. I've worked in another mansion before and was not even treated half as well as I have been treated at Forestedge. I've worked here four years now and I really cannot complain."

"Truly, such a good master, he is."

"But he keeps having a hard time upholding his good reputation due to young Master Arthur. I heard how supposedly the master had to pay big amounts of monies to servants, to prevent them from breathing a word about a certain scandalous event that took place here."

"What really? Because of Master Arthur?"

"Complete and utter silence. No one is allowed to talk about it, Mr Francis will admonish anyone whom he catches even alluding to it ... but they say he was involved with a maid!" The elder maid said, half-whispering but still loud enough for me to hear.

"A maid? You don't mean he put his hands on her?!"

"I don't know ... but really I wouldn't mind if he was to put them on me."

And they laughed. Dirty, uninhibited laughs.

Father was too kind to the household staff for them to have the audacity to blather like that within the manor. I alerted them to my presence with a heavy stomp and went to stand in the door frame. They both were startled, only the older one daring to turn around. With a hoarse voice she greeted me and bowed deeply. Then urged the other to do the same, even though she was frozen in the motion of holding the linen up. Finally, she too, was able to turn around and do as bid without lifting her eyes. I quietly glared at them and nodded. Both swiftly turned their backs towards me again, unable to think about what the best course of action would be. While leaning in the door frame I looked on, as they wordlessly and frantically attempted to work. Like witless, little mice they scurried around the bed, continuing to change the linen. Even though they had finished the task before my appearance. After feeling that I've intimidated them enough, I went my way. No other sound than that of maids pursuing their work left that guest apartment thereafter, while I walked over to the main landing.

Thankfully, I went to the doctor's quarters readily changed in my walking attire, for I could not bear to stay a second longer in these stuffy halls. It wasn't only Evangeline who was weighing negatively on my mind, it was the whole household. My sentiments towards this place hadn't changed even one bit. Quite the opposite, after the military service I hated it even more. It was hardly comfortable. I hated having to be indoors, because while the servants were never visible, they were somehow still omnipresent. With their omnipresence, they furthermore seemed omniscient: about our lives, our habits, and the good and bad qualities all of us bore. Whereas I knew nothing about those that lived and thrived off the Clarence name. Not even most of their faces. For that reason, I truly detested being served or waited on. What would they do after observing my actions and demeanour? Gossip in their servant's hall, in their quarters, and apparently even in our living area. Gossip about how 'Young master decided to wear these clothes today' and how 'Master

Arthur said this and that to the miss and mister.' The only purpose of this practice being to dispel their boredom in this remote place, and to bond within their class against the hand that fed them. The awareness of their inability to ever bite it was in the back of their heads. In truth however, they knew as little about us as we did about them, as they only observed and served but never interacted with us as people. Especially with regard to my person, it seemed that nobody was putting them in their place. However, that was already the case before I left.

As I walked through the lobby, I came across Evangeline who was wearing a crème coloured, long-sleeved tea gown. A green sash tightly fastened around her waist emphasised her waistline, showing that she was not wearing a corset beneath it. She greeted me with a cheerful smile, which I found unusual. Yet, I could not help but feel refreshed by it. We chatted briefly about how the preparations were going and how she was looking forward to seeing her friend again. The friend about whom we haven't talked at all since she last mentioned her to me in the reading room.

Then, looking at my attire she asked, "Are you going out for a ride in that dress?"

"No, I will only be taking a walk." I replied hastily, as I finally wished to leave.

"I've been so busy these past weeks, I was not able to talk to you at all," she said, looking at me shyly, then inquired, "and it would be nice to get some fresh air. Do you mind if I join you?"

"Evey, you never take walks beyond the garden of the manor." I rebuked her, impatiently.

"Isn't that where you are going?"

"I am not."

"Then where are you going?" she asked, wonder in her face.

"It does not matter where; you are not appropriately clothed for it either."

"I could change! I was … when you last asked me to join you for a walk, I was waiting for you to do it again … but you never did. Can I really not join you?" she said eagerly and looked at me with imploring eyes.

When was it that I invited her? It must have been almost one month or more already, and she was patiently waiting for me to ask her? It was typical of her to say nothing. To not to state her desires. That was however for the better. Better for me.

"No, I'd rather be alone today." I answered, avoiding her gaze.

"I see … I'm sorry for imposing on you." She replied, despondently.

"Maybe some other time." I responded without thinking, as I beheld her. I disliked seeing her with a dejected expression on her pretty face, "I'll take you along some other day."

She then smiled again and bid me an enjoyable walk. Of course, it was an empty promise. The last thing I wanted currently, after being the object of gossip within the house, was being alone with Evangeline. Alone, in some place where there was nobody watching over her.

5
A Sibling Rivalry

The scenery was growing ever verdant, it became a good time to visit the lakes and fells of Cumberland as we were at the beginning of the third week of May. It was the time for the stay of the Thompson siblings that would last three days. Daniel Thompson, I faintly remembered. He was one year younger than Harold and they both visited Eton. Despite that they were never more than acquaintances through connection. He was of moderate height, significantly shorter than me. Nonetheless, Thompson stood upright and assured, not intimidated. As Thompson senior was a dandy, Daniel Thompson must have internalised his father's habits. Thompson junior was a man that paid attention to aesthetics in himself and others, noticeable by the way he scrutinised both, Evangeline, and me. He was wearing the most fashionable sack coat with matching waistcoat, trousers that had creases, a silken cravat, and finely polished oxfords. Beneath the light-grey felt hat, the dark blonde hair was carefully groomed backwards. He was the perfectly outfitted gentleman, but unbefittingly dressed for the countryside. His overall appearance was so contrasting to my own, who chose to be in a tweed Norfolk jacket with matching breeches, cap, and riding boots all day. Equally contrasting were the two ladies: while Evangeline attempted to look her best in a green, French-silk reception dress with chic leg-of-mutton sleeves, Miss Violet Thompson sported casual wear. A plain blue and white cotton ensemble with a boating hat on top of her light-brown braided hair. However, this was not where their differences ended. Although of same height as Evangeline, Miss Violet had the chin raised, sharply gazing through her gold-rimmed spectacles. Her air of confidence and complacence highlighted her ungraceful posture. It slowly dawned on me what Evangeline meant with 'not to my liking.' Despite that she evidently had a handsome figure.

They greeted Father first, and we did our formal introductions, shaking hands as was appropriate. Even though his gentlemanly smile suggested otherwise, I could sense within the firmness of Thompson's grip a trace of hostility towards my person. Deciding to ignore it for the moment, I then greeted his sister, who in contrast to him seemed to weaken her gesture the longer I looked her into the eye. Not anymore expressing her previous confidence, her gaze shyly wandered over my shoulder. What was furthermore curious to me was that along with the customary flowers for the hostess, Miss Violet decided to gift Evangeline a poetry anthology by a French author. It was a very flashy choice, in my opinion.

The guests retired to their quarters and remerged refreshed from their abode to the private dinner. Even then one could see the contrast between the Thompson siblings, for the brother aimed to look his best while the sister put in the minimum effort. At least in that point both of us seemed alike. I was in informal attire, but Thompson was wearing his full formal evening suit, and Miss Violet was in something that looked like an old demi-toilet which had lace added to it. To honour the importance of our visitors and mark her first time as hostess, Evangeline wore an exquisite golden dinner gown with extravagantly puffed sleeves and a finely rhinestone embroidered bodice. It matched her blonde hair and made her shine. A thick layer of yellow organza covered her up to the neck, exposing less skin than I had expected to see, but it drew the focus onto the curves of her waist. Although it suited her well, she appeared insecure wearing something so lavish. I as well, found it hard to get used to her mature appearance.

For the occasion, Doctor Armitage who usually preferred to take meals alone, joined us for dinner. Thus, we all were seated, with Father as the host at the top, Evangeline to his right and me to his left. Thompson was choicely sat next to her, and Miss Violet insipidly to my right, with the doctor next to our female guest. As the hostess, Evangeline unfortunately struggled to uphold conversations and so the topics often shifted between the estate, the weather and other trifling matters, until it finally hit my person.

"Mr Clarence, I heard that your rank in the cavalry was that of a Lance Corporal. I am not very learned on military ranks, but it is not a commissioned rank, is it? Even though you went to Sandhurst?" Miss Violet said, rather intrusively.

"Miss Thompson, Arthur did not complete his stay at Sandhurst." Father answered for me, embarrassment written all over his face.

"Oh, you did not? That is quite curious for someone of such an esteemed house. Do you mind my asking why?" inquired Thompson.

It must have been a grand piece of gossip — a true delicacy for the higher circles — when I petulantly ran off. Hence, I was uncertain whether the Thompson siblings were being ignorant or brazen with their inquisition, or even both. Especially considering the close business ties of my family to the Thompsons. I masked my annoyance and went along with their pretence.

"I was an impatient youth, therefore I enlisted and started off as a Trooper with the 21st Hussars." I said, for in truth I refused to go to Sandhurst altogether.

I failed entrance on purpose. After escaping from conflict within the mansion I secretly enlisted and stayed with my cousin until my conscription was irrevocable. It was the final act of rebellion of my adolescence. If I was going to join the military, I decided that it would be on my own terms. I refused to be later paraded around for prestige. Father, yet again upset by my out of line behaviour, refused any financial support for me, and I received my just deserts for this naive move once the basic training started. A spoilt upper-class whelp such as I, was shocked at how little 1.2 Shillings pay a day in actuality were. The pay dwindling away with lacking care for equipment and surroundings, I was forced to pull myself together if I did not want to be disrespected and penniless. Ironically, I was thus spurred on to aim for good-conduct badges and to undertake extra duties, all leading to my promotion.

"A Trooper, yes … of what rank … ?"

"A Private."

"A Private? With the mean people?" Miss Violet exclaimed shocked. She was obviously ignorant.

"I can understand young Clarence's sentiments. I as well enlisted right after I graduated and was deployed into action during the *Indian Mutiny*. Some men simply are men of action." Doctor Armitage said sympathetically, even though having been the family physician for that long made him know what the true reason for my hurried departure was.

"However, isn't the skirmish at *Omdurman* the first time the 21st Lancers actually saw action. You were in India before. The involvement in Sudan was in retrospect not the best thing to happen to your regiment. Without wanting to offend you Clarence, it was an unnecessarily costly and antiquated thing, this full-scale cavalry charge. It could have been altogether avoided considering the modern technology at our Army's disposal." Thompson said brazenly.

The room fell silent as this challenge was thrown onto the table.

"Having Gordon revenged is not something that can be weighed up with money." I answered, hardly concealing my offense. For several reasons this attack appeared to me personal. To have it labelled as 'unnecessary' and 'antiquated' made the red badge I had carried away from that day sting even fiercer than usual.

"Indeed, young Clarence's regiment was crucial in restoring our honour. This comes at no price." Doctor Armitage insisted with cordiality.

However, it was Miss Violet who interjected in what I could only assume to have been an attempt at being as much involved in the conversation as possible: "Oh, I did read about this in *The Contemporary Review*. You say revenged, but did Baron Kitchener not go too far with his revenge by slaughtering the wounded enemy?"

As I was already goaded on by her brother, I shared my unchecked opinion with her and everyone else, "Miss Thompson, it is easy to criticise if one did not throw their own weight against the desperate *Mahdists*. It was a carnage that resulted in the loss of several of my brothers in arms. If you had experienced the valour their faith gave them, you would know that they needed to be snuffed out then and there, all in order to avoid future resurgences. And with the way most of them were maimed, ending them was an act of mercy."

Miss Violet, intimidated, averted her gaze while Thompson appeared unimpressed. A profuse cough cut through the strained atmosphere.

"Gentlemen, Miss Thompson, please! This is a topic for the smoking room. Ladies these days seem very keen on politics, however I think it is best discussed over a drink and cigarettes without people of delicate disposition among the listeners." Father urged, hinting at Evangeline who was wordlessly listening to the discussion and casting a disturbed look at me in particular.

Thus, there was no further discussion on political affairs, and dinner was eventually concluded a short time later with port being enjoyed along the planned evening programme.

For the evening entertainment afterwards, Evangeline decided to play some tunes to welcome the guests and we all went to the music room. Conscious about Father's presence she did not play anything romantic like she would play every morning. The solemnity of the final piece she played contrasted the raw emotions expressed in the daily nocturnes, as it carried a hint of melancholy. The low rising accords and technical trills that required minute control made Evangeline as well appear different from when I last observed her play.

"Sublime!" Thompson said as he clapped. It was the word that would not come to my mind. He stepped up to the piano and casually lent onto it to look at Evangeline.

"If I am not mistaken then this was the *Sonatina* from Bach's *Actus Tragicus*. You played it from memory even though it usually is a duet, that is very impressive." He said. While his tone was mild and courteous, the intensity of his body language kept me on edge.

Smiling politely, she answered, "You are right Mr Thompson, I as well am impressed that you knew."

"I told you that she liked *Bach*! It is so befitting of you Evangeline. Although, it is so very, hum … pastoral … quite tepid. Is that really the type of music you enjoy?" Miss Violet interjected, rudely.

"It is what I like to play the most." Evangeline replied, blushing.

Thompson, keeping up his gallant smile reprimanded his sister.

"Now Violet, is that really something you should say to our hostess? I can only wonder as to how you treat a friend. To criticise her so …" He pointed out. It appeared that he was used to chiding her, as he sounded more annoyed than embarrassed.

Straightening her spectacles, she faced her brother and said, "She is my friend, and therefore I think it is very well for me to state my opinion. Do you disagree, Evangeline?"

"Yes, you are right, Violet." Was her quaint answer.

Father, the doctor and I were silently observing the scene from our seats. While Father seemed to take joy in watching a group of young people engaging in trivial chitchat, the event further laid out to me that both Thompsons would not be pleasant company. Not pleasant to me, that was.

"See, Daniel? Evangeline is a sensible person that is open to criticism. Say, would you know how to play a piece by *Tosti, Satie* or *Debussy*? Papa wrote us that you cannot go into a *Salon* in Paris without hearing their tunes."

"No, I can't. I do not have any sheets of them either. I apologise."

"Oh, of course. It would be hard to come by them here, would it not? Maybe I should have brought some as a gift. I am sorry for being so negligent." She apologised, sounding more condescending than sincere.

"Maybe you should have, after all you have not touched the piano in years. It's a shame. You have no other accomplishments." Thompson remarked and thus seemed to hit a nerve with Miss Violet, who then went off to argue petulantly, "Well, let our sisters have a go at it. I do not think any modern woman needs to be confined to her piano as a sole piece of accomplishment. After all we are capable of intellectual reading, and of daringly riding horses, just as well as you men!"

Yet again it sounded to me like an insult towards Evangeline.

Thompson smiled amused upon hearing this statement and then turned to look at me, asking, "What do you think Clarence, is she right?"

Knowing his sister, he skilfully deflected her energies.

"On the matter of reading, I would agree. Evey, for example, is well read as opposed to me. On the matter of horse riding: I cannot tell." I answered slowly, contemplating on how to not further get into their argument. Miss Violet ignored the first part of my answer and readily reproached me, as though she was waiting for an opportunity to do so, "It is because you are a cavalryman that you would not think much of female equestrians, am I right? Evangeline surely is just as capable!"

An uncomfortable tension rose in the room as Miss Violet was trying to prove her dominance. Then finally, Evangeline spoke up.

"Pardon Violet, as you know, I have not ridden a horse in almost three years. As a matter of fact, I would rather we did not talk about it altogether." Ever the graceful hostess, she retained her warm smile, the stress only visible in her hands.

"Oh— oh, of course! I am so sorry. I do apologise for upsetting you." Our guest stammered, flustered. Her confidence was whisked away, as she remembered the importance of Evangeline's remark. Beseechingly she alternately looked to her and to Father, only briefly glancing over to my person. Exercising his usual jovial bearing, Father attempted to soothe our guest's anxiety.

"That is quite all right, Miss Thompson. You were not aiming to upset any of us." He assured her. I was in doubt of this observation. In the least she was aiming to challenge me and possibly attempting to incite Evangeline to join into an argument.

"I am enjoying this carefree atmosphere. Speaking of Paris, how is your father's business fairing?" Father inquired.

"Very well, sir. Thank you. He is busy liaising and arranging with all the partners for the next *Paris Exhibition*." Thompson answered.

"*Paris Exhibition?*" I interjected, a faint memory springing up in my mind.

"Yes. It is less than a year but there is so much to do." He replied, with a look that questioned how I could not have known about the next *Exhibition*.

"Is it in Paris again? I forgot all about it being next year. I remember that we went the last time it was there. It was such a wonderful experience." Evangeline said excitedly, then beaming happily at Father and me.

"Indeed, it was." Father agreed, returning her smile. He seemed quite pleased.

"Oh, you did, Evangeline? Did you ascend the Eiffel Tower then? How was it? It must be like seeing one of the *Wonders of the World*. It must be magnificent!" Miss Violet prattled on with childish enthusiasm. For the first time that day she seemed genuine.

"I only managed to go up the first level, which was already quite frightening. But Arthur went all the way up, he even received a medal for reaching the top." Evangeline elaborated and eyed me with admiration.

"Did I receive such a thing?" I wondered aloud.

It was hard for me to sort through all those memories of the multitude of impressions that we took away from the visit to the Exhibition.

"Yes, you gave it to me. Don't you remember?" she insisted eagerly.

"How was the view, Mr Clarence? I so wish Papa would take me to Paris, too." Miss Violet interjected agitated, before I could answer the previous question.

"It was … spectacular … I suppose." I answered.

I hardly remembered the view from the tower, as I was exhausted from walking all day and climbing all the stairs. As soon as I reached the top level, I too was starting to feel anxious about the height and did not stay long enough to take in the view properly.

"Is that it? You are not very well versed, are you, Mr Clarence?" Miss Violet said with a disappointed sneer.

"Well, as the doctor pointed out he seems to be a man of *action* rather than *words*. Isn't that right?" Thompson noted merrily, looking over to me.

"I am." I answered, plainly staring back at him.

The talks about the past and upcoming exhibition continued for a while until it was time for the ladies to retire to their chambers. As always, I would go to the smoking room and invited everyone out of courtesy. For obvious reasons Father would decline, and Doctor Armitage who was not keen on drinking, did not join in as well. It was only Thompson and I that eventually went there. Fortunately, it was old Francis who was minding us, as I would have been twice as cross if I had to have his son in the smoking room with me. As we sat down Thompson noticed the family portrait.

"What a superb work of art. It must be made by a master. Your brother looks just like I remember him from Eton. He was such an admirable student. Especially watching him play cricket made me regret my choice in sports. I would have liked to join him. I was on the rowing team, however."

"He had that quality. He made things look enjoyable, no matter what he did." I said. After all, as a child watching him ride made me enthusiastic about it, too.

"Does that mean you played cricket at your school?"

"No, I was on the polo team."

"As expected of someone who joined the cavalry. Do you still play?"

"My injury does not permit it at present."

"It is quite a shame to become an invalid. What use is there to a cavalryman that cannot ride his horse?" he commented casually, yet I could clearly discern his ill-intent.

"Thompson, it seems to me that you are not particularly good with words either, or are you plainly insulting me?" I asked while setting down my whiskey tumbler.

"Did I? Please accept my apologies. I seem to forget my manners when I am exposed to my sister for too long. Violet is so straightforward it's contagious." He answered, again with his mannerly yet snide smile.

I knew them too well these types of upper-class sons, as I was surrounded by them in boarding school. Shrewd, arrogant, and calculating; attempting to provoke their opponents until they revealed a weakness, eventually inciting them to do a misstep. Had I been younger, I would have been provoked enough to start a physical altercation. But age did make wiser. To what end he was doing it, was yet not clear to me. Thus, I stayed silent.

He then continued, "Violet has always been rambunctious, especially with her lofty dreams of taking up undergraduate studies. It makes her interfere. Yet, she has her good qualities, too. She is more delicate than one would think. I hope the two of you can get along."

"I will be mindful of that."

"Miss Hollings, it seems, was a sweet little angel then." Thompson noted, looking at the portrait again.

"She is." I answered without thinking.

"You cherish her, Clarence."

"Of course, I do."

"Yes, of course. You are family. I can relate. Even I value my sister."

With this ambiguous statement, there was nothing more of importance for the two of us to discuss, and we finished our drinks and cigarettes discussing trivial things.

After Thompson retired for the evening, I as per usual stayed on. Shortly after the long case clock chimed eleven, the door creaked open. It was Evangeline, of course. Having hitherto lied stretched out on the méridienne I simply turned my head to look over to her who was once again taking a seat in the armchair next to me.

"You again? What are you doing here?" I asked, not rising. She carelessly waltzed in, only wearing her nightgown and dress.

"I wanted to see the portrait." She replied. Her face was turned towards the painting opposite the chaise longue.

"At this hour?"

"A poem in the volume Violet has given me made me think of it." She answered, and I then noticed the book she had brought along.

"Your eyesight will deteriorate like hers, if you read in your room at night." I chided her.

"Ah, but you used to read fairy tales with me in bed and your eyes seem fine." She laughed.

It was peculiar to hear her laughter because there was a hint of sadness within. Growing impatient I asked her if she was taking pleasure in bothering me with poetry in the smoking room.

"And if I did? Would you let me read it to you then?" she teased.

Not declining, I had become curious in what made her come all this way. Evangeline understood my cue as I closed my eyes to hear her read the poem called 'Semper Eadem.' The purpose and meaning of it completely failed me, and saying so to her, she simply chuckled.

"Hearing it once is not enough, I suppose."

"Once is more than enough for me." I answered irritated.

Opening my eyes to look at her again, I saw that she was still staring at the portrait. Silently, pensively, sad. The young woman in her white nightgown was a stark contrast to that round-faced little girl in the frame.

"It is odd, but before we talked about it, it had completely escaped my mind that we had such an enjoyable time at the Paris Exhibition. It is like a dream, just as phantasmagorical as the painting." She mused; her gaze forlorn.

The portrait was made the same year. I, as well, only then remembered the trip to Paris. Our first and only travel abroad as a family. We reminisced about the days we spent there, running around excitedly to see everything but never being able to see all. She was but a small child that easily grew tired, and I carried her on my back for long stretches. However, I was just as much of a child as her, in view of all the wonders we experienced at the Exhibition. An ever-shifting vista of sights, sounds, and tastes. Machines and structures that towered over us like giants. Cultures that were so alien and strange, but still part of the same world we inhabited. The exposition of all achievements past and to come. We were full of unadulterated wonder for what the future would hold and what infinite possibilities lay in front of us. And I saw the future borne onto us that day in Sudan. Men slain worse than cattle. It did not matter if friend or foe. They were all maimed, shredded, and then expired. All by the accomplishments of the past, then present. It was a terrifying vision. The memory of the exhibition let me faintly remember a forgotten feeling of enthusiasm. But that feeling would not last. The present had deviated too much from what I envisioned as boy. It was the same with Evangeline. As I saw her past and present selves juxtaposed in front of me it became more apparent than before: I cherished her in the past, and I cherished her in the present. But somewhere along the way I forgot how to do it with sincerity.

"I was not a burden to you then, was I?" she asked.

"Of course not. You never are." I answered.

With a pleased smile on her face Evangeline rose from the armchair.

She bid me good night and vanished just as fast as she had appeared. Looking again over to the portrait of the happy and proud family, the only words which I could retain from the poem, came to mind: 'To live is a curse! a secret known to all.'

6
Inclination

In the morning of the second day of the Thompsons' visit, we set out for a hillwalking trip to Windermere. The small town that had grown around its railway station was not very far situated from the estate. The boarding school that I used to attend was around the area, as well. The prospect of seeing another familiar landscape other than that of the estate's again invoked a feeling of nostalgia. Our starting point was the Windermere Hotel from which we would ascend Orrest Head to get a view on the Windermere Lake, and the fells nearby. It was an easy enough walk of 2.5 miles that any urban dweller could manage. Afterwards, we could enjoy refreshments at the hotel while we waited for the train. Or at least that was the initial plan.

Evangeline was wearing a subtle hiking dress which still made her look refined, and as to highlight its impracticality, Miss Violet wore an ensemble of almost the same fabric with knickerbockers. Thompson as well, was wearing hiking attire, in which he appeared to be uncomfortable. Setting out as a group, I let the three of them walk slightly in front of me.

"What a lovely day for hillwalking! The weather is quite beckoning." Thompson exclaimed while looking into the blue sky.

"You say that, brother, but you never seemed to feel beckoned by similar weather in Edinburgh. Even though there is a hill to walk up, and *I* have invited you several times to join me."

"'A hill for magnitude, a mountain in virtue of its bold design.' It's hardly somewhere you just go for a morning hill walk, Violet."

"As per usual you use magnificent phrases, because you are too ashamed to admit your own indolence, Daniel." Miss Violet teased her brother who was evidently annoyed.

Their bickering went on. All the while, Evangeline turned to the side and snickered stealthily behind her hand at the sibling squabble. She appeared to take great joy in their company.

"Do you do a lot of hillwalking, Mr Clarence?" Miss Violet asked, turning around.

"I don't." I answered curtly.

"He walks the estate grounds for hours almost every day, but no one really knows where he is until he returns. It's a mystery." Evangeline chirped, falling back to walk next to me.

Watching the Thompson siblings must have animated her to act more sisterly again, and it was pleasant.

"I never thought that anyone would wonder where I went off to."

"But I do wonder … with your health."

"It's best for my health if I stay physically active. Doctor Armitage, agreed. He even encouraged me to."

"I see, so that's why you are roaming around. *The lone wolf of Forestedge.*" She said first smiling, but then seemingly remembering something unpleasant, she became flustered.

"Maybe I will take you to my den someday." I said with a playful yet sarcastic grin, which made her blush.

Wordlessly, Thompson looked back to observe our interaction, while Miss Violet admired the scenery. Following a path that led us through a young woodland, it was Thompson who noted that we must be going through private property.

"Oh no, it's all right. I asked permission of Sir Heywood in advance. I thought it would be nice if we could enjoy a walk in private." She said smiling at him warmly.

"That is very mindful of you, Miss Hollings." Thompson reciprocated he familiarity.

And from that point on we were broken up into pairs: Thompson and Evangeline in the front, and Miss Violet and me at the rear. I was keeping pace with her who was walking at a slower speed than I expected from her previous boasting about being a regular hillwalker. Not paying much attention to the scenery, I was watching the pair in front of me for a while, as they seemed to get along well. They exchanged smiles and sensible chuckles, making me honestly wonder what they were talking about, until finally, Miss Violet addressed me.

"Say, Mr Clarence, don't you think they look lovely together?" she asked, as she must have noticed me observing them.

"A brother's feelings may differ from those of a sister's watching that scene." I answered, deciding to be as vague about the matter as possible.

"Hm … I wonder what my brother thinks when he looks back at us," she mused, "I wonder why he was so insistent on us becoming acquainted. After all …" and then she broke off.

She adjusted her spectacles. Brows knit as in deep thought, she did not finish the sentence. Her heavy trot continued as she crunched onto the pebbles on the road.

"After all?" I urged her to continue.

"Evangeline was often writing about you in her letters. Praising your good qualities."

"Is that so?" I asked, surprised by the change of subject, but also at hearing such words for the first time.

"Indeed, she was saying that you were a considerate and kind person, Mr Clarence. However, I must admit that I heard otherwise from a friend of mine."

"What did they say?"

"That you are an amoral animal." She answered plainly insulting me. What was she thinking so long for if she dropped common decency anyway? I requested her to repeat and elaborate on the matter.

"Well, Mr Clarence, I think that neither of us need to pretend that you do not have a certain reputation. Even though you have been out of the country for near to five years, there are certain things that will not be easily forgotten," she started out blunt but became increasingly nervous the longer I stared at her, "An intimate friend insisted that I must be careful around you."

"I can only wonder if this friend is mutual?" I asked her straight to the face, which shook her even more. Then I added with a smirk, "Don't you worry, Miss Thompson. I am not an adolescent anymore, and the military service has straightened me out … so, there is no apparent danger to your physical wellbeing."

Hurriedly she turned away from me to admire the scenery again. For a while we continued to silently walk along each other. Having left the woods and farmlands behind us, we were quickly ascending the hill. At the top the four of us re-joined. Lazy clouds had gathered to lie low. Here and there, the lake was glistening as individual rays of the sun hit the surface. This highlighted the fells in the background. It was a very tranquil and romantic view.

"Marvellous! You have my thanks for choosing this spot and taking us here Miss Hollings." Thompson said, looking at Evangeline with fondness.

"My pleasure, Mr Thompson. I am pleased that you feel that way." She replied and graced him with a lovely smile.

"It is very nice indeed, but the view from Arthur's Seat is even more impressive. You should come and visit us in Edinburgh sometime, Evangeline. Maybe then Daniel will be inclined to join us up the hill." Miss Violet pointed out with her usual blatancy.

"Certainly, if Miss Hollings will join in so will I."

Excluded from the conversation, they continued to chat, and I only listened in. So, these were the people that she found friendship with while I was away, and I could not say that I felt comfortable around either of them. I went to stand slightly apart from the trio to take in the serenity of the landscape by myself. While I was in India and Africa there were rare times in which one could admire their surroundings, and it was always awe-inspiring but also strange. Sometimes I did think back fondly to home and the climate that I was used to. But overlooking it then I realised that there was a certain desolation to this place as well.

We decided to head back to the hotel and again, Thompson and Evangeline went ahead of us while Miss Violet slowed our pace, what I then knew was out of courtesy to her brother. For that action, she had slightly piqued my interest.

After reaching a waypoint I asked her, "Miss Thompson, may I ask how long you have been friends with Evey?"

"Oh, hum … it must have been some three odd years. Your late brother came to my coming-out ball, naturally through our fathers' connection. He invited my brother and me to the estate … and that's where we became acquainted." She said.

"I wasn't aware that you knew my brother."

"Bless his soul, he was such a fine gentleman. It's a true loss … that he should pass so young. My sincere condolences." She verbosely declared.

"Thank you for the considerate words."

"I could tell why my brother admired him so. However, I think he was a bit … how do I say this? Watching him and Evangeline, it made me feel sorry *for her*."

"Pardon?"

"Well, you see, this is not an attack towards your brother, his soul may rest in peace, but he was very, well … complacent. Yes, as though it was the most natural thing in the world for Evangeline to marry him one day." She stated bluntly.

"What do you mean? Of course, it was natural that they should marry one day." I asked without making any effort to hide my agitation.

"Oh, Mr Clarence. Don't *you* think that there should be more to marriage than the promises made by our elders? Of course, those two were affectionate towards each other. But that affection did not seem any different than that between Daniel and me," was her conceited reply and she went on further, "Besides, it is a real pity. Evangeline is such a bright lady. I have asked her before if there was nothing else, she wanted to learn other than those *traditional accomplishments* expected of us. But she said she was content. To think that she would not strive for more than becoming someone's wife. Pitiful. It must be because she has been confined to a countryside estate all her life. I can only mourn all those of my sex that have been groomed by their family since birth to fulfil no better purpose."

This was her complete and unapologetic statement. Clearly this woman was mad to boldly say something like that to me, insulting not only Harold and Evangeline, but also our family. On second thought, she was not mad. She was naive and oblivious. The Lord only knew how much she was spoiled by her family to reach that point. Having been a social failure herself additionally embittered her. She was with no apparent options after three years of her debutant and on the best way to becoming a spinster. Worst of all was that *I* was considered the last resort for a boisterous child like her. The child that no one had put in its place before. We *did* have more in common than I thought, and I knew exactly the treatment for this kind of behaviour.

"Is that really what you think, Miss Thompson?" I asked passively.

"Of course, any self-respecting modern woman would agree."

"Miss Thompson, you said it has been three seasons since your coming-out. Can I infer that there were no offers then?" was my straightforward question.

I would not put up any pretence for her anymore.

Befuddled she adjusted her spectacles and stammered, "No— Certainly. There weren't, Mr Clarence. Not as if they were needed. After all I have different plans for the future."

"I heard it from your brother, you are planning to pursue studies at a college?"

"Yes, that's right! A scholar needs to focus on their studies. There would be no time for romance anyway."

"Don't say that, Miss Thompson. There is a certain charm that only intelligent women possess. I'm sure a romantic affair will find you quicker than you think." I said, putting on my best, my most charming smile.

"I know that you are pulling my leg Mr Clarence, after all I know myself that I don't have the charm that a man would appreciate in a woman. Not like Evangeline has, for example." She replied slowly.

As her cheeks reddened, I could tell she was mesmerised. And as luck would have it, she tripped and stumbled, which gave me the opportunity to stop her from falling. Making sure that Thompson and Evangeline were at a far enough distance, I gently held back her arm and took off her spectacles. She was instantly flustered and alternately looked at me and then the grove around us. Admittedly, Violet Thompson's face could be as handsome as her figure. It was a lot more pleasant without the spectacles, and the insecurity of a virgin made it shine more attractively. Looking at her like that made my blood boil.

"You know, Miss Thompson. You mustn't put yourself down all the time." I suggested warmly. Firmly holding her arm I edged closer and added, "You are prettier than you think."

Then I made her look deeply into my eyes. Uncertainty and excitement made her quiver. She closed her eyes and lifted her chin, inviting me: in expectation. In anticipation. This was the pivotal moment. If I kissed her then she would have submitted her body to me later, and I would have enjoyed it. I would have enjoyed every bit of that pretentious creature, and I would have degraded her in every heinous way that came to my mind: for the way she irked me; for her condescending attitude towards Harold, Evangeline, and my family's way of life; and to spite her brother. I could have, but I did not. For one, because Evangeline held this morose wallflower in some sort of esteem, and for the other because it would have been a Pyrrhic Victory. Thompson was aiming for this. For the sake of utilising my misconduct for his gain, he banked on me going for this easy prey. So, he was the type to remorselessly pander his own sister for his profit. Both Thompsons made clear that they thought of me as being an unreasonable beast. They were wrong. Thus, I instead decided to humiliate her a little. I leaned in, my breath mingling with hers. Our lips not quite touching. Then I pulled away to laugh at her. First cordially, then maliciously. She opened her eyes and was taken aback, her sight confused and unfocused.

"Surely, you did not wish to tame an amoral animal like me. Or was I to be the tamer that would *work you*? You are pretty, Miss Thompson," I said while releasing her, "Pretty full of yourself."

Her cheeks were crimson and strained, the eyes watery with indignation, and the shoulders lifted in infuriated tension. Miss Violet snatched up her spectacles and slapped me across the face, with all her might, I supposed. Then exclaiming "Y–you ratbag! *You are a villain!*" she dashed down the path and passed the other pair.

I was amused at having pushed her far enough to use actual insults. Evangeline and Thompson turned around to look at me in confusion. Then she set off after her humiliated friend, while he remained where he was. I knew Miss Violet's pretentious pride would not permit her to tell a living soul about the moment in which she revealed her ugly vulgarity. The stupidity of wanting a taste of that which her friend warned her of, that which made other women readily discard their honour and reputation. Rubbing my cheek, I concealed a smirk from Thompson whose expression spelt out discontent. Then he turned away to set off after the ladies.

Eventually, we went home with Miss Violet putting as much of a distance between her person and mine as she could. In the train, she and her brother went to a different compartment and Evangeline accompanied them, only reappearing in front of me on one occasion.

"Whatever did you do to her?" she asked me reproachfully.

"Nothing that would explain her making such a scene." I replied looking her straight into the eyes.

She almost unnoticeably fidgeted with her hands but otherwise hid her nervousness perfectly. I turned my view outside the window, observing the passing countryside.

"I really worry about us having to sit in the carriage together on the way home. Mr Thompson seems to be quite cross with you as well." She noted with a hint of anxiety.

"Don't you worry, I sent out a telegram from the hotel requesting that the coachman bring my steed with him. They don't need to suffer my presence."

"Are you sure that you will be fine riding back?"

"Why shouldn't I be?"

"Very well." She said after a moment's pause. Then she turned back to return to the Thompson siblings.

Sure enough, the coachman was awaiting our arrival at the train station with an extra horse for me. I was loitering at a distance until they had left and then took my time riding back to the estate. It was still too long of a ride, for the sensation of the injury shifted from being uncomfortable to aggravating. An instant punishment for the small sin committed. As I entered the driveway the carriage was already out of sight and the horses in the stables. The groom took my mount from me, and I could feel him eyeing me with suspicion.

Entering the lobby, it was old Francis who greeted me, "Mister Arthur awaits you in the study, sir."

I figured as much. Bidding him to lead the way, I could feel a familiar atmosphere of disdain impregnating the space as I passed the corridor, even though all servants kept out of sight, as they should. After having been announced I went in. Father was standing with his back to me, his frail figure hunched on the cane. Inhaling the musty air of the multitude of volumes that were gathered in the tall and dark bookshelves, somehow transported me back to all other instances in which I was summoned. He did not ask me to sit down, and I stood as straight as an arrow with my hands behind my back, awaiting his scolding.

The matter of me ordering my steed to the railway station already evoked a sense of foreboding, and naturally seeing Miss Violet upset ... in fact, shaken made it clear that I, again, had done a misdeed. It could not be hidden. However, none of the returning party could or would say what it was that I'd done and instead it should be recounted by myself. I knew very well that I acted petty towards Miss Violet, and yet I could see as little wrong in my action as she did in her words. Therefore, I only mentioned that we had strong differences on certain matters and that I may have overdone it slightly when laying out my opinion. Father quietly listened to what I had to say, and then shook his head in disappointment.

"Arthur, you are not of an age anymore at which there would be a point in beating some sense into you. I really thought that the military service changed you for the better. It is disheartening to see that you are still lacking common decency." He sighed.

"I am truly sorry, sir." I replied without sincerity.

This was immediately noticed by him who became slightly agitated.

"Do not apologise to me, boy. It is Miss Thompson and her brother whom you must apologise to. We owe the Thompsons, and this is what you do! You make things hard for Evey, too. It's disgraceful. You should think about other people for once."

Not having the same energy anymore which Father possessed when I was younger, the scolding was unexpectedly brief. Instead, I was barred from dinner like a small child, and expected to meet Thompson personally afterwards in the smoking room. Lying on the cushy bed in my own bedchamber only made my flank hurt worse. I was contemplating on what to say to Thompson as I truly hated having to apologise, especially for things that I did not in the least was sorry for. Yet, I felt some excitement in seeing what change in countenance this event would bring forth in the prospective suitor. It was old Francis again that came to me and let me know that our esteemed guest was awaiting me in the smoking room. As I entered, Thompson was sitting in the same armchair as before, once again admiring the family portrait. Having changed into his usual dandy attire, he looked more confident than he did in the morning. He already had a tumbler set next to him on the gueridon table. This time I seated myself in the armchair opposite of his, putting a

82

certain distance between us and crossing my legs. After old Francis had tended to me, he discreetly left the room.

"First of all, let me apologise, Thompson. I did not mean to upset your sister and if she finds herself able to face me, I would like to apologise to her personally, as well." I began, not even attempting to give my voice any semblance of genuine remorse, nor getting up to hold out my hand.

"Violet would not tell me what happened. The years with the cavalry must have brutalised you for you to upset a lady so. I can only wonder what you actually learned?" he answered coldly.

"It is just as you said, your sister is straightforward, yet delicate. I may have overstepped the line by sharing my genuine opinion with her."

"And what opinion would that be?"

"That as a prospective match she was intolerable. Especially to the likes of me."

I wasn't at all surprised to hear Thompson snicker at this statement.

"I see that this is a laughing matter to you as well."

"One brother to another, I can tell that you care just as much for Miss Hollings as I do for Violet. Miss Hollings is very lovely and fetching, Violet on the other hand … it almost seems like a horse-trading to the Clarence's disadvantage. I am aware that my sister is quite a handful, but I did sincerely hope that the two of you would have gotten along. After all, both our fathers would have been happy to have their nuisances out of the way. As for me, I would like to think that Clarence senior will be able to see in me the son he has lost."

Thus, the snake revealed his true colours. I remained seated and glared at him, cracking my knuckles.

"Thompson, you really *are* curious as to what the years with her Majesty's cavalry have taught me. I can assure you that stupidly riding my horse all day is not the only thing."

Without averting his gaze, he chuckled and then said, "Clarence, you do not actually want to attack me, do you? Did I say something that could upset you? The *enfant terrible* of Forestedge really needs to work on his temper."

"The same can be said about you, Thompson. Your mask is slipping. For what reason?"

"Out of respect to you and Miss Hollings." He said with his vexing, polite smile.

"Pardon?" I asked dumbfounded.

"After the recent end of the mourning period, Miss Hollings has still rejected my advances … on the grounds that she cannot spare any thought on courtship or the like, unless you had returned safely. She seems to hold you in great regard as she stated that reason, instead of continuously mourning your late brother, which … honestly, I would have been more sympathetic towards. She was forfeiting her own future for some vague event that may not even come to pass. But who would have known that you would return so soon? I'm glad for that. She seems more open to the idea now … and for this reason I do not wish to hide my intentions from you, Clarence. I will court Miss Hollings. Seeing that you declined the succession to the estate, I may assume that a part of the Clarence shares will come into my family's custody. As dowry per chance? Anyway, I was of the opinion that you should know in advance." He laid out to me arrogantly.

"And you think challenging me like this will not be to your disadvantage?"

"What can and will you even do, Clarence? Will you meddle with Miss Hollings' future for the simple reason of disliking me? My affection is genuine. I will treat her the way she deserves, so do not fret. Are you going to dissuade your father then? I am sure, you yourself know that he is very much in favour of this connection."

Thompson wasn't only arrogant but also impertinent. His calculations went two ways, either I would make a ruckus then and there, and turn things to his favour, or I would limply stand down saying nothing. I may not have been an eloquent speaker but after composing myself I finally let him know that there were facts he could not get around dealing with.

"Out of respect for what your family has done for mine, I will ignore what you just said. Thompson, you seem to forget several things: *I still am* a Clarence, and part of this family. My reputation does not matter here. *I still am* Evangeline's foster brother and have a connection with her. Maybe not through blood, but through affection. And furthermore, it is up to Evangeline whether she wants to wed you, *neither of us nor my father have a say in this.*" But if I could help it, I would surely stop her from marrying a sly fox like him.

"Indeed. It is up to Miss Hollings whose regard she is more inclined towards: a suitor that respects her, or troublesome relations that upset her friends."

Concluding with this ambiguous notion, there was nothing more to add to the conversation. Thompson did not finish his drink and courteously bid me a good night, retiring to his apartment.

As the long clock chimed eleven the door creaked open just as the night before. Without rising I knew who it was.

"Is it already time for the haunting of the White Lady of Forestedge?" I asked while lying fully stretched out.

Evangeline's light laughter rang through the room. Instead of the armchair, she this time squeezed herself down at the edge of the méridienne, right at my feet.

"You kept your humour." She said, still giggling.

"Aren't you cross with me?" I asked, not looking at her.

"Why should I be?"

"I upset your friend."

"That you did. But I know exactly that Violet is quite eccentric. Therefore, I wanted to hear from you what happened."

After a brief deliberation whether I should tell her the truth about Miss Violet's tirade against Evangeline and our family, I decided to state only that which was necessary, "She annoyed me, so I taught her a lesson."

"Is that it?"

"…"

"It's fine then. You do not need to talk about it if you do not wish to." She said, and further inquired whether I was feeling all right.

"What do you mean? Aren't you concerned about the wrong person?" I inquired, then half-rising to look at her as I was surprised by the question.

"Uncle Arthur scolded you, did he not? And you had to apologise to Mr Thompson, too. For a fact, I know those are two things you truly hate."

"You know me well, don't you?"

She smiled without responding to my question, simply awaiting my reply.

"I am all right. Now be on your way and return to bed."

I fell back onto the long side, folding my arms behind my head and closed my eyes.

"I see," she noted plainly, "Don't indulge in drink too much, and sleep well."

Rising from the edge, she bid me good night, and in passing lightly brushed against my face with the cuffs of her gown. After the door closed, the warm scent of lavender lingered on. It was like a phantom presence that tortured me with immutable desire.

7
The Philosophy of a Base Animal

It was the third and final day of the visit of our esteemed guests. The morning curricular reported of the World Goodwill Day, announcing the first 26-Nation Hague Peace Conference, and as the Thompsons departed early I — ironically — did not have the chance to have any amicable exchanges with the siblings anymore. I doubted that any of us had the desire anyway. Out of courtesy and, in fact, because it was the most mature thing to do, no one further mentioned the incident of the previous day. Miss Violet resorted to pretending that I did not exist. There was a persistent unwillingness to hear an apology. While saying their goodbyes, she repeatedly invited Evangeline to come and visit her in Edinburgh, and Thompson reinforced his sister's proposal saying that it would be a joy to have Miss Hollings there. After they had finally gone things went back to the way they were. I kept out of sight of Forestedge's inhabitants, going out for short rides and roaming around as per usual. While she was not openly avoiding me, I was not spending any time with Evangeline either. I felt slight disappointment at our relationship reverting to each of us going through their own daily motions without anything else to say or any activity to share. At the same time, I knew it was better if things remained that way. I still could not look at her without having tainted thoughts. When Thompson challenged me in the smoking room I truly, for a second, held the petty sentiment that I should let him know how I was one step ahead of him. I had kissed his desired bride not once, but twice. Aside of defiling her reputation, what would that have proven? Only that I was even more despicable than they all thought I was. I hadn't forgotten this fact.

After a week had passed, even Father's enmity subsided. He calmed down quickly because this was not the worst thing that ever roused his anger. The weather was good and for once I joined in for lunch which was set outside on the patio. Arriving at the second course, Evangeline and Father were already conversing. I went over to my allocated seat.

"Oh, there you are, Arthur," Father greeted me, "I was just talking to Evey about the ball which the two of you will be attending."

"A ball?" that was my first-time hearing of it.

"Yes, at Miss Mirren Fawcett's … my acquaintance. You met her before. It's a private ball. The invitation came in yesterday. I'm sure you received one too." Evangeline explained shyly.

I then remembered an unopened letter with an unfamiliar handwriting distinctly addressed to 'Mr Arthur P. Clarence, Jr.'

"This could not wait very long, therefore I told Evey to reply for the both of you. Of course, you will be her escort," he stated plainly towards me and then turned to Evangeline, "Have you sent your reply yet?"

"Not yet, Uncle Arthur."

"Good. You should rather ask Aunt Gwen whether she could come to be her chaperone."

"As her brother you would be best to chaperone her, don't you agree?"

"Are either of you sure that you want me to join her after what happened with the Thompsons?" I inquired dispassionately.

Both fell silent. Evangeline helplessly looked at Father who in consternation knit his brows with his bony fingers and shut his eyes for a moment. Opening them again, he sternly looked at me and insisted in a harsh tone, "Why does it always have to be an argument with you? I instructed you before to accompany her to social activities, and I do not take 'no' for an answer. I am expecting your best behaviour, boy!"

"Yes, sir …"

"Excellent. Then it is settled."

And so, it was by the command of the brittle patriarch that we would go together, no matter what. There was nothing much I could say, and

Evangeline became engrossed in preparing for an exciting evening. While I did not find the prospects riveting at all, it did fill me with a sense of contentment to see her for once acting like a normal carefree lady of her age. She did not talk much to me about her plans, but I could often see small smiles flicker over her face which let me guess that she was imagining her dress, or she would hum waltzes that she probably looked forward to dancing to. The ball drew ever closer as it was turning mid-June. During meals I would receive the preparation updates: the dressmaker had come to the mansion to advise her on her gown and take her measurements, and her and Eilers went over several types of make-up and hairstyles. Finally, the only thing missing was her shoes. Ladies always seemed to have problems with those damned things. I could only wonder why they put so much effort into choosing a nearly invisible item of clothing that would draw the least attention of men. After breakfast and before I could make my escape from the premises Evangeline caught me and requested a brief chat in the parlour. I went with her, however without sitting down. I wanted to quickly get the matter solved and directly asked her what it was that she needed me for. She did not sit down either and instead stood close by.

"I would like for you to go with me to Carlisle the day after tomorrow. I would like to have a look around for shoes."

"All of a sudden? Wouldn't it be better for your lady's maid to join you on your quest?"

"Yes, well … she will come along, too."

"Then I really needn't join you, do I?"

She suddenly grabbed my hand, startling me. Squeezing it tightly she then looked up with imploring eyes that I remembered from childhood.

"Please, Arthur! You owe me this favour. After you have upset her, Violet has not been responding to me anymore. The least you could do is join me for a nice outing to the city. You should get off the estate, too. And besides, Uncle Arthur said you must join me for enjoyable activities!" was her insistent plea.

I still did not feel remorse for what I did to that pretentious wallflower, but Evangeline's words made me feel guilty towards her. After not having minded me for several weeks, she was suddenly insistent on us spending time with each other. Did she need that long to work up her courage? There was no point in arguing with her when she looked at me that way.

"If I must." I replied, surrendering.

We arrived in the city in the late morning. The railway station was dyed in a muted light. Through the iron latices beneath the glassed roof the caged grey skies were visible. Submerged in their daily businesses, droves of people were hurriedly scampering across the various platforms, while trains headed in all directions. As we emerged from the station, a familiar voice called out to me. It was Thornton. He gave his greeting to our party and explained to us that he was out for business in the city as well.

"Clarence, you make yourself scarce these days. We didn't even have the chance to properly talk at Irvine's place. Why don't you join me to the coffeehouse?" he said with a good-natured smile, and then looking over to Evangeline, "That is of course, if the lady can spare you?"

Before I could reply that she insisted on me joining her, Evangeline instead told him that he was free to take me along. After all, it was true that we did not have time to talk at our last meeting and she found that it would surely do me well to be with a friend for a change. However, I was to promise that I was back at the station in the early afternoon and that we were to have refreshments together. Gratefully, I accepted Thornton's invitation as I was not at all keen on looking at lady's slippers. It may have been that she did it out of courtesy towards Thornton or because she had a change of heart, but I still wondered why she was so insistent on me coming along if she was sending me away, nonetheless. Thus, I went along with Thornton to a coffeehouse on Castle Street close to the nearby

Tullie House, a Jacobean mansion that had been converted into a museum and art gallery in recent times. Had the weather been any better, I would have suggested sitting down in its gardens, instead. I did not appreciate the atmosphere of coffeehouses as the ambient noise was always that of self-important talks on business. The waiter had brought us coffee as soon as we were seated.

"You are all holed up in that dreary manor of yours. I invited you several times to come and play a set of tennis, and you always declined. Be careful, or you'll become an embittered misanthrope." Thornton admonished me warmly.

Sarcastically, I stated that I may already have become one. Then, I apologised to him and recounted what had happened. The whole incident with the Thompson siblings made me less keen on seeing other people, and I preferred to keep to myself. He laughed heartily at my story.

"Ah, you still are the same old Clarence. What a relief! You almost had me worried that an imposter came back. The melancholic gentleman act does not suit you at all, although I'm sure that some ladies will be drawn in by it."

"You would know where to find them."

"Well, if you are bored, I am sure that Jenny has some nice friends to introduce to you."

"I'll keep that in mind." I chuckled.

"Oh, and while we're at it, Mrs Irvine was complaining to me that you were not visiting at all. I guess you already had enough of her after the boat shed?"

"So, you were in on that?"

"She missed you so and begged me to help her. You see ... she is quite *articulate*." He said with his sly smile and an unmistakable wink.

"Good grief, James should put a leash on her." I sighed, and leant back into my chair.

"They are married. There is no tighter leash than that if you ask me."

"And still, she's such a wagtail. Jumping up every handsome man that crosses her path ..."

"What does it matter as long as everyone has an agreeable time? *You*, of all people, ought not be one to complain," Thornton laughed, then mused, "However, I do understand you, Clarence. Why should you leave the estate if you can enjoy the company of a beautiful angel such as Miss Hollings every day?"

I glared at him and then came to a realisation.

"If you *did* know about it, why did you let James send Evey after us?"

"What reason could I have stated to stop him from doing so? It's not like you've been caught red-handed." He shrugged.

"No, it's not." I denied.

Of course, I wished it was true and that Evangeline hadn't seen us.

"See? Even though it would have been more entertaining if you were." Thornton noted merrily.

"..."

"Goodness, Clarence. Can't you take a joke anymore? I must say, military service has made you a bore."

"It made me different."

"Right, so we merely need to wait around for a while longer than usual until you can provide us with a scandal?"

This was his final mischievous remark on the whole topic. We shifted into others for a while, talking about people we knew and things that had changed in my absence, ending on the note that we must meet up for that set of tennis. The morning had passed quickly, and we said our goodbyes, each going their own way.

As there was still some time left, I strolled along Castle Street to pass by the cathedral. Upon entering the imposing Gothic monument, a feeling of awe intruded me. Not only due to the solemnity and heaviness of the interior, but also because Mother, who was a devout worshipper, habitually forced us into it whenever we were on outings to the city. I specifically was urged to repent for my wicked ways. And under her watchful eyes I was made to repeat the *Lord's Prayer* out loud and clearly, on my knees. Over and over.

Since my return, I had not joined Evangeline and Father to the local parish church on Sundays, except for High Feasts. Not because I was not a man of faith, but because I disliked being watched when we were standing in our pew. The return of the wayward Clarence son was still a miracle the parishioners wanted to behold with their own eyes. No, I had faith. I saw it for myself in the fervent moment of battle, within the Mahdists and even within me: faith in righteous deeds was that which would eliminate all fear. Principally the fears of being torn apart, suffering and of dying. The only fear that it could not take from a person full of vice, was the fear of never being reunited in the Kingdom to come … for I knew I was unable change my ways. It was something I came to believe after having grown more faithful during the time of recovery in the field hospital. As I beheld the vaulted ceiling of the choir, the magnificent canopy of stars, I thought back to the clear nights spent beneath the African sky. There, I remembered those of my comrades that perished. With my eyes fixed on the intricate stained glass of the East Window which presented to me the illuminated *Triumph over Death*, I prayed. I prayed out loud as I used to, hoping that the humble offering of a lowly sinner like myself would suffice for those departed to the heavens: Harold, Mother, and my brothers in arms. I wanted to somehow reach them, even if I was not to join them later on.

In the early afternoon, as promised I met up with Evangeline at the train station again. Apparently, she had found what she came to seek out in the city. However, after I re-joined, the lady's maid excused herself and went away. Evangeline explained to me that Eilers was asked to do some shopping errands for other servants that had no opportunity to come to the city.

"You see, it's only the two of us all afternoon." She said with a sweet smile.

"Really, I'm not interested in sightseeing, and it looks to be raining soon. What are we even going to do?"

"Well, firstly we could have tea! You haven't eaten either."

"Very well, then let's head somewhere."

I took the small parcel which she had purchased from her and carried it. The streets were busy with all the shoppers, promenaders and errand boys rushing around. Heavy carriages, carts and buses clambered across the packed streets. The busy atmosphere created unrest in both Evangeline and me, as neither of us were used to the bustle of a city, being confined to our own small corner in the countryside. Evangeline was helplessly trotting beside me, not knowing where to look or step as people came our way. I took her hand, hooked it underneath my arm to link tightly.

"Arthur, we cannot walk like this. What will people think?" she reprimanded me and blushed.

"It is only an issue if you make one out of it. When you were little, I always *held* you by your hand in the city."

"But ..." She meekly protested and then gave in.

Both of us felt more comfortable as we walked at the same pace with no space separating us. For once I did not have any impure thoughts, and instead was reminded of the times when we had family outings to the city. She enjoyed walking with me the most. Evangeline never pulled or tugged like an impatient child but would always be well-behaved, just as she was in that moment. It was the same with viewing the windows of shops we passed: she only briefly paused with her eyes and not with her whole body in order to look at things she found interesting or pleasant. I matched her habits and eventually it appeared more like I was the one being walked by her.

As we passed by a millinery, a familiar figure stepped out with her maid and looked at us.

"Oh, what a treat! If it isn't my dear Arthur and his foster sister Miss Hollings."

"A good day to you, Celia." I saluted her, tipping my hat lightly.

Evangeline, as well, greeted her with courtesy, but I could feel her fingers grabbing onto me tighter.

"What a wonderful weather to come across you!" Celia exclaimed.

"It's about to rain." I noted.

The clouds had darkened the sky.

"So, it does. Perfect, to huddle together as it seems," she replied, severely scrutinising us, and then added, "Where were you two headed to?"

"We were about to have high tea, Mrs Irvine." Evangeline answered honestly.

"My, how lovely. Incidentally, that is what I was planning to have. Now. You don't mind my joining you, do you? I know just the right place that serves lovely sandwiches."

To my disbelief Evangeline accepted her proposal. She really was too well-behaved for her own good. Even though I attempted to ward Celia off, she wouldn't have it and led us along. We entered a tearoom, and our guide sent her maid away to tell James at his office about her whereabouts. The three of us were seated. Looking around, the place it really suited Celia's sense of aesthetics. There were big bouquets of fresh flowers in amphoras that stood on half pillars at each door. The bits of wall which were visible were of a garish colour and had pompous baroque plastering. In the middle of the high ceiling there was a lavish chandelier hanging from the glass dome. A multitude of mirrors dressed the remaining parts of the walls, increasing the lighting to blinding brightness. The waitress came and Evangeline and I ordered, Celia however sent her away without requesting anything.

"You drag us all the way here and yet you order nothing?"

"Arthur-Dearest, to tell the truth the scent of tea is a tad overwhelming for me right now. I lost my appetite. You see, I'm *enceinte*." Celia enlightened us while putting the gloved finger to her mouth, as though she was to become sick.

Despite that, she still had a malicious twinkle in her eyes.

"Well, congratulations." I said passively, and Evangeline joined in sincerely.

"Oh, there would be no harm in showing more enthusiasm, Arthur. I can promise you that it will not be your bastard."

"I hope for James' sake that it isn't Thornton's bastard, either."

"Hah, there you are, Arthur-Dearest. Lovely! Back to your usual self. I was already worrying that I'd receive a tepid response such as 'Don't say something distasteful in front of my *dear sister*!' again."

"I've given up on that. You are a foul-mouthed trollop, after all."

Celia chuckled, shifting around in her chair. As always, she was taking pleasure in being insulted by me. Evangeline became pale at our exchange, scanning the room for something else to look at. I did not intend for her to witness a scene like this, but there was something about Celia's attitude that always drew out the worst in me, and with regard to the fact that Evangeline had seen us at our worst already, I discarded the quality of reticence. She started to fidget with her hands underneath the table, which did not escape Celia's observing eye.

"Dear me, I am so sorry, Miss Hollings. Of course, I mustn't forget that you are delicate. *Your dear brother* told me so. Let's change the subject, shall we? After all, I know that I am just stealing away the attention our Arthur should be showering over y—"

Just then our tea and snacks arrived and were placed generously on the table. Hurriedly, Celia produced a handkerchief and held it to her mouth appearing genuinely unwell.

"Mrs Irvine, are you all right?" Evangeline inquired concerned.

"Aren't you a dear to worry about me? Yes, as I said: I become nauseous at present. Do let me catch my breath." She replied, her tone of voice had become strained, and she gagged.

I silently drank tea and ate a sandwich while watching her, and to Celia's credit the sandwich was good. Eventually, she overcame her nausea and started anew.

"You are so hard to get a hold of, Arthur. But I see now that you must have such a great time with Miss Hollings inside and outside the estate that you forget about the rest of the world. You could have at least notified James about your plans to go to Carlisle. He would have been glad to see you. What exactly brings you to the city?" Celia asked, a certain forcefulness in her voice.

"We went to shop for something she needed." I replied bluntly.

"Gosh, you are always so vague. Is that parcel it? I can tell it must be shoes, perchance? The size betrays them." She chided me, all the while intensely staring at Evangeline, who couldn't withstand her and nervously answered, "I … I … bought dancing slippers, Mrs Irvine."

"How wonderful! An occasion to dance? Where?" Celia continued to interrogate.

"At the Fawcetts' place. Does that suffice now?" I interjected, having had enough of her.

"Fawcetts'? To where Dinah Fawcett lives? And are you going to accompany your dear sister, Arthur?" Celia said amazed, an ominous smile growing on her face.

"Dinah … Fawcett? That name sounds familiar. As a matter of fact, yes. I will escort Evey." I confirmed and then looking at Evangeline asked, "Your acquaintance is Miss Mirren Fawcett, isn't it?"

"Yes, but Miss Dinah Fawcett is her older sister." She replied.

A faint memory remerged from the depths of my mind. There was a Dinah Fawcett. Celia started to cackle, which made the ladies at the table next to ours look at her disapprovingly. Then after recollecting herself, she smiled at me, slyly.

"Oh, dear me, oh Arthur. You do have a weak memory, don't you? It is too unfortunate that I am not invited I would have loved to see Dinah's face again," and turning to Evangeline, "Miss Hollings, Miss Fawcett will so love to see him. Then again, there are also other ladies that will be pleased by his presence."

"Are you done yet, Celia? You look rather pale; we wouldn't want you to be sick. You'd better get out of here."

"How considerate of you, Arthur-Dearest. I think I do see the maid over there. James must be done and ready to head home," she then put her hand on Evangeline's and patted it lightly, "I know that I was disturbing the quality time of you siblings."

We said our goodbyes and relaxed back into our seats as soon as Celia was out of sight. After taking a sip from her lukewarm tea Evangeline started to speak again. She appeared relieved as that strumpet's forceful aura had dissipated from the room. Yet, Evangeline still was flustered.

"She is … quite … she is quite the character."

"Don't pay her any mind. Celia has always been malicious like that. Even as a child."

"You must really … uhm … you love her, don't you?"

"Love? Me? Celia?" I started to laugh heartily to the dismay to people around us. The thought was so absurd, "Is that why we had to go along with her? Because you thought I wanted her company?"

"But— I mean, after all you are still friends, and you did … you …" she stammered befuddled.

She shook her head to ward off an embarrassing memory. It must have appeared absurd *to her* that I would be in any way involved with a rotten person like Celia if it was not for love. Especially after watching how we treated each other. At some point, Celia must have loved me, for I remember her to have had slightly more temperance and delicacy around me in our adolescence. However, my interest in her never exceeded my basic needs, and she was a good sport about it.

"But … then why?" she asked meekly.

"Evey, do you also think animals copulate out of love?" I replied after having regained my countenance. I was not expecting an actual answer. She narrowed her gaze; the cheeks and ears were shining scarlet with embarrassment.

"To ask me— How can you say something so vulgar in public? Besides, humans are not animals, Arthur." Evangeline protested.

"That is where you are mistaken." I scoffed and thus terminated the discussion.

When I was younger, I too believed that affection and physical intimacy were an inseparable institution. After all, I was always watching my parents and their conduct towards each other. In comparison to many other families, they were openly showing affection. Even if it was not overt or passionate, it was at all times present. However, in my fifteenth summer I learnt otherwise. Tending to my horse in the stables one of the maids came to find me. Mary, that was her name. I did not know how long for she had been employed with us, nor did I know where her hometown was. All I knew was that I found the mature body of the older girl exciting. The calloused work beaten hands that would firmly press onto my youthful chest all the while the sinewy thighs straddled my immature frame. She was evidently quite versed in the art of pleasing men. In turn, she showed me how to please women. Caught up in the flurry of these novel sensations, I for a while mistook lust for love. And so, I asked her one day after one of our encounters if she loved me. Her laugh at that moment sounded precisely like that which I had thrown at Evangeline in the tearoom.

"Oh, Master Arthur, you are precious. Do you love me?" she responded.

I denied, because in the moment in which I heard that laugh, I knew that I did not.

"I too, do not love you," she stated plainly, and furthermore, "I do however think you are quite handsome and wild. It would have been a shame not to."

To a hot-blooded adolescent like myself the simplicity of the answer was oddly satisfying. I stopped pondering on the deeper meaning of sexual intercourse, and we carried on as before. Until we were caught in the act, and it was by Father at that.

That was the last time I saw her, as for the next day she was turned out of the estate. But not before that wench received her thirty pieces of silver hush-money. Under tears she claimed that I coerced her — not forced her — she had that much decency. That the young Master would relentlessly pursue her, and she eventually gave in because she did not want to jeopardise her position. Father, with his lack of faith in me and his strong love for the underprivileged, believed her. So did Mother, and even Harold. Everyone believed her, from the scullery maid to the footman, because they all knew that Master Arthur was troublesome. Maybe old Francis did not, as he in truth was a good judge of character. However, the head butler did not have the spine to stand up against a mob led by sir and madam themselves. They had all made up their mind: I, and I alone was culpable for this scandal. This was detrimental to my existence at the manor. Servants then would talk about me, hands covering the mouths: hushed whispers. Like rats they would scuttle around the halls, never to be seen but always to be heard. *Young Master Arthur is a villain.*

As for me, I received the beating of a lifetime, and took it without protest. What use would there have been in fighting, for no one believed a word I said? The bruises were still visible when I returned to boarding school, and it was decided that I were to go to Sandhurst for me to be reined in. This punishment was for nought. With my reputation evaporated and the prospect of a toilsome military career, I decidedly became the promiscuous scoundrel that all of Forestedge thought I was. Keeping my hands off the servants, I would instead go on to take the honour of every beautiful young lady that was fair game. Ironically, offers increased with my notoriety. The whole experience taught me three things about women: their bodies were addictive; they were sly by nature; and finally, that they were base animals, the same as men. I was justified in treating them like such thereafter.

8
A White Peony

Aweek after our outing to the city, the evening of the private ball had come. R.F. Doherty won the Wimbledon singles championship for the third time that day, which reminded me of how I still needed to have that promised set of tennis with Thornton. Thinking of him in turn made me recall Celia and her ominous mocking. I was not too sure if I would not be a nuisance to Evangeline who was still very much looking forward to the prospect of society, dancing, and an overall merry time. I donned the same black swallow-tailed coat combination that I regularly wore six years prior. While it was the males' good fortune to have one standard outfit and not requiring purchasing new ones every season, the suit itself had become tighter in my absence. It made me feel more uncomfortable than I already was. I would have much preferred to wear the dress uniform of my regiment, the only type of high-quality attire tolerable to me then. Having waited in the parlour for a time, Evangeline was finally ready to make her entry: her neckline exposed, she wore a grey-blue and turquoise wrap dress that accentuated her slim waist. Silver-threaded flower embroideries were abloom along the hem, and the long trail made it look hard to walk in. The bodice was at the décolleté and shoulders covered by an intricately embroidered grey tule fabric that allowed for bare skin to shine through. Except for pearl earrings, a matching necklace and two peonies fastened into her top bun, she wore no decoration. Waving the matching rigid fan with her gloved hands, she asked, "What do you think?"

"Divine." I stated sarcastically, even though I sincerely thought it.

She graced me with a pleased smile either way.

"But why are you not wearing your dress uniform?" she asked, inspecting me from head to toe. There were notions of disappointment evident in her voice.

"We are not heading to a Royal Ball, are we?"

"No, of course not. It's merely that … I truly would have liked to see you in it … I mean not as in the photograph," she stammered, "And, it is odd to see you so well groomed."

A tender blush illuminated her cheeks. Hating to be waited on by any footman, I personally put an actual effort to be clean shaven for once and to have my hair properly arranged.

"As opposed to what everyone may think, I do know what is expected of me when partaking in a social event and I know how to take care of myself."

I went over to her and offered her my arm, which she hesitantly took. In passing my gaze wandered into the parlour mirror and looking back at me was a complete stranger that led along an exquisite lady. Father met us in the lobby, with young Francis standing behind him, unable to hide his admiration for Evangeline's beauty. The valet helped her into a delicate evening cape, while old Francis handed me the gear necessary to complete my ensemble. Tedious.

"Look at the two of you," Father said beaming with pride, "I should have had an artist preserve this moment in a painting."

We smiled back at him.

"You look like a proper gentleman in that attire, Arthur. I am sure it will let you remember that you should be on your best behaviour." He said complimenting me and at the same time admonishing me like a small boy.

"Sir, I will."

"I hope you have an enjoyable time."

"Thank you, Uncle." Evangeline said and gave him a peck on the cheek before we exited.

The ride to the Fawcett estate took less than an hour. I watched the scenery pass by wondering if I had travelled that way before. Thinking back to the beginning of adulthood, the seasons of social events which one had to go through were so long and strenuous that, especially an aloof person like myself, would have forgotten all the paths travelled and all the people met. Even as we entered the driveway and the Palladian villa came into full view, I could not quite recall whose face I was supposed to assign to this place. Arriving fashionably late, Evangeline and I entered the hall to greet the Miss Fawcetts' who were standing next to their mother. The lanky Miss Fawcett that I had met earlier in the year was wearing a crepe-and-gauze ball gown of a yellow colour. The puffed sleeve let her already thin arms appear even thinner. As we saluted her, I saw a figure hovering slightly aside, and upon seeing Miss Dinah Fawcett, it all came back to me. The pointed nose and sharp chin. The thin, sleek dark hair. A bony figure that made the clothes wear her rather than the other way around. Unsure about what Celia was referring to the last time we came across each other, I was then relieved to see that the matter was not of a more indecent nature. Even though it was admittedly a petty affair: Miss Dinah Fawcett was obsessed with me for a while. She tailed me at social events, hoping for me to chat her up, which I didn't. Then, I received letters almost daily, which I ignored initially. Only once did I reply asking her to leave me be. Miss Fawcett must have taken this as an incentive and would go on to send me the longest and gaudiest love letter I would ever receive, declaring finally that 'surely her love would correct my ways.' Being fed up with her antics, I showed this letter to Celia and asked her for advice as she was the only lady our age I could consult with. I should have known better, as for the next social event she gathered her entourage in order to pounce Miss Fawcett like a pack of wild hounds. Probably, as foolish as I was, I was aware that something would happen but did not care enough to consider what … and I never got to hear what exactly they did or say to her. In the end, Miss Fawcett did not appear in society for another six months. Harold reprimanded me severely for having disgraced a lady and her feelings, and for having incited other ladies to act out for me. I could not place when exactly these events transpired, but it must have had a lasting effect on her, as Miss Fawcett was clearly shaken by my sight. I felt her gaze drilling into my back as I escorted Evangeline to the seating area. However, it wasn't only her eyes that I had on me. Upon having a quick look around, I did recognise a number of familiar faces. It was to be expected, after all this was the countryside. Equally many gazes were directed towards Evangeline, who unaccustomed to so much attention by the opposite sex, started to strutter as to not lose confidence. I withheld laughter. As soon as my partner was safely seated, I intended to move out.

She stopped me however, asking anxiously, "Are you not going to sit with me for a little while?"

"Of course not, no one will ask you to dance if I hang around you."

"What about the first dance?"

"Evey, you will have more than enough men to ask you for that honour."

"Then you are going to ask other ladies to dance with you?"

"This is a ball after all, I shall as well have some fun, shan't I?" I said and left her side.

I went around and extended my hand to the pretty flowers that were strewn out in the seating corner, and I especially darted for those that sat in groups looking over to me as though they were gossiping. It was enjoyable to watch them become more flustered as I came closer, and to subsequently behold their surprise at whom I would ask for a dance. It only needed a faint smile paired with an unwavering meeting of the eye, and my name would be marked down on their dance cards. Nothing much had changed in the ballroom, it was still a place for the unspoiled ladies to join hands with a man and be held close enough to feel his virile energy, without having to fear that they will be overpowered by it. It was all strictly ordered, carefree fun. Therefore, they easily chose to forget whom they were facing. Having been out of the country further pushed my bad reputation into obscurity, foremost among the younger ladies, as there were enough seasons to accumulate gossip about the wrong doings of other people. Upon returning one of my dance partners to her seat, someone called out to me. I turned to look and went over to a group of ladies who were all around my own age. The caller that caught my attention was leaning deeply into the backside of a brocaded crème-coloured couch, that was contrasted by her wearing an elegant silken evening toilette of burgundy. The low neckline exposed the fine, undecorated structure of her clavicles and softness of her chest. The gentle waving of a feather fan made her auburn curls flutter in the breeze. Her dignified posture did not waver when I came to stand before her. Juliet Graham used to be a lady in Celia's entourage. However, it turned out that rather than a follower of hers she was her love rival.

"If it isn't Mr Clarence!" she said, smiling at me.

"Miss Graham, it has been quite some time." I said, bowing to her.

"It is Mrs Kendall now."

"Congratulations. It appears that all the ladies I knew ventured into the safe waters of matrimony."

"I wonder if we actually are safe there from you, Mr Clarence."

"It depends on your vigilance … If you are free now, shall I have the honour of dancing this set with you?"

"For old times' sake and to honour your service to the Empire, I really should, shouldn't I?"

Thus, accepting my invitation, we headed to the dancefloor, and her group whispered as we went away.

"Celia was right, you have become more handsome."

"Well, I'll be damned! You two are talking to each other?"

"You didn't think that she would pass on the opportunity to brag about having been with you."

"Indeed, she doesn't know discretion as opposed to you, Juliet."

In dancing it really was like in coition: the joy one would find in the act depended on how well the lead was and if the couple properly connected. A bad lead would create a jumbled mess, an aggressive one would lead to an exhausted and overwhelmed lady. I pressed my hand firmly onto Juliet's waist, digging deeply into her ceinture, to which she squeezed my hand tighter. As I looked into the big brown eyes, she turned her face to the side laughing softly. There was still compatibility which was important for both.

"The same old excellent dancer, I see."

"The body does not forget how to move once a skill is mastered."

"Hum, is that true? I would like to see for myself. I wonder if you could pay me a visit and converse with me about it?"

"And to make the acquaintance of your husband?"

"Oh, Mr Kendall will be down to London for business, come July."

"Then I will consider it."

The set ended and I led her back to her seat, kissing her hand as a farewell to another day. Then, I returned to where Evangeline was sitting. She had been joined by a young man who had just entered adulthood, still of awkward posture but otherwise appearing decent. Her face shone with relief as I drew close.

"There you are, Arthur— Uhm, you met Miss Laura Everett before, at Forestedge. Uhm ... this is her brother, Mr Paul Everett. As I told you before, I do apologise even though I promised you this dance, Mr Everett, but I really must take a break right now," she explained, then glancing over to me insisted, "And surely Arthur would like one too."

I concurred grabbing a nearby chair and seating myself next to her. Mr Everett and my eyes met, and he easily understood. Moving on to look for another lady to dance with, Evangeline sighed as he went away.

"Are you all right?"

"Yes, I truly wanted a break." She said, waving the rigid fan profusely at her reddened face. The gust of the fan drew my attention towards her bosom which was glistening with the fine pearls of sweat.

106

"You look flushed, do you need any refreshments?" I asked, looking away.

"No, I'm fine. I've been continuously offered drinks."

"Evey, you are aware that you are allowed to reject them, aren't you?" I said, glancing over to check if the redness wasn't due to too many drinks.

"Am I? I forgot." She answered giggling softly.

"It's unlike you to forget your etiquette training."

"It is, isn't it? Maybe you are a bad influence."

"Bold words."

She continued to giggle and started to waft air my way. Her merriment was catching, and I chuckled too.

"Are you having an agreeable time?"

"I am. More than that. Enjoyable!" she huffed, then turning to me, "And so do you as it seems. This has been your first break in over an hour. Isn't your injury bothering you?"

"No ..." I only noticed the stinging after she pointed it out to me. "It did not bother me. You are right, I was actually having an enjoyable time for a change."

"And to think you did not want to join me at first. There you go." She smiled happily ... innocently.

"Then, I should show my gratitude." I said rising from my chair, holding my hand out to hers, "Shall I have the honour of dancing this set with you?"

"I thought you'd never ask!"

She gracefully took my hand, and we went onto the dancefloor. I initially intended to avoid dancing with her at all. However, the vivaciousness of the ball let me lower my guard. It made me think of the days I spent learning all those moves. Among the many things required to learn to enter society, dancing was one that I truly enjoyed, because as my teacher confirmed, I had a natural talent for it. Evangeline used to peek in when I had to practise in the mansion. Knowing how modest she was about her own wishes, I invited her in, and my teacher helped her learn a few steps. At first, she continuously stepped onto my feet, but she was stubborn and would not stop until a song was finished. I did not mind; her treading was so light I barely noticed. As we continued, she quickly improved. It was a warming memory of a pastime that we used to enjoy together. But I instantly regretted having asked Evangeline to dance with me as soon as I held her. The fast-paced Viennese Waltz commanded the confident lead of the male, and she was giving in to me. The back elegantly curved to be firmly held; the face turned away blushed cheeks with a delighted smile, putting emphasise on the defenceless neckline and a heavily heaving chest, the hurried movement of the lower body that had to keep each other's pace … gazing down from above it was the kind of salacious outlook every knowing man was aiming for in a different setting. The dancefloor truly was a place for unspoiled hands to connect with those that were already tainted. I wanted her more than ever. The never-ending rotation made dizzy. It was tantalising.

Finally, the set finished, and I would be able to safely return Evangeline to the seating area. When we came to our seats where the hostess, joined by an unknown lady of middle-age, was awaiting us.

"There he is. Mr Clarence!" Mrs Fawcett called out to me.

I bowed and took a better look at the stranger, who was wearing the most lavish Parisian style toilette and delicate, gem studded jewellery. Suddenly, I could feel how all eyes had turned on me, readily awaiting a scandal. Evangeline as well, glanced at me with curiosity.

"Lady Alcott, may I present to you Mr Arthur Clarence, the younger." She presented me, and hastily my foster sister, as her presence seemed of no importance in that moment.

"To what do I owe this honour?" I asked, after kissing Lady Alcott's outstretched hand.

The ladies went to take a seat.

"It is *my honour* to meet you. You are in fact Lance Corporal Arthur

Percival Clarence, Jr of the 21st Lancers, yes?"

"The very same."

"You see, Lieutenant Gerald Henry Feversham is my godchild and he told me all about you."

"Lieutenant Feversham? How is he fairing?"

"He is readjusting to a life with his injuries, but he is well. To repeat his statement: 'Thanks to the Lance Corporal it is only a part of my hand I forfeit, and not my life.'"

"What is this? Please do elaborate." The eager hostess asked, and with her the seating area was all ears.

Lady Alcott recounted the charge at Omdurman: as everyone already knew, we were surprised by a thousandfold Dervishes suddenly emerging from a dried watercourse. All lances were positioned, there was no other option than to increase speed and clash with them head on. Yet, it was not enough to trample the enemy. Piercing deeply, right to the hilts of our steels, lances became useless, and the swords were drawn. Shots flew in all directions while my own section was annihilated, as they were torn down from their horses, hacked and slashed. Upon retreating I spotted the Lieutenant close by, the Dervishes had his bridles in their hands, one attempting to cut his stirrup leather as well. The rush of adrenaline made the memory of it hazy. How I did it, I couldn't recollect, but I quickly cocked my Martini–Henry, shot the fiend that damaged the stirrups, and rode over to the Lieutenant's aid as he was already being hacked at. They were still too much to take on for the both of us and the last conscious memory was of a fish-hook spear ripping at my left side among other injuries sustained. The summary of twenty-one minutes of one day in my life were enough to shatter my comfort and confidence, for I could not hear others talk about them without becoming nervous. The jocundity of the ball, as well as guilt of desire melted away in face of this terror. Faintly, I could hear 'Oh's and awestruck whispers as they commended my bravery. Everything became muted and I did not really follow the conversations anymore, nodding and acknowledging whatever was said, until I felt a gentle hand tugging on my fingers.

Evangeline looked up addressing me in a hushed voice behind her fan, "You never told us," and, "Your face lost all colour, are you all right?"

"Of course." I wasn't.

Then, I excused myself to everyone and headed for any space that I could find which was empty. In solitude, I took my time to recover, holding my side as the wound felt like it was ripped open again. Desperately I tried to forget it all: the roaring thunders of anguished cries, as merciless metal hit the frail flesh; the disgusting feeling of warm liquids touching the skin — a moist sensation that was anything but a refreshment from the dry suffocating heat of the desert — to have lived where other human beings perished; and the days and nights in which I felt like I'd rather wanted to die than suffer the torture of a healing body any longer.

I was unsure how long it took me until I found my composure, but I was eventually able to hear the music properly again. Remembering that I left Evangeline all by herself, I returned to the seating area, but she was gone. However, glancing around the dancefloor, I could not make her out either. A lady sitting near her seat advised me that she may have wanted fresh air, and thus I went to look for her in the direction of the patio. Traversing one of the outer hallways I was suddenly stopped by an unfamiliar gentleman, a bumbling Duke of Limbs, who appeared to have waited for an opportunity to get me alone.

"Mr Clarence, I demand that you apologise to Miss Dinah Fawcett."

"And who are you to demand that of me?"

He explained to me that he was a dear friend of hers who could not stand that someone who abused Miss Fawcett's feelings was nonchalantly attending a party at her parents', in summary: he was an admirer that wanted to impress her. As I was already agitated, I bid him think twice about challenging me and noted: "I can only wonder what you wish to do if I don't comply with your request. Unless you would prefer to settle this with bare knuckles."

Apparently, he was intoxicated enough to consider this option. Before he could lunge at me Miss Dinah Fawcett herself intercepted, having jumped out of a hidden corner in which she had concealed herself. She looked at me with a wary yet somewhat pleased expression, and then turned to her 'dear friend.'

"Mr Fenton, you mustn't pay attention to Mr Clarence and his petty ways. This matter was settled a long time ago," and then turning to me, "Did you know, Mr Clarence? Your brother personally apologised to me on your behalf."

"I am aware."

"He truly was his brother's keeper. In retrospect, I can say that I was infatuated with the wrong Clarence brother. Mr Harold Clarence was such a sweet and sincere man, it is a shame that we lost him and are left with you." She said with a sneer, and yet her eyes lingered on.

The two of them departed in the opposite direction and I was left alone in the scarcely lit hallway. What a pathetic revenge. Stirring up the memory of my deceased brother to insult me was a dirty trick only a coward or a woman could come up with. Not anymore enjoying the place, I decidedly had enough of the ball and hoped to find my partner as soon as possible for us to leave.

Further heading down, I noticed the familiar blue and turquoise dress outside on the balcony. As I thought, it was Evangeline, a young gentleman just standing next to her. Moving closely to the slightly opened double-winged doors, I peeked out. The gentleman, who turned out to be Everett, offered her a glass of champagne to toast with him, which she gracefully declined. Suddenly, he became tense and set down the glasses onto the balustrade. It was not my intention to eavesdrop, but it would have been wrong to simply disturb the scene either.

"Miss Hollings, you danced with several men, but you rejected me saying you were tired. However, I did see you dance with Mr Clarene instead. You could at least have done me the courtesy of one dance." The suitor said, his face in folds of frustration.

"I am very sorry Mr Everett. You are the brother of my acquaintance, but I do not want to raise any wrong hopes within you."

"Did you not say you would consider my interest once Mr Clarence returned?"

"No, I did not say so, sir. I said I would not entertain *any idea* of romance until he returned."

"Isn't that the same?"

While Everett adhered to a standard of manners, Evangeline appeared visibly intimidated. I would not wait long enough for things to turn another way. However, before I could move in on my own, she had noticed that I was standing at the door and called out to me.

"You summoned me?" I said, as I dramatically opened the double-winged doors.

It was a boisterous type of entry, and I wondered if my previous encounter had made me more irate than usual. Apparently, it had a strong effect on the unwelcomed suitor, for he stepped back from her. Young Everett was clever enough to catch on, and with a curt bow to his object of admiration he excused himself, quickly scuttling past me into the semi-dark hallway.

I went over to Evangeline who hid her lower face behind her fan, her cheeks red from drink. Clearly, she was suppressing laughter.

"Thank you for coming to my aid, Sir Arthur." She said, finally.

"Anytime, my lady."

She explained that at first, she went to look for me, but then upon spotting young Everett, Evangeline had gone away from the ballroom to specifically avoid him who had been darting for her all evening. Picking up one of the untouched glasses that were left on the balustrade I emptied it in one gulp.

"You should just have waited and declined. Apparently, I'm quite useful to you for warding off pests. After all I now see that it is not only

Thompson but other suitors that you told this excuse." I said languidly.

The bustle of the party and finally the run-in with Miss Fawcett and her pet had tired me out. Evangeline wore a strong expression of hurt.

"It is not like that," she protested, "It is not like I 'use' you. I earnestly did not want to entertain any idea of romance when you were away. I was sincere when I told him that I did not want to spare any thought on it until you had returned safe and sound."

"And why is that?" I asked. Would it not have been usual for woman to do the opposite? Bask in affection when they were downtrodden.

"Because, you see—" she said, thinking carefully, "It is obvious, is it not? You are … you are my family."

Evangeline as well, took a big swig, emptying the champagne. Her face crumpled for a second due to the bitterness. The blue hues of the dress made her merge with the starlit evening sky, her golden hair shining in the light of the moon.

"And you? Why are you always so secretive? You never made any mention of your heroics. You should have been awarded." The alcohol must have quickly heated her senses as she became quite agitated.

"Heroics?"

"You risked your life to save another!"

"When a dog jumps into a pond to save a drowning man, do you give it a special reward afterwards?" I asked her matter-of-factly.

She looked at me confused.

"I did my duty in aiding a brother in arms. I do not expect or want any type of award for it. It was natural. Besides, I eventually needed saving too."

In her muddled state it took her a moment's time to process my statement.

"Why do you keep likening yourself to animals? It's distasteful. You are a person. A human with a heart!"

Her speech began to slur slightly at this haughty argumentation as she said, "Really, you are being so modest … the full evening suit does make

113

you a different man!"

She turned but stumbled over her trail. I swiftly caught her arm.

Looking up to me, she said with an unbridled laugh, "See! You make me fall for you! Like all those ladies inside waiting for you to ask them to dance."

Her eyes sparkled with the gaiety and carelessness of too much drink. It was adorable and made me smile. It was dangerous.

"You had enough for today. We should head back to the manor." I said, and hooked her arm under, gently placing my hand onto hers.

We discreetly exited the hall, missing supper and the hostess as well. Evangeline's movement became more laboured with the heaviness of spirits circulating through her blood. The coachman and I cautiously lifted her into the carriage. The steady rat-tat of the vehicle carried her swiftly into sleep. She must have had a pleasant dream, for she smiled occasionally. Having not been fastened properly her cape came undone on one side. As her head rested against the carriage side, her neck was yet again exposed and along with a peony, a golden strand of hair came loose falling over her bare shoulder. I wanted to bury myself into that dainty and defenceless flesh. Taking off my glove, I leaned over, took the peony, and gently brushed the hair aside to readjust the cape. My fingertips burnt upon contact with the heated skin.

The black and white uniform of the Gentleman never sat well with me. The rules were manifold and confusing, and my temperament would get in the way of acting as was expected of me when appearing in society. Despite the anxiety which I still felt at the recollection of the battle, I was more comfortable in my field uniform, because I knew that it fit me and that I fit with the people who wore the same alongside me. There was really only this one rule to remember: you fight together, you live or die together. I was sure that this was all I needed to know.

Tired, I fell back into my seat. While turning the flower around in my hand I contemplated on how tedious society actually was, how things between me and Evangeline would not revert to the way they were, and how much better it would be to return to my regiment, rather sooner than later.

9
Wednesday's Child

After the ball, there was a change in Evangeline's attitude toward me. She had become more open and familial again. Every other day, she would request my time for simple things like playing card games and listening to her piano practice. As it was only a little time of each day she requested, I did not feel that there was any harm in it and gave in. July began and we sat in the parlour one afternoon, chatting over a game of *Écarté*. She was telling me how Thompson and his father had to travel to France again, and how Thompson junior was writing back and forth with her from there.

"He always has so much to write me. Even though I don't really know what to respond, he keeps replying instantly to every letter I send … " she said, slightly troubled.

"Then stop writing him."

"You know perfectly well that I can't."

She blushed at this statement, which irritated me greatly. I did not want to further talk about Thompson and instead asked if she was receiving letters from Miss Violet again.

"Oh yes, she calmed down. Can you imagine? She is in Paris right now with her brother and father! And it's all because of you."

"Did she write that?" I asked.

As expected of her she had no one to boast to and decided that she *must* write Evangeline.

"No, but one can only assume so, seeing that you upset her so much that both suggested she come along to lift her spirits. At least that is what she wrote."

"I made her wish come true for her then. She should be grateful to me."

"You are awful." Evangeline reproached me yet couldn't stop herself from snickering.

After playing quietly for a while, it looked like I was going to win the game.

"Arthur, let's put in different stakes, shall we?"

"Different stakes?" I asked surprised.

"If I win this game, you have to take me to the stables and help me ride a horse again."

"I refuse. I don't think that's a good idea."

"I knew you would say that, which is why I proposed to change the stakes."

"And if you lose?"

"Then you can ask *of me* anything you want, obviously." She said smiling, and suddenly the game had become precarious.

'Ask of her anything,' how could she innocently tell me those words? Did she forget my warning already? I started to think of things I had pushed into a dark corner of my mind. Recollections of the view of her during the ball flashed in front of me. My imagination was running wild. And there was a strong urge to win the game, at the same time I endeavoured to calm myself down and not to take her words seriously.

Not knowing if it was luck or providence, she did turn the tables and won the game. Relieved that I did not have to face temptation, I was instead forced to take her to the stables. I did not like the idea either, but she insisted that a "Gentleman has to keep his word."

Thus, we made plans for the next morning, to see if she could overcome her fear. I personally thought it was not the time for it yet, as she would still show signs of anxiety when she was only near the animals that pulled the carriage. Evangeline however was very insistent, even mentioning our plans to Father over dinner. He as well was worried, but at the same time considered it a good opportunity for her to become slightly more independent again. As always, he demanded of me to be especially considerate and careful when I was to lead her in this venture. With his demand leading my thoughts, I asked the coachman if there was a cold-blooded horse in our stables, and the only one he said we had was a Clydesdale. While they were well tempered, I was worried about the height of the horse and thus instead chose a good-natured Anglo-Arabian mare. The first morning we only went to observe the animals in the stables, while I was getting ready to ride out. Evangeline had a look of disappointment as I left her. After five days, however she seemed calmer around them, and I decided that we could give it a try. In the morning of the sixth day, the groom had her old side-saddle fastened to the mare. With a proud face she wore an old riding habit. Why she had held on to it I was uncertain of, but the lady's maid did her best to alter the dress and make it fit. Nevertheless, it appeared tight around *a certain area*. The groom led the horse out onto the lawn where I helped Evangeline mount it. As I still did not feel perfectly confident about the whole venture, I was on my own Thoroughbred trotting next to her, while the groom led her by the bridles in front. At first it seemed like she was enjoying it, however the longer the trot continued the more nervous she became, almost agitated. Evangeline's breath became erratic and instead of properly holding the reins she started to fidget with her hands. The Anglo-Arabian was not very used to riders, and Evangeline's uneasiness even stirred me up. I reprimanded her with great concern, telling her to hold on and calm herself. As though my own words startled it, the mare suddenly bolted. The groom was hurled onto his back, and by the abrupt rush the hapless rider was thrown backward, caught with her skirt onto the saddle. With the danger of her being dragged around I swiftly rode after them and caught the reins. I stirred the dumb beast into a circle that became ever smaller until it came to a halt. Hurriedly getting off onto her side, Evangeline was a dishevelled mess that barely hung from the saddle: the hat and veil lost along the way, the hair almost fully down, pale and shivering. Holding her by the waist, I loosened the buttons of her safety skirt, and she quickly flung herself at me. We both fell onto the ground. Sobbing frantically, she pushed her face into my chest, and I helplessly put my arms around her. Her shaking frame was so incredibly light and yet weighed heavily on me. Gently stroking the messy hair to calm her down, as I could feel the fabric of my habit become drenched in her tears. All the while there was a repeated whimper between the sobs: it was the name of my brother. There was not one good thing to be found in this harrowing moment of physical closeness.

We returned to the lobby and Doctor Armitage was instantly called from his quarters. While there was no major injury, Evangeline did have a sprained wrist and was to refrain from playing the piano for two weeks. Of course, the whole event upset Father, and it came as no surprise to me that I was the one to be blamed for how things unfolded. After all, I chose the horse she was to ride and decided when she seemed fine enough to try. It was not only him who thought that way, it was what everyone in the household thought, including myself. *The poor Miss. She loves the piano so. That's what happens when one relies on young Master Arthur.* I should have known better. Always the humble angel, Evangeline did not blame me at all, which was more upsetting than it was consoling.

The subsequent days I avoided her and the manor altogether, escaping to Juliet's. She happily received me with open arms as married life must have left her bored and unsatisfied. I was repeatedly consoled and comforted at her place. Yet, I could not truly come to feel better. To my misfortune one of her older brothers turned up for a surprise visit … a surprise to Juliet in particular. Someone must have let him know that they saw me there. On the evening three days after the riding accident, I returned to the manor. It was late at night, and I was relaxing in the smoking room with a glass of whiskey when Evangeline entered and seated herself in the armchair as she already had during her previous visits.

"Oh, I was sure I heard you. You did not even join us for supper. Where have you been?"

"None of your business."

"Don't say that. I was worried about you ... and so was Uncle Arthur."

"I wonder about that."

"What happened there?" she asked, got up and placed herself beside me.

Coming closer to inspect my face, she reached out to the cut on the lower lip and the light bruise. I, however, waved away her hand.

"This? Never mind that ... I overstayed my welcome. That is all." I answered taking another stinging sip from my tumbler. Then she also noticed the scraped skin on my knuckles, taking my empty hand into hers.

"Even here? Truly, what *did* happen?"

I pulled it away and instead took hold of her injured wrist, which startled her.

"What about your wrist? Does it still hurt?"

"Slightly."

Then I squeezed it gently and she instantly flinched with an agonised 'ouch' escaping her.

"Slightly, you say ... it's still painful enough for you to react that way. Why were you so insistent on riding a horse again anyway?"

"This Friday is your birthday ... therefore ..."

"Therefore. Therefore, what? I told Father and you that I did not wish to celebrate." I retorted, sudden anger rising within me.

"But ... But it would have been so nice if we could have ridden out. Just us, like we used to."

"Like we used to? It would not be the same, for various reasons." I told her, almost shouting.

"Arthur, I know that—"

"Leave me alone! Now!" I demanded cutting her off, finally losing my nerve.

She immediately obliged and bid me a good night.

Yes, we used to ride out on my birthdays. All three of us, Harold, Evangeline, and me. It was all I ever wished for: to be with the two people dearest to me, doing what I liked best on the one day of the year on which everyone voluntarily forgot that I was troublesome. Five sets of reproachful eyes were staring down on me from the frame across the chaise longue. One of them judged me more than the others. This year would mark the end of my twenty-fourth year. I would turn the same age that Harold was when he passed away. There was nothing to celebrate, I would grow a year older that year and every consequent year. Living on and surpassing my brother in age, but unable to surpass him as a person. The dead were sanctified. He had become so perfect that I would forever be unable to measure up to him. Even worse than that was that I was low enough to lust after the woman that would have been his wife. Him being dead made my desire more attainable. There was nothing happy about my birthday.

The following day at breakfast Father did not make any mention of my disappearance nor did he inquire about it. Neither did he make any remarks about my injuries. It was only Doctor Armitage whom I visited afterwards, that somewhat cheerfully commented on how my sudden disappearance made him nostalgic. Especially the tending to my wounds, which were undoubtedly sustained in a scuffle, made him grin inappropriately. He still reprimanded me for my behaviour.

Everything went back to its regular course with me indulging in my habits and activities, and Evangeline somehow passing the time without being able to play her piano. By the time of my birthday, I had gotten a hold of myself again. Right after breakfast old Francis handed me all the letters that had arrived for the occasion. Before I could go away to read them, Father summoned me into his study. I instructed for the letters to be brought to the reading room and wordlessly followed my father as he walked ahead of me through the corridor. His pace was slow and laboured, continuously joined by a steady tapping of his cane. We entered the study, and he went to sit in his chair behind the massive ebony desk, offering me to take a seat opposite of him. The last few times, I was too distracted to properly look at it, but I noticed the new miniature bust on the desk. It could have been a semblance of my brother, although I was unable to tell, as it was slightly hidden behind the desk lamp and facing Father.

"Are you well, Arthur?"

"Sir, of course I am."

"And your injury?"

"Better by the day, sir."

There was not much for us to discuss, and he shifted in his chair uncomfortably. He opened one of the drawers of his desk and produced a small box, setting it on the table in front of me.

"This is for you. It's good to have you back. Happy Birthday." He said plainly.

I was dumbfounded. Taking the box into hand I opened it to find a golden Double Hunter pocket watch of exquisite quality. It appeared to have been custom-made. Wondering when and where he acquired it, as he did not leave the house except for necessary matters, I looked for the maker's mark. However, once I noticed that he was observing me, I became self-conscious and instead placed the timepiece back into its box. Then I thanked him for his generous gift. With nothing more to say, he suggested that I could go ahead and read all the correspondence that I had received in private.

After I left Father's study, I went to the reading room. The letters and cards were a multitude of well wishes from friends, family, and my regiment. Evangeline peeked in and then entered without asking my permission. She nonchalantly went to sit next to me and for a while watched me as I read my letters.

"Oh, what is this?" she asked, picking up a postcard with a painted view onto a walled city and its orange tiled rooftops. The predominant feature was a grand cathedral with a dome atop. Intently she gazed at the postcard which said 'Firenze.' She respected my privacy and did not turn it around to read its message.

"It's a card from Rosalind. She spends her summers there with her half-Italian Gentleman." I said, without looking up from the letter I was holding.

"Shouldn't you be calling him by his name by now?" she scolded me.

"Why should I?"

"How long have they been cohabiting?"

"Four years now."

"See, four years! A common-law marriage. It's so scandalous!" she asserted, with a hint of admiration in her voice.

"Rosalind has the fortune from her mother's side to live on, therefore she can live as freely as she wishes."

"I have my family's inheritance too … do you reckon I could also live like that? Maybe with a *half-French Gentleman*?"

"Don't you go and aspire to be like Rosalind!" I warned her, finally looking up from the letter I was reading.

Evangeline snickered upon seeing my feathers being ruffled over her silly comment.

"Is there a letter from Aunt Gwen as well?" she asked, scanning the discarded envelopes.

"There wasn't. But there was a telegram. I suppose she wanted to surprise me; she apologised for not being able to come in person and asked me to visit her soon, instead."

"Will you be going?"

"I haven't decided yet."

Not minding her, I let her leaf through the different envelopes. She studied all the handwritings.

"Why are there some addressed 'Master'?"

"It's what the *old sweats* called me. They did not have much regard for a wealthy young master that ran off to enlist as a private. While they were initially using it dismissively, it eventually became my nickname."

"Old sweats?"

"Veterans."

"Oh … I see. You must have had a hard time then."

"The hardest. I was constantly beasted, and they worked me to the bones."

I recounted to her the many things I had to do. As I never had specialised training beyond my schooling that prepared me for academia, I became a maid to all those around me, in order to prove my good conduct and to earn a penny: being tasked with cooking, cleaning, shovelling trenches … and latrines, tending to the animals and many things more. All the while I was gloated at for being incapable of the most menial tasks, never having done any of them even once in my life. Of course, no one would have had the gall to act that way toward me, if they hadn't perfectly known that I was on my own without the backing of my family. Even the superiors were drawing some joy out of it because they resented my attitude. I had to swallow down my pride and literally get off my high horse. But the reward for all those troubles was respect and true appreciation, and it made me content.

"Why did you never write any of this in your letters?" she asked, looking at me with a mix of awe and admiration.

"To be honest … I was truly ashamed."

"Ashamed?"

"Yes, after all I brought it upon myself by acting out and I did not want anyone to know that I did get my comeuppance." I laughed, having become able to laugh about this matter, for in truth the shame was deeply ingrained. Among the many things I learned, the greatest one was humility. I came to the realisation what an awful son, brother, and man I had been. How much unrest and trouble I truly had created, and how many things I had taken for granted. When I was lying in my sickbed, I saw how my obstinate pride was a jagged knife that had torn through the relationship with my family, and that there were things that could not be mended anymore.

"That's why you've been more careful around Uncle Arthur?" Evangeline mused.

"Yes, and also for reasons of his health. How could I aggravate him now?"

"What about when you insulted Violet then?" she asked gravely.

" … I at least try to do better, don't I?" I said, a bit sheepish.

She laughed and conceded. Sometimes I wondered if she ever genuinely felt upset on behalf of Miss Violet or if she had decided to take my side. It did not matter, for I enjoyed seeing her laugh.

A different thought entered her mind as she asked, "If you had so little money for things, how were you able to send me a birthday present every year?"

"I asked Rosalind to lend me some. I still owe her for that and other things."

"She has a soft spot for you, doesn't she?"

"I think in retrospect she felt guilty for letting me enlist and harbouring me at her place, all the while."

"I was cross with her for that reason too, you know?"

"Well, don't be. Without her I would not have been able to meet ends at times. You also received nice birthday presents, did you not?"

She smiled without a word and patted my thigh, then she went over to a table near the door and took a small parcel that I had hitherto not noticed. Evangeline returned to sit next to me.

"Speaking of birthday presents, I have one for you as well."

After handing it to me happily, I opened it. Her present was a golden, single Albert pocket watch chain with a fob.

"Did you know that Father was to gift me a pocket watch?" I asked surprised.

"I did. He was holding onto it for five years after all."

"What do you mean by that?"

125

"Did he not say anything? He had it fashioned five years ago … I think Harold told me once that it was meant to be a present for you entering Sandhurst…"

Feeling overwhelmed by this information, I did not say anything. She continued to look at me eagerly as I took the chain out of its box. Upon inspecting it properly I saw that the fob was the small medal for ascending the Eiffel Tower that I had supposedly given her all those years back, and it was gilded.

"You actually still had this?"

"I kept it safe in my treasure box." She said giggling and explained that she secretly had it made to order when we went to Carlisle, "I thought you could use a lucky charm."

"Do I look like I need luck?" I asked.

It was the type of sentimental gift that only a woman could come up with.

"One can never have enough of it. Here is another gift for luck."

Then she leant in to kiss me on the cheek, her lips so very close to mine, yet still far away. The scent of summery lavender tickled my nose as she broke away.

"To many happy returns." She said, beaming at me.

Sentimentality took hold of me as well. I embraced Evangeline, holding her tightly. She returned my embrace and rested her head onto my shoulder. Only for the occasion of my birthday I wanted to indulge in this moment: I wanted to savour her warmth, brush my face against her soft hair and feel the breath that would moisten my neck. Releasing her slightly to have a glimpse at her, I beheld a look of anticipation, that which I knew too well. I wanted to indulge in this moment … but just then our peace was broken by the lady's maid that intruded the scene.

"I'm awfully sorry, sir, miss! I did not mean to … I—" Eilers stuttered as she saw us arm in arm on the sofa. We parted then.

"Not at all. There is nothing to be sorry for." Evangeline answered, sitting in her perfect posture, and showing neither signs of fear nor embarrassment.

She rose from her seat, and asked what was the matter. The maid explained that it was time for the doctor to have a look at her wrist. The young miss excused herself for having to leave, and again wished me a happy birthday, thus exiting the room with her maid. Once the door was shut, I took out the new pocket watch and fastened the corresponding chain to it. Looking at it for a while, I decided not to wear it just then. I had completely grown unaccustomed to wearing something so precious on my person. Then I pulled out the one I was wearing from its confinement in its allocated pocket. The window of the Half Hunter pocket watch was obscured by a piece of paper making its function pointless: there were numerals with no indicator of time. Pressing on the mechanism, the hinge of the already beaten and bruised casing popped open exposing the inside of the cover. A familiar face glanced at me with big innocent eyes, and an endearing, carefree smile. I meditated on whether I should remove the crinkled and worn photograph and place it in the new pocket watch. However, I decided against it. It was better left where it belonged. Then I returned the worn timepiece into the left pocket of my waistcoat.

10
A Cobbled Path

Wanting a break from the estate, I wrote Aunt Gwen that I would come to visit her in Edinburgh where she had been living ever since she married. Before she was wed, Aunt Gwen lived with us at Forestedge, in the capacity of Harold and my governess. Not lacking prospects but unwilling to entertain any thought of marriage, she was a spinster until the age of twenty-nine. This always put her at odds with Father. He insisted that she should marry for a husband to take care of her, as her lungs were weak due to asthma, and he had his own family to mind. She however protested that as the eldest he might as well take on responsibility for her, and 'hold on to the dowry.' In truth, Father was as little compatible with her vivacious nature as he was with my rebellious one. While she was able to form Harold into a fine gentleman, Father blamed her for failing to control me. This was a gross misjudgement on his side, for what I was like without her control they came to see after she did marry. Two years before Evangeline entered our family, Gwendolyn Clarence met the dashing but considerably older captain of the Royal Navy, Sir Ian Robert Murray, and she finally moved out of her ancestral home. Still a child, I was truly upset with that change because I had spent more time with her than with my own mother. Not very long after Aunt Gwen's departure, I was sent to boarding school and there I was truly unmanageable, being expelled from one to be enrolled to another that was closer to the estate.

Widowed and childless, Aunt Gwen grew excited about the prospect of having family visit. After all, she was the female relation closest to me next to Rosalind and Evangeline. Dropping the letters completely, she sent a quick staccato of telegrams, hurriedly arranging for me to come to her place as soon as possible. To my dismay she insisted that I bring Evangeline along. Even though he said he would be lonely, Father too, welcomed the idea that she should join me. At least, when taking her along I would not have any run-ins with the Thompson siblings, as they were still in France.

Not even two weeks after my birthday we headed over to Edinburgh. Aunt Gwen made all sorts of plans for us: sightseeing, the opera, and the museum — having an overall good time. My initial attempted escape from the estate ended in my wishes being completely ignored. Despite her title, Aunt Gwen's household was very small, only having an old parlourmaid, an even older butler — who was mostly out of sight even before the passing of his master — and a cook. Thus, with a social schedule and with Evangeline coming along, our travel party increased to four, as each of us was to bring a servant. Of course, for her it was her lady's maid Elaine Eilers. I brought along some young footman who had recently been put into the position. It was a tedious business. The journey up North was uneventful, with Evangeline and I sitting opposite each other and exchanging trivialities. At some point she produced a collection of short stories, *The Jungle Book*, which she read out loud supposedly to entertain me. Or at least that was what I suspected, as it was the last thing, we had read together five years prior. Instead, to my annoyance, it drew in a gaggle of children, crowding our first-class compartment. I then opted to close my eyes and sleep, eventually failing in an attempt to do so. We arrived at Aunt Gwen's town house in York Place long past midday. Yet, we were treated to a luncheon which she had prepared, barely giving us the break, we needed to refresh ourselves. While the maid and butler were there to greet us, they seemed to fade into the tapestry as Aunt Gwen whirled past them.

"Oh, my dears!" she said, meeting us directly in the hallway.

"Aunt Gwen, you look well." I replied.

"Oh, I'm so sorry that I was unable to come to the estate for your birthday, my dear. It's always those weak lungs forcing me to drop my plans suddenly. But look at how you have grown! Such a strapping man," she said kissing me on the cheek, and then turning to my travel companion, "And look at you little Evey! What a refined lady you've become. How can half a year make such a difference? I'm feeling quite a lot older seeing the two of you!"

However, she still looked considerably young for her age. The youngest sibling of Father, she had the same traits that almost all Clarence's had: a sharp face with hazel eyes, flaxen hair, a tall and slender stature. Only the way she addressed us indicated the great gap in our age. Another trait of the Clarence's was pushed to the extreme: the charm. Her engrossing nature was so enthralling that one could not escape it.

"Now come in, sit, and eat!" she instructed us, while the servants rushed to take away our things.

As soon as we sat at the table, Aunt Gwen's aged maid, Agnes, waddled in with the first course of the meal, a light consommé.

"Gosh, Arthur! What the deuce were you thinking?!" Aunt Gwen exclaimed slapping her hand on the table, which startled both Evangeline and me.

"I ... pardon, what do you mean?" I asked, almost dropping my spoon.

"Running off to the Army like that! And all the way to India. I've been wanting to ask you this to your face. I thought I had taken better care of you and that you would have confided at least in me."

"I know, I'm truly sorry. But Edinburgh really was not far enough from Forestedge to go through with my plans." I stated, for it was true. While Father did not personally make the attempt to stop me, Harold surely would have come and dragged me to Sandhurst if he had caught wind of my just being under his nose. After all, he made his way down to Brighton where Rosalind lived. Although, it was already too late by the time he caught up to me.

"That Rosalind. We should have expected it of you ... two peas in a pod. Out of all the nephews and nieces I have, you two are my favourites! The rest is just so boring ... " and then turning to Evangeline, "Of course I don't mean to say that you are boring, pet. It is merely that you are not a Clarence, and all Clarence's have the tendency to either be as boring as tepid water or as wild as raging rivers." And then she smiled at me.

"Which one are you, Aunt Gwen?" I asked, humouring her.

"Is that really something you need to ask, Arthur?" she answered with a puckish grin.

Then, throughout lunch, we continued to chat about recent events. It was mainly Evangeline who talked about how the Thompsons visited us, the ball we went to, and the riding accident of which her wrist had already recovered. Aunt Gwen was listening attentively, changing her expressions accordingly to each event: a mischievous one for the way I upset Miss Violet, a pleased one for our apparent enjoyment of the ball, and a despondent one for poor Evangeline's injury.

"What eventful few months the two of you had!" she exclaimed, "I was looking forward to having you play me something, pet. You don't mind, do you? I especially had a tuner come to take care of that dusty old piano of mine."

"Naturally, I would be pleased to play for you, Aunt Gwen. I would just like to rest for a little if you would excuse me."

"Oh, of course. Go ahead. Arthur, dear, you will join me for a coffee in the parlour, won't you?"

Thus, Evangeline did retire to the quarters assigned to her and I went with Aunt Gwen into the parlour.

As soon as we sat down her air of nonchalance shifted into a slightly more sombre tone. Looking me straight in the eye, she asked, "The Thompson boy, is he little Evey's suitor?"

"Yes ... one could say that." I answered hesitantly.

It came as no surprise how observant she was, noticing Evangeline's blushes, even though she never once mentioned that she was still in close correspondence with Thompson.

"My, how tedious. Of all families it must be them. How dull." She sighed, shaking her head.

"You know the Thompsons?"

"Of course, I know the Thompsons, my dear. I don't know them well, especially not the children. But we inhabit the same city after all. And while I am not involved with my brother's business, I do know his closest associate. After all, he had Mr Thompson senior himself court me." Aunt Gwen noted, and dismissively clicked her tongue.

"I never heard of this."

"Why would you? It was before your birth. I rejected him as I did many. He was such a bore. Is this one a bore too?"

"I wouldn't say that he is boring." I pondered, thinking of Thompson's sly attitude.

"Is that so? ... but I really can't believe my brother. He was pushing it back then with me and now he is pushing it onto our little Evey. He's such a hypocrite, marrying for love himself but expecting others to do it for duty. I am in the right mind to have a word with him."

"There seems to be affection on Thompson's side, at least." Was my honest reply.

"Well, and little Evey ... what does she think?"

"How would I know?"

"True, how would you? And you? What do you think of it?"

"I don't enjoy his person, to say the least ... "

"My, when have you become such a diplomat, Arthur? Just tell her straight that you don't want him around her."

"I don't have the right to. Evey is an adult now." I said, remembering all the moments that I was dangerously close to Evangeline.

"You have every right to, after all she is dear to you, is she not?"

"Of course, she is *dear family*." I insisted, flustered.

132

"How about you? Is there someone who caught your eye? I'm curious!"

Aunt Gwen's barrage of questions was an unbridled assault for which there never was a complete defence. It was for this reason that I shied away from visiting her sooner and for which I was secretly grateful that she hadn't ambushed me at the estate yet. Despite all the affection I felt for her, I was daunted by her keen observation skills. To my relief, Agnes then entered to serve the coffee, distracting my aunt as she insisted on presenting me with the 'very best pralines' one could get hold of in Edinburgh. Raving about how well they tasted she completely dropped the topic of courtship and talked with me about our plans for our four days stay in the city. Her schedule was for us to rest on the day of the arrival, look at the most prominent sites the day after, then go to the opera on the third day — for finally a company had come to visit the city and she just could not pass the opportunity — and then we would already be leaving again. A very short stay but knowing her health we did not wish to impose on her too long either. The rest of the afternoon passed in a flash, as Aunt Gwen overwhelmed us with her charms.

The following day, however, showed how much her asthma had worsened. Her health was easily affected by her excitement, as leaving the bed was already an issue for her that morning. Thus, she let us know that she needed some time to recover and that it would be impossible for her to climb the inclines of the Old Town. Instead, the two of us should have a wonderful time and meet up with her in the afternoon for a visit to the National Gallery just atop the Princes Street Gardens. I wanted to escape Evangeline by coming to the city, and yet again I was alone with her. However, I had to admit that seeing her excited about the most menial things filled me with a sense of joy, as well. We took the tram over North Bridge towards the Old Town. She darted for a seat atop the vehicle as we were lucky to have sunshine that day. Happily, she watched the sandstone cityscape pass us by during the short ride. Our starting point was just behind the bridge at the junction of the Royal Mile.

"Which way should we go?" Evangeline inquired eagerly.

"You shall decide. I do not really care for sightseeing. Why are we even doing this? We've been here so often."

"Don't moan! Just because you've seen it before, does not mean that it's not nice to see it again. If you really don't mind, then let's go to the castle first."

"You lead the way." I answered and turned towards the incline all the way up.

"Are you not going to offer me your arm this time?"

"Would you want me to?" I asked without expecting an answer.

But to my surprise, she was not as embarrassed as she was that time in Carlisle and instead naturally placed her arm into mine.

"What will people think, Evey?" I reprimanded her, startled.

"You said it was only a problem if I thought of it as one." She replied with a teasing grin.

Captivated, I let her do as she pleased. While we walked up the craggy, cobbled road towards the castle, we passed the many multi-storeyed edifices, that were stacked up to four levels. Seamlessly the grey tenements merged into each other. Only here and there, they were broken up by the steep closes that would lead down to a lower level of the city. It would have been quick walk, but we went at leisurely pace. Finally reaching our destination, we were treated to a marvellous outlook onto the city in the late morning, stretching beyond the densely built new town towards the Firth.

"We never went up that hill ... Even though we've been here so often." I mused, having turned towards the view on Arthur's Seat.

"No, we haven't."

"The hill was just around the corner, Sir Ian enjoyed taking us out to Portobello for swimming and sailing more. I liked it better too." I said, after all a beach was refreshing sight for someone who dwelled in the countryside.

"Would you like to?"

"Go to Portobello?"

"No, I mean: would you like to go up Arthur's Seat?"

"You are not wearing appropriate frock. Besides, how would Miss Thompson feel if you betrayed her like that. Going up with me instead of her?" I laughed.

"She needn't know."

"Does she even know you are here? She'd probably be cross with you for coming all the way without her being home."

"Oh yes, I wrote her in my last letter that I was coming here with you."

"You did? And Thompson?"

"No, I did not write him about it."

"Not about *visiting* or not about *visiting with me?*"

She blushed and did not answer, thus I did not insist on continuing to talk about it. While I never repeated to her the details of the exchange I had with Thompson, the offense against Miss Violet and Thompson's coldness towards me made it apparent that the two of us would never become friends. We would not even become friendly with each other. Even though they were in France, us being in Edinburgh made the Thompsons a recurring theme of our conversations. It made me feel twice as annoyed than before for not having been able to come all by myself. We took in the view for a little longer and then headed back down the Royal Mile in the direction of the George IV bridge. Evangeline insisted on her regular pilgrimage to *Greyfriars Bobby Fountain*. As though she had never seen it before she studied the brazen Skye Terrier with delighted smiles.

"Your obsession with this statue escapes my understanding … Why do you have to look at it every time we come?" I asked while watching her circle around it.

"It's just such a lovely story of loyalty and love, don't you agree?"

135

"Evey, it's a dog …"

"It doesn't really matter if it's a dog or not. The important thing is that there was true dedication."

"Aren't you a romantic …"

"Love, loyalty, and dedication are important in life, Arthur. For dogs and men, alike." She said and hooked her arm right back into mine.

We continued our promenade through the Old Town and around midday went to have a light lunch. Forgetting the time, we were pressed to walk promptly down Cockburn Street, as any type of steep and insecure closes would have been too difficult to descend for Evangeline in her constricting attire. As we arrived late at the National Gallery, we were both flushed. Aunt Gwen was already awaiting us on *The Mound*, at the foot of the imposing ionic pillars of the neo-classical temple building. We were able to discern her from the crowd as she was wearing a ridiculously broad straw-hat with a green band, which was decorated by a whole turtle dove lying wings-spread and face down on the brim. As to make it an even more gruesome spectacle the hat was fastened by a dangerously long hat pin with a heart-shaped head, creating a picture of the poor bird having been apprehended by an arrow mid-flight.

"Oh, look at you two dears being all sweet together." She said smiling.

I had not noticed anymore, but we were still walking about arm in arm. We instantly broke away from each other, which made Aunt Gwen chuckle.

"Don't be shy about it, you silly geese. Now come along!"

I did not understand more about fine arts than any other layman, only enjoying those artworks that appeased my sense of aesthetics. Due to my education, I was at least able to discern the broadest themes and periods. However, fine arts was something that was likely to be appreciated by more sensible beings, such as my female company. Thus, I let them walk around the galleries as a pair, while I would traverse it by myself, occasionally stopping to look at something that caught my interest. I was pausing in front a religious painting of a scene that did not seem familiar to me. It showed a group of people clad in colourful robes, in a sort of celebration. A wedding perhaps? The focus being on a couple that were crowned with floral wreaths, their hands joined. Maybe due to the talks of courtship I was drawn to the image. The solemnity of the scene invoked an emotion of despondence within me.

"There you are, dear!" Aunt Gwen came up to me from behind, ripping me out of my contemplative thoughts, "Were you looking at that painting?"

"Yes, somehow … I just felt compelled to."

"You have a profound taste, don't you?" she said smiling mysteriously, and added, "We were thinking of leaving soon and having tea somewhere."

"That's a wonderful idea. All these artworks are overwhelming my dull senses."

Aunt Gwen sympathetically patted me on the shoulder, leading me to where Evangeline was. In the distance, I could see that she was viewing a painting with a more profane topic: a scantily clad woman being embraced by a man in armour. At the foot of the woman's ornate skirt there were a child and a dog. It appeared lavish and vulgar. I really could neither understand nor appreciate the imagery and wondered what exactly had drawn her to it. Suddenly, a gentleman came to converse with Evangeline. She greeted him with surprise, but also with warmth. By his perfect and prim get-up, the gestures and vexing smile I could instantly tell who it was: Daniel Thompson. In the flesh.

"Thompson! Fancy seeing you here …" I promptly called out.

"Clarence, the same could be said of you." He answered, glancing over to Evangeline.

"Oh, so that's the Thompson boy." Aunt Gwen whispered under her breath.

We greeted each other with a customary handshake. The tension between us must have been palpable, as Evangeline looked slightly troubled. Before she could formally introduce him, I made sure that I presented him to Aunt Gwen who was eyeing him with curiosity. I could tell that this irked him even though there was no visible crack in his veneer. What he was doing in Edinburgh, even though we thought he was still in France? He alone returned because there was an urgent matter that needed settling at their office in the city. What he was doing in the National Gallery all by himself then? Having tirelessly worked for the past days he felt like relieving his senses and enjoying something pleasant. In short, it was for some pretentious reason that we chanced upon him. He inquired about our plans for the day, and Aunt Gwen graciously — or in my opinion rather mischievously — invited him to come along with us to have high tea. Thus, in a party of four, we made our way through the Princes Street Gardens for a place of Thompson's recommendation that was close to *Jenners*. The flowers were in full bloom, and for us to enjoy them we walked slowly. While Thompson and Evangeline were ahead of us, conversing and smiling at each other fondly, Aunt Gwen and I kept a distance, observing them.

"If we give them their space," she said, "maybe we can see what little Evey actually thinks of him."

"Wouldn't it be easier to ask her?" I suggested, annoyed at the pair trotting in front of us.

"You haven't asked her yet either, have you?" she retorted.

I was caught out and didn't answer.

"You are an established man now, Arthur, and she is a gown woman. You don't need to tiptoe around Evangeline. You should admit to her what you truly want." She said encouragingly.

I was stunned by her flagrant statement. Was my desire for Evangeline so evident? Yet, that was not the actual problem. I could not believe what Aunt Gwen was insinuating. I sincerely doubted that she was aware ... no, I was sure that she was mistaken about what kind of emotions Evangeline did stir in me. She would not have said something so outrageous if she knew that I was suppressing the basest of all impulses. That I really wanted to bed my foster sister, without any meaningful emotion.

"What are you talking about, Aunt Gwen? Evey is my ... she is like a sister to me."

"Arthur, why is it that you and my brother keep forgetting that *Evangeline is not your sister*? Neither is she a Clarence." She admonished me.

"If I am not supposed to think of her as a sister then what should I consider her as?"

"That is for you to decide, dear." She said, again wearing the same mysterious smile as in the gallery.

Truthfully, she was not one of the tepid Clarences. I could not understand her way of thinking. At the steps toward the Scott Monument, Evangeline halted to wait for us. Once caught up to the pair, it was Thompson who initiated a conversation.

"Miss Hollings told me that you will be visiting the opera tomorrow. I did not mark you down as a man of culture, Clarence."

"..."

"Are you fond of the opera, Mr Thompson?" Aunt Gwen asked.

"At times I am, Lady Murray. You see, our family has a private box at the theatre as my mother loves such cultured activities. In fact, I was planning to watch tomorrow's performance as well. I was to join Mama, but she is unwell. It is really nothing to be enjoyed alone."

"A private box? Why don't you come along with us then Mr Thompson? Or maybe we could join you?" she suggested nonchalantly and with a conscious lack of modesty.

Of course, the sly fox would not let the opportunity slide to spend more time with Evangeline and to impress her. Certainly, he must have been overjoyed by the fact that he could play the attentive suitor, and all in front of me. Thus, he became an accessory to our plans. In honour of Miss Hollings' visit, he insisted, he could make some time and join us for at least that one day of our stay. It was irritating to have him around, and I could not quite figure out what Aunt Gwen herself was planning, especially with regard to her previous comments. And I began to wonder, as Thompson was in all respects a clever man, if he as well had caught on to me. I wondered, if in fact, all his snide remarks and provocations had their origins in some sort of insecurity, maybe the idea that I was a potential rival. However, it did not make a difference to me. Whether he saw me as a rival or not, he made clear that there was enmity, and I would not let him walk all over me. The next day would show how much or how little Evangeline cared for him.

The afternoon and evening passed by, and I was glad to finally have some rest in my room. I still felt uncomfortable in soft beds, but the pain of the injury had significantly decreased. Surely, I would soon be able to return to service, and while thinking about it I fell into a shallow sleep. A light rapping at my door awoke me. I switched on the electric lighting and without asking who it was, I opened the door to find Evangeline standing in front of me, requesting to enter. Before I could turn her away, she walked in to stand in the middle of the room.

"Disturbing me at night has become a bad habit of yours." I said, as I remained at the door.

"I'm awfully sorry— It's ... I needed to talk to you about something."

"My guess is that you want to talk to me about Thompson?"

She blushed but shook her head and nervously started to fidget with her hands.

"What is it then?" I asked annoyed.

"No ... I ... I think ... it can wait. Uhm— Sleep well." She stuttered without looking at me.

As I barely had the time to close the door after she entered, she quickly rushed out through it again, and bolted towards the bedroom adjacent to mine. By the life of me I did not know what her visit was about. Or rather, I did not want to think what it could be about. So, the white-livered rat was on her mind after all. I did not like it one bit. Lying back down in bed I meditated on what she had told me earlier that day: 'Love, loyalty and dedication are important in life … for dogs and men, alike,' and I weighed up Thompson and myself, and in what respect either of us expressed any of it toward her. Too tired from having walked all those inclines and cobbled pavements that day, I fell back asleep without coming to any conclusion.

11
Ascension

As announced, Thompson had sent over a servant with his calling card to proclaim that he would be coming soon. Because the weather had remained fair, he wished to join us for our walk up on Calton Hill. We had finished our breakfast as the butler delivered this bit of news to the table.

"Calton Hill ... I suppose that's the best he can do." I said dismissively.

"What do you mean, dear?" Aunt Gwen asked with curiosity.

"He's an indolent cad." I explained, to which she chortled.

Evangeline was taken aback and berated me, "Arthur, don't be rude!"

"His own sister said so herself."

"No, she did not. Besides, isn't it fine? We were heading there anyway."

"It will be tedious to have him around."

"Why, on the contrary! Listening to the two of you, it sounds to be interesting to have Mr Thompson join us!" she exclaimed, and I knew what she was referring to.

"Will you be fine joining us as well, Aunt Gwen?" I inquired concerned about her health.

"Today I am as fit as a fiddle! It would do me good to have a little exercise every now and then," she ensured us, then playfully looking over to Evangeline added, "And I also would not miss the view for the world."

Around an hour later, Thompson arrived and was seated in the parlour. The ladies, of course, had not yet finished with changing into appropriate frocks. I thought it uncommonly intrusive for someone as so mindful of etiquette, but he must have felt alleviated by the extraordinary grace of being allowed to visit in the morning. Addressing him from the door frame in which I stood, I did not bother to enter the room.

"Thompson, you are here already? It's indecent to rush ladies so."

Even though his seat was facing the door, he did not rise and barely even looked my way.

"I'll keep that advice in mind, Clarence. I'm sure that you would be the expert on indecent behaviour towards ladies." He replied coldly.

"Speaking of which, how is your sister doing?"

"Very well, she is enjoying her time in France. It is good that she does not have to be here and suffer your presence in our hometown."

"A true shame. You could just have dragged along one of your other sisters for my enjoyment then. I hear they are more fetching, but maybe just as gullible."

For once, his cold facade slipped and to my entertainment he darted me a glance, fury in the eyes. So, he had favourites among his sisters. Before I could hear any sort of reply, Aunt Gwen had bumped into me. Then she ushered me into the parlour by tapping her closed parasol against my calves. Her flamboyant walking dress was just as loud as her exclamations that I should not loiter around. Evangeline trailed behind her for she had finished dressing, as well. She was in a simpler get-up than I anticipated, with all the time that took both to change. Wearing a plain shirtwaist with a bow, wool skirt and felt hat was a refreshing look for her, especially as she was continuously wearing those suffocating toilettes that made her look older than she in truth was. Just as quickly as Thompson had an emotional burst, as quickly did he regain his sense and put on his elegant airs again. He rose and greeted the ladies courteously.

"It took you an hour to change into simple clothing like that?" I asked.

"I simply could not decide, and seeing that we will walk up Calton Hill ... is it really that plain?"

"Oh, not at all. The subtlety of the dress only emphasises your natural beauty, Miss Hollings." Thompson said with his gentleman's smile, even though I could tell that he was disenchanted with her not putting more effort in the way she looked. He was even more dismayed to see that upon leaving she was wearing a similar Norfolk jacket to mine. Knowing that women put so much mind into clothing, I wondered what message she was trying to carry across to him, but quickly brushed off any useless thought of it.

Not long after, we took two hansom cabs to the foot of the hill, even though it was not very far away from York Place. Thompson and I had the displeasure of sharing one, as upon her insistence Aunt Gwen and Evangeline rode in the other. The ascension was unspectacular and did not take particularly long either. I paid attention to Aunt Gwen, as it still was a steep incline. Thompson and Evangeline walked far in front of us.

"This reminds me so much of the times when the three of you came to visit, only that it was Harold that hung back with me and Sir Ian, and you and little Evey rushing in front of us. He was always such a mindful boy, my poor dear." She reminisced.

"He really enjoyed Sir Ian's company ..."

"... and Sir Ian really did enjoy his. My Darling, he held all three of you dear, as though you were his own. I'm sure he would have been proud of the merit you have brought to the Empire."

"Even though I am not a commissioned officer?"

"That did not really matter to him. To be honest, you are right, Arthur. Would you have stayed with us; you would have been found straight away! When you ran off, my brother and Harold came personally to look for you here."

"They did? What happened?"

I was surprised. Yet again something that was never mentioned to me by anyone, neither orally nor in writing.

"Sir Ian told them off. He was of the opinion that you should be given agency over your own future and that you mustn't do anything you did not want to do. One would think that a service man like him shared their sentiment about your disobedience. However, first and foremost he was a free-spirited Scotsman."

"He would not have chosen you otherwise." I remarked.

"Oh you!" Aunt Gwen said, becoming bashful.

"I wonder if he actually was aware how foolish my actions were."

"I don't think he considered you foolish. He always ensured me that 'You'd come out of it a better man.' when I voiced my concerns after receiving your letters. And after all, he must have seen that the role my brother envisioned for you, was not a type of role that'd fit you. You are contented the way things are, aren't you?"

I agreed. Sir Ian was always a very wise and perceptive man. While he indiscriminately displayed a jolly demeanour towards us children, he was still a man of conviction and had a keen instinct for judging people's characters. He must have been aware that a ne'er-do-well like me needed to experience hardship to be humbled.

Seeing the couple ahead of us I mused, "I wonder what he would have thought about Evangeline being courted by the likes of Thompson."

"Probably the same thing I do."

"And that would be?"

"That with regard to status and looks they do appear like a good match, but that everything else about them is very mismatched."

"Mismatched?"

"Just look at them."

But aside of the difference in attire, I could not deduce what exactly she was alluding to. We closed in on Thompson and Evangeline, who were already waiting at the summit. With excitement she quickly walked back to me, and almost ran, completely forgetting her surroundings. Upon dragging me towards the National Monument, she asked if Thompson would like to join us in standing at the edge of it. He declined, watching on bemused at her childish glee. There it was, the 'Pride and Poverty of Scotland,' the unfinished Parthenon-like-structure. Evangeline was impatient and did not wait to walk around to the steps that would make it more accessible. Instead, she had me scale the foundation of the tall portico and help her up from above. I suspected that this was the reason for her plain attire, as she had always taken joy in climbing up the monument. However, I would not have guessed that this childishness remained within her, so much that she forgot her usual refined mannerism over it. The magnificent panoramic view of the whole city was even more imposing than that which one could enjoy at the castle, especially because it included the castle. In spite of that, our focus was on the Firth. As the wind was billowing with big clamour, making it hard to even understand another, we silently faced the view towards the body of water. The sun rising towards its midday height made the surface shine. Glancing over at Evangeline, her expression was wholly content, and I felt satisfied at seeing her that way. Aunt Gwen and Thompson were waiting at the slightly elevated ground. Carefully Evangeline descended, holding on to my hand all the while. As I was about to climb down to the ground to help her from there, Thompson to my disdain took the opportunity to extend his own hand towards her. She graciously accepted, and he firmly pulled her down, momentarily catching her to hold her in his arms. They exchanged shy smiles.

"You really do love the view from here, don't you, Evey? That excitement of yours never changes." Aunt Gwen commented coming up to them.

"Yes, it's a wonderful view. It always makes me remember the first time I saw the ocean."

"Is there any semblance to the Indian Ocean and the Firth of Forth?" Thompson asked quizzically.

"Oh, well not exactly. It's the dense city suddenly being broken off by the water, and the many ships coming in and out of a port that makes me think of it. It was so very impressive, it made me forget about all the fears that shook me before the passage."

"A young, orphaned child, having to leave everything it has known behind … It must still be heart-breaking for you to think back to India." Thompson said compassionately.

"No …" she replied slowly, contemplating, "I barely remember the place that was my home … and I don't remember my parents all too well, either. It's been such a long time. And … after all, I found a new family here. A family that cared for me so well and that loved me just as much."

She glanced over to me and smiled, so innocently, so earnestly. It was a smile that pierced me like an arrow through the heart. A reminder of the shame I should feel for my wrong thoughts and actions.

Thompson left us after a luncheon to return to his office, and then to change for the evening, meeting us later at the Theatre Royale where the opera would be performed.

As I again was finished before the ladies, I browsed through an *Opera Guide* in Aunt Gwen's reading room. I was not at all familiar with the performance we were going to watch. Squirming around in the armchair, due to having been forced again into the constraining black and white evening suit, I read the synopsis. *La Forza del Destino* by Verdi was one of those melodramatic stories about star-crossed lovers and vengeful family feuds. It was a lacklustre setting: a woman eloping with her lover, who accidentally murders the father, then the lovers are split up and the heroine's brother ventures on an odyssey to kill both. Some war somewhere happens, there are misunderstandings and as always it ends with the destitute woman being undone by the villain who eventually also dies, while the tragic hero must live on with the miserable knowledge that his lover perished.

"That's quite commendable. You are reading up on the opera."

Evangeline had entered wearing a modest mauve coloured evening toilette that gave less exposure to her neckline than the ball gown she had worn at the Fawcetts. Her hair was elegantly pulled up, revealing her fair neck that was adorned by a glass-beaded choker necklace. The long white gloves blended with her pale skin, folds and frills hid her bust and a plain violet sash that closed at the back in a bow was draped around her dainty waist.

"If I'm forced to sit more than two and a half hours through it, I may as well know what exactly they are shouting at each other for."

"The plot is not the main thing about the opera, it's the music." She said, leaning over the backrest of the chair to peek into the *Opera Guide*.

"That's like saying the plot of a play does not matter as long as the set and outfits are opulent."

"No, it's not."

"It is."

"What are the two of you bickering about like an old married couple?" Aunt Gwen asked, as she entered in her ornate evening gown.

"A trivial matter." I replied.

Finally, all of us were ready to depart. As the Theatre Royal was barely a five-minute walk away from Aunt Gwen's place, we took an evening stroll. The sun had yet to set as we passed the many new electric streetlamps, that provided security for those who would promenade much later in the evening. Thompson already awaited us at the entrance to the theatre, greeting me and Aunt Gwen customarily, however kissing Evangeline's hand as she reached out to shake his. Her cheeks instantly turned crimson, while our aunt covertly hooted behind her spread feather fan.

"Your beauty is dazzling tonight, Miss Hollings." He said and gazed straight into her eyes.

"I— thank you, Mr Thompson." She answered, the blush not having faded yet.

Thus, without a moment's hesitation he draped her arm under his and led her in, while she followed like a docile lamb. Aunt Gwen who observed the pair quietly, hid a grin behind the fan. She was taking decidedly too much joy in Evangeline's courtship with Thompson.

"Aren't you going to say something to him?" she asked, suddenly turning to me.

"Why should I?"

"Don't you be boring, dear!"

"Whatever do you mean by that?" I asked flustered.

"Ah, there we are!" she exclaimed with a whimsical smile, rudely pointing her finger into my face.

However, we did not delve deeper into this topic as we entered the theatre, following Thompson to his family's private box. Just as I anticipated, the opera was as convoluted and nonsensical as the description in the guide made it out to be. I personally did not find the music appealing, yet Aunt Gwen seemed to have an agreeable time. And Evangeline? She too was trying to focus on the stage but appeared to be distracted by Thompson's presence to fully take in everything. Occasionally they would exchange words and gesture to the stage. Finally, after more than an hour it was time for the intermission, and I excused myself from the ladies as I needed to smoke a cigarette. Unfortunately, I was thus stuck alone with Thompson in the smoking lounge, and he unexpectedly paid attention to me by starting a conversation. A sense of foreboding made me more aware of his pretentious mannerisms: the way he stood with his chin up and his arms crossed, that vexing grin on his visage — clearly, he was burning with the desire to rub something in my face.

"I haven't said this before but Clarence, for once you look like a genuine gentleman."

"I'm only one on the outside." I said, after puffing my cigarette.

He smiled wryly.

"Are you enjoying the opera?"

"I can't say that I do. It's a drab story."

"It has very common themes to please a broad audience. For example, *a brother that is the undoing of his sister*, very tragic but not uncommon."

Thompson said, gazing at me condescendingly.

"I see. Although, there would be no tragedy if it wasn't for *a mongrel interfering with family business.*" I retorted, reciprocating his nasty look.

"While we are speaking of family business, I must thank you again Clarence. If you had not decided to visit your aunt in Edinburgh, I would not have been treated to such a lovely evening with Miss Hollings."

Instantly, the scales fell from my eyes. With this statement it became apparent to me why we had run into him. Coincidentally being at the gallery, coincidentally having a ticket for the same performance … It was no coincidence; it was Father's doing. Surely, he knew before us that Thompson had returned from France due to business. They are business associates after all. As we had to bring servants with us, Father probably instructed the footman to spy on our schedule, so that it could be passed on to Thompson. The rest played out just as both had desired. Their joined duplicity was appalling to me.

"I assume you have been exchanging telegrams with my father?"

"Oh, you are surprisingly quick on your feet, Clarence."

"That's another thing I learned in the service."

"Amazing," he said with a sardonic smirk, "As you helped me reunite with Miss Hollings sooner than anticipated I'll tell you this out of gratitude: I received your father's blessing. Therefore, there is nothing in the way of me proposing to her."

It was a low blow, and I physically felt it. So, this were the odds I was going against, and yet against in what way? I disliked Thompson and did not want him near Evangeline. But Father appreciated him, and Evangeline … appreciated him? I still was not certain about it. However, where was I in this picture? I grew evermore uncertain as to why exactly I did not want her to be engaged to him. After all, she was a woman and not a girl anymore. What I told Aunt Gwen; I did mean sincerely: I had no right to meddle. Not with the way I viewed Evangeline. I was being worse than her suitor, but I would never concede to him.

"I told you this before, but you seem to have forgotten, Thompson.

Therefore, I will repeat it for you. Slowly and in simple words: only Evangeline will be the one to decide on her future."

"And she will share her decision with me tomorrow. You shall anticipate it, Clarence." He said coldly.

"I shall. Eagerly." I answered.

We exited the smoking lounge to be met by Evangeline who was agitated, urging us to come along into the foyer. Aunt Gwen was sitting there surrounded by some other ladies of her acquaintance. She had to take a rest for recovery as she suffered a dizzy spell and was short of breath.

"It's just too suffocating in here. I cannot stand it much longer" she apologised, "I ruined the evening for you."

"Don't worry about it, I was not particularly interested in the opera anyway." I assured her.

"We'll take you home." Evangeline said and was about to set off to the cloak room, but Aunt Gwen stopped her.

She insisted that she should enjoy the rest of the evening, and that it was more than enough if I accompanied her home. With her acquaintances as witnesses, she turned to Thompson asking him to take good care of her little niece, and to send her home right after the performance. He happily accepted. In spite, of Evangeline's protests of not wanting to impose on him and worrying about Aunt Gwen, she eventually gave in. Thus, our party split into two pairs as I headed out with my aunt on my arm, and Thompson back to his box with Evangeline on his. It was still not fully dark, for there would always be a dim light brightening the Scottish summer night. The night was made even brighter by the streetlights, as we set off on our brief way back to York Place. Once we arrived, Agnes immediately ushered her visibly shaken mistress into her smoking room, in which there were always datura cigarettes prepared in case Aunt Gwen should feel worse. While she inhaled the calming smoke, she commented in a dejected voice:

"How boring, Arthur. You did not even contest it."

"What is it?"

"You let Mr Thompson walk off with Evey."

"Were you trying to incite a feud between Thompson and I?"

"Are you implying that there isn't one already?"

I did not deign to answer her provocation and she simply sighed.

"Where's your grit, dear?"

"Aunt Gwen, the opera in combination with your cigarette must have excited your imagination too much."

"That's no way to talk to your elders, dear. Anyway, we'll hear from little Evey how the rest of the evening went. The second half should be well on its way."

"I'm not going to stay up that long. The opera drained me of all my vital essences."

As soon as I was sure that Aunt Gwen was feeling well enough, I retreated to my room and shook off the detestable evening attire. For a long time, I lay in bed to contemplate. It almost appeared to me as though Thompson was right after all. Maybe Father did in fact see in him a semblance of Harold, for he had become so eager on uniting Evangeline and him. Mrs Daniel Thompson of Edinburgh … no, surely Father would try to find a way to have both live with him in the mansion. After all, once Evangeline left … once I left for service, he would be all alone, and that would be unbearable. What would remain in the halls for him? Yet, I liked none of it because I disliked Thompson. Instead, I pondered on what it would have been like if Harold had wed Evangeline. Would it have been better? Mrs Harold Clarence of Forestedge? It sounded right to me. But this future was lost almost three years prior. Whichever outcome Thompson's proposal would have, on the long run it made no difference, as there was the certainty to Evangeline one day marrying a man, starting her own family, and becoming happy, as I hoped. I truly wanted her to find happiness, and that would only work if I finally let go of my petty and unseemly desires for her. They were standing in the way of my sincere wishes for her future. 'I must let go' and 'I must move on' were the things I was sure of, and those thoughts would only be realised as soon as I put a physical distance between the two of us. Finally, I had calmed myself. With the resolve of reining in my desires, I lay awake in bed. However, a light rapping at the door ripped me out of my meditation and should hoist me back into a precarious reality. The reality that would prove to me that I was deluding myself. The reality that showed me that there was certain futility in my thinking that I could truly become a better man. Without turning the lights on, I opened the door to find Evangeline standinginfrontofme.

12
Folly is in the Heart of Children

Evangeline walked in without asking my permission and darted towards the bed. Her legs flopped up as she let herself bounce onto the edge. With a hint of brightness yet remaining outside, her features were made visible. She was only wearing her nightdress, not even a gown to cover herself up. The hair was tied loosely together with a ribbon. I was glad that I did not turn on the light to have better look at the arousing outlook. She seemed quite perturbed, shutting the door behind me I walked over to stand in front of her, hoping that the matter could be quickly settled.

"What are you doing here again? You are becoming more callous by the day."

"I ... I really need to talk to you."

"Is that so? I'm sure it can wait until tomorrow."

"No, it cannot."

And she started to nervously fumble with her hands, the only bad habit she ever had. For the first time I found it extremely disconcerting, because it was a sign of excitement, a sign of feelings that she attempted to mask. It always had been. What was it that unsettled her so? I wanted to grab her by the wrist and make her stop, but I did not.

Instead, I asked her again, "What is it that you want from me now?"

Then she explained to me what happened after I left with Aunt Gwen, that from the moment we had exited the theatre Thompson expressed his happiness about her being in town, that he was singing praises to her person and her beauty, so much that she was not even able to follow the opera for a second any longer. He insisted that he was sincere about her and — boldly for his character — professed his love. Evangeline overwhelmed and alone, did not know how to handle the situation and silently nodded, thinking of a way to escape from the theatre. Insisting that this was neither the right setting nor the right time to deepen their relationship, and with the distraction of Aunt Gwen's health always in the back of her mind, she lamented that she really should have joined me in taking our ailing elder back home. Without watching the finale, Thompson returned Evangeline safely to York Place at her bidding and said his goodbyes for the evening, with the promise to meet again before she leaves. Only Agnes and Eilers were there to welcome the young miss at the door. Despite what she told me, Aunt Gwen must have been too exhausted and had retired to bed. After changing her for bed, both servants also retired. Everyone in the house was asleep and thus she came rushing to me.

"After today, well … he said that he will call on me tomorrow in the morning. I think he means to propose." She finally said, unsettled.

"And what is the issue here? Do you not like him?" I asked. I could not tell her that I was aware of it already, neither did I think that I should mention anything about Father's and Thompson's conniving ways.

"Of course not! I … I mean not like that. As a friend, yes," she answered, thinking out loud, "He is pompous and pretentious, and thinks he is hiding it well. Violet I can forgive for being that way because she is also naive and sometimes has something entertaining to say. But him … he is quite the schemer. And that is nothing I appreciate in a prospective partner."

She shook her head, putting into words a thought that had lingered in my mind. That was her level of perception. She had a firm grasp of all the people around her. There had not been any reason for me to be worried for her. And yet, I was somehow taken aback.

"Then why did you entertain him? You are making no sense." I demanded, remembering all the smiles and pleasantries they had been exchanging during his visit to the estate and in the past days.

"It is undeniable that the Thompsons were a great help to Uncle Arthur. Therefore, I felt obliged to at least give him a bit of my attention. I— I … don't know why he would think that I was infatuated with him. However, I would not have thought that Uncle Arthur would come as well around to thinking that him and I were a good match."

"Did Thompson say that?"

"We would have never run into him if they were not conspiring with each other." She said, half-loud and seemingly annoyed. I would have never guessed that she had both figured out. Evangeline was full of surprises.

"Aunt Gwen and I, as well, were thinking that you were a good match, looking at you from afar." I said, omitting the rest of her statement and hoping to put an end to the discussion.

"Is … Is that really what you think?" she asked, still fidgeting with her hands. She did not look up.

"Does my opinion even matter?"

"Of course, it does, after all … you … I don't have the courage to reject him on my own, or to tell Uncle Arthur that I do not wish to marry him. You … you have to …"

"What exactly do you need me involved for? I cannot ward Thompson off, nor can I truly support you when facing Father. He and I are not on good enough terms that he would weigh in *my concerns* in the matter of *your future.*"

There was no instant reply to my reproachful speech. The silence pressed heavily on the two of us, and I hoped that she was finally ready to leave it be for this night.

However, after a few deep inhales, she began anew, "We — you and me — we were enjoying ourselves before we ran into Mr Thompson, weren't we?"

"Yes?"

"It's ... our relationship improved again, and yet ..."

"Evey, I really have no idea where you want to go with this."

"I need your encouragement." She uttered with determination.

"Well, certainly. Go ahead and decline any proposal. Break it off with Thompson straight away. Tell Father why you do not want to. You are of marriageable age ... you have your own inheritance to claim later ... therefore, you have a choice. And afterwards, if you are upset, you can come and cry to me, if that is what you need." I said impatiently and asked her to once and for all leave me at peace.

"If I am an adult in your eyes, and if I do have a choice, then ... then I want you to treat me ... as an adult ... woman." She insisted.

Then she firmly took hold of my hand, finally lifting her gaze.

"What are you doing?" I demanded, avoiding raising my voice.

There she was, relentlessly peering up to me, her eyes a shining layer of expectation that was gleaming in the semi-darkness. *That* was the type of encouragement that she wanted. The strength had left my hand making me unable to shake her off. All her words, they were mere excuses. Pretences leading onto a certain path, that once treaded on would make the world behind us crumble away. I quietly laughed at this madness. In the short time since my return, had I rubbed off on her that much? With the past tragedies that she had faithfully borne, did she feel encouraged to act out by copying the only role model that was around: me, the wayward son? Encouragement. Yes. If I only had accepted that our relationship was deteriorating to a point beyond repair, this would not have happened. I feared repulsion. I did not want her to hate me. Instead in my desperation I overstepped a line and kissed her pushing it into the opposite direction from which as well there was no return: obsessive attraction — not only mine for her, but hers for me. Still firmly holding my hand and shifting on the bed, her eyes never broke their fixation on me. I asked her why ... why she was so persistent? Why me?

"When I watched you ... I really thought it was unsightly." She said slowly, incoherently.

Even though she had resolve moments ago she was fighting for words.

After seconds of quiet deliberation, she admitted, "That was a pretentious sentiment because you are right. We are animals, aren't we? I was fooling myself; it was excitement and I ... Every day, I thought about how you kissed me, longing for it more and more ..."

More and more. The crescendo of the sensual impulses had become immutable for her too.

"Have I been on your mind all this time?" I asked, my throat all dried up.

She nodded.

"This is my final warning to you Evey. If you invite me to do things, I will not stop." I insisted, hiding my pain.

I truly wanted it to stop then and there, simultaneously there was a strong pull to advance. The strength of her resolve fed on mine. It absorbed the energy from the thoughts that held me awake just mere minutes before she entered this bedchamber.

She kissed the palm of my hand, the soft lips travelling from its middle to the tips of my fingers. Fine moisture clung to them. A touch that unleashed a tempest within me. The vicious emotions that I had hitherto desperately tried to mute were spiralling out of control: the wrath that I felt whenever I was mocked; the greed to monopolise her company and envy over not being able to do so; the desire to do impure things to her from the first time I saw her in the morning not even to be shaken off in my shallow dreams; and finally the vainglorious pride I felt in this very moment that she asked me to do them. Now that she had unfastened the lid to my heart, I thought, she should as well bare all that poured out.

Pinning her down onto the bed I wanted her — I wanted Evangeline, to make her intention clear. Her steady breathing did not change. There were no signs of fear. I looked down on her and saw the pink hues of her pale flesh shining through the thin chemise.

"You want me to kiss you then?" I asked her, moving in for our lips to faintly touch.

A licentious whisper resounded in the room, "Yes."

Yet I did not, because I knew it would not be the end of it. Because I knew, once this threshold was crossed there would be no return to sanity.

"Do you know what will happen to your reputation if we were to be found out?"

"I don't care ..."

"Then your chastity ... Is it mine to take?"

My chest was painful with palpitations that made me feel faint and invigorated at the same time. Following a strenuous silence, her quivering fingertips brushed against my cheek, easing the angry tension that had hitherto drawn every sinew of my body.

"I'll give it to you."

I surrendered to her, and the greatest grace was bestowed upon me. The thin layer of temperance that held me afloat was torn asunder. For all those months that I had dreamed of this moment, I felt delirious, unknowing as to how exactly it had come to this conclusion. Her inclination was towards passion rather than reason, choosing the foster brother that craved her body over the suitor that was ready to look after her for life. The heart of maiden stained with an obsession over the games that adults played. Casting away my conscience as I did our nightclothes, there truly was no way back. I granted her wish before mine: I pressed my lips onto hers, opening to reunite with the tender tongue. The muscles remembering our previous encounter, she reciprocated, pushing, tugging, eventually lightly biting into my lip, the sensation electrifying my whole being. The current passed back to her, making her twitch with excitement as I mapped the contours of her naked body. I kissed her along the slender neckline to the firm breasts, and she flinched every time at a touch that was unbeknown to her. My fingers venturing to that secret spot beneath her golden fleece. Her hips moving in accordance: a paradox movement, as her hands were raised to hide her face in shame. She was sensitive and quickly moaned in delight. Not waiting any longer, I parted her legs and entered her, my body heavily weighing onto her dainty frame. A brief and stifled cry escaped her. Not pushing me away, her hands went to cover her mouth to muffle the sounds of delectable agony. I lost all reason, as I indulged her with all my other senses: her feminine scent, the softness of the narrow flesh enwrapping me, the taste of her sweat, her sounds of pleasure. Perceiving the silver glitter of tears in the corner of her eyes made me pause. A new wave of guilt swept over me, strong enough to almost tear me away from her. Sensing my alarm her arms reached around my neck, and she spoke an anguished but sweet whisper that she could bear with the pain, if only I talked gently to her. Yet, I only kissed her and caressed her. My movement becoming more conscious. More considerate. I had neither thoughts nor words, as I frantically tried to recall the last gentle words, I had imparted to her. To anyone. And what came to mind was that which I would never admit to another woman, "I need you."

Upon opening my eyes, I realised that day had long come. With a start I sat up, but I was alone in bed. Evey had left my room at some point in the night without even waking me. Whilst I was dressing myself, the footman knocked to bring me warm water and told me that the ladies were already downstairs waiting for me to join them with breakfast. I hurriedly got ready. Both looked up as I entered, I instinctively avoided staring at Evey. An unfamiliar shyness overcame me. She, however, smiled at me as I went to take my seat. Aunt Gwen did not notice, for as soon as she saw me, she reiterated that what I already heard from Evey in the night before. Then she let me know that Thompson had in fact left his calling card just prior to my coming downstairs.

"I thought it'd be more sensible to wait until Arthur joined us to ask you, as he also seems quite interested. Will you accept his proposal?" Aunt Gwen inquired, beaming with curiosity.

"I will reject it ... of course"

"Of course? So, you never were invested in this courtship?"

"No ... I ... I never saw him that way. It was merely that he helped Uncle Arthur ... and—"

"He'll be heartbroken about it. Little Evey, you are quite coy and callous!" Aunt Gwen cut her off as she said this in jest.

However, Evey was taken aback and cast down her eyes in disgrace.

"There is no need to upset her further." I interjected.

"Well, aren't *you* happy about this turn of events? You have been sitting there all the while, grinning like a Cheshire cat ... as if you had known!"

I went to cover my mouth with my hand. I hadn't even noticed it.

"I ... I told Arthur yesterday already, a- after I returned." Evey bumbled.

"Ah, I see. You two were *secretly consorting* with each other?"

We were both stunned, and I could feel my heart stop for a moment. Surely, she did not mean it the way we interpreted it.

"How disappointing, so I was the last one to find out ..." Aunt Gwen sighed.

"You certainly aren't. After all, Thompson will be receiving the news soon."

"Oh my, yes. Of course, I will be sitting in with you Evey. Although, I will not have you sit in with us." Aunt Gwen warbled while she turned the teaspoon in her cup.

"Why not?"

"First of all, I'm the chaperone. And second, as much as you dislike the fellow, I think you should at least have the decency to not watch him walk into his doom and frolic in it. Especially not with that gormless grin of yours."

I turned my gaze somewhere else.

"How exciting! To sit in when you reject a suitor for the first time."

"Aren't you the one who is frolicking in face of his humiliation?" I reprimanded her.

"Hush! I am not. It's simply so very exciting. Arthur, you don't know how nerve wracking the first time is for a maiden. The anticipation of the deed alone makes one shake. Aren't I right, Evey?"

"C–certainly. Yes." She answered, the tips of her ears crimson, and I too felt my face become hot.

Thus, it was decided that Evey would give the news to Thompson in the parlour, and that she should at least wear the finest and most appropriate dress she had brought along, for a woman should look her best when breaking a man's heart. Then, we talked with Aunt Gwen about our departure schedule and that we should maybe take a later train, due to us not knowing when Thompson would show up on the doorstep. Aunt Gwen called for Agnes and Eilers and told them to get everything ready so that Evey may be changed. I was reminded of the previous day when she took so much joy in watching Evey and Thompson, and then she was taking just as much in the prospect of him being crushed. I truly sometimes could not fathom what was going on in the heads of the 'fairer' sex. As we had finished our breakfast, Evey slowly rose from her seat and paused for a few seconds. With cautious and slow steps, she walked towards the door.

"Are you feeling all right, pet? You seem a tad unsteady today." Aunt Gwen asked with a quizzical smile.

"Oh— oh, it is merely, that we walked so much these past days. I'm not used to it ... and besides ... I feel very exh—. Very anxious." She stammered, and then darted me a shy glance.

"Oh, the nerves! I do relate. I too felt my knees give in when I was in your situation in my youth."

Evey left the room and I attempted to go after her before she would be in the hands of her lady's maid, being dolled up for who-knows how long. I felt that there was an urgency of talking to her before she had to face Thompson. However, I was stopped dead in my tracks by Aunt Gwen, who squarely blocked my way.

"Now, you wait for a second, young man!"

"Wait? For what?"

"Did you say anything to little Evey yesterday to influence her decision?"

"Her mind was made up as soon as she came to my room." I answered honestly.

"Hum … yes, I'm not surprised. All the same … something is different about her today." Aunt Gwen mused.

"It's the nerves, like you said. I doubt that Father will be happy about this outcome."

"Yes, indeed. I did not take that into consideration. Oh, poor dear!" she nodded understandingly, "as a responsible brother, you know what you ought to do, don't you?"

"What would that be?" I asked, slightly perturbed.

"Obviously, to support her when she will talk to your father. Dear, you are a tad slow to catch on at times." She sighed.

"There is nothing else I could do, is there? I should talk to her before she rejects Thompson." I insisted, hoping that I would have the opportunity to send the lady's maid away.

"Everything you could have said on that matter, you had the opportunity to say yesterday. Leave the poor dear alone to gather her thoughts and courage. The last thing she needs is for you to belittle poor Mr Thompson, and thus make her feel worse about herself … because I know that's what you want to do."

She was wrong, the last thing I wanted to talk about was her discarded suitor.

"In any case, you are not to be near the parlour while we receive Mr Thompson. Is that understood?" she ordered sternly, having reverted to her governess persona.

"Shouldn't I at least see him out afterwards?"

"To gloat at him? Absolutely not! You must stay out of sight. Where is my 'yes, madam!'?"

"Yes, madam."

163

"Now off with you to the reading room, or any place where you won't disturb us. And remember to be a good boy: I neither want to hear nor see you"

I was foiled, and without a chance to talk to Evey. As I could not disturb her while getting ready, I went off into the reading room, just as Aunt Gwen suggested. After all it was not too far from the parlour away and everything in the main hallway was in earshot. Because I did not know what else I should be looking at, I picked up the *Opera Guide* again and leafed through it. Soon after, I heard Thompson arriving and being shown into the parlour. He came much too soon, even though the day before I told him that it was indecent to rush ladies. He'd be sorry for not listening and for his impatience. About twenty minutes later, I heard Evey and Aunt Gwen descend the stairs and enter the parlour together. For some reason, this felt like an ordeal to me as well. Even though I detested Thompson and his ways, as a fellow man I could not help but feel a hint of sympathy. He would never know the actual reason for her rejection, even though he was infatuated with her. He was so very sure of his success. I wondered how he would react if he knew that all his animosity towards me was justified but came to the conclusion that there was no point in being considerate towards someone who received their dues for having been exceedingly arrogant and shallow.

While reading the entry on *La Traviata*, and without even taking in what the summary said, a memory from our childhood resurfaced. It was the summer in which Evey had entered the estate and she had been with us for merely days. Whenever spoken to, she would simply smile and nod, and I was mystified upon watching her, for this type of behaviour seemed to me just a compliment to her doll-like appearance. I could not stop observing her. It was a behaviour beyond my comprehension, and I felt that a girl her age ought to play like all the little children did. Therefore, on a rainy day when the nanny was preoccupied and nowhere to be seen,

I incited her to play hide and seek with me within the manor's east wing. She was very good at it. It was becoming continuously harder for me to find her, until through a loud clatter, I was made aware of her presence. Evey had accidently broken a delicate and expensive gift my mother had received. A gift of which I don't even remember what it was. I could not forget her frightened face when I found her, because it showed awareness of a misdeed. An expression, that to that point was not ever to be seen on my face. A maid came upon hearing the noise and saw the remnants of the expensive object. *Without a doubt, it must have been our Master Arthur who again would not pursue a quiet activity.*

I was reprimanded and she said that this could not be hidden. The head butler must be informed, who in turn would directly pass it onto my father. I unapologetically stared back at her and simply stated that with the rain I needed something to do and that now with her there, she would have something to do as well by clearing it up. As the servants had the permission to drag me away when I was misbehaving, she angrily pulled me to where old Francis was, whilst Evey was helplessly trailing behind us. Then Francis took us along to my parents. The doors were shut on Evey and she was taken away by Mother. My punishments were ten cane strikes to each of my palms and being sent to bed without dinner. Having experienced it often enough at that point it did not mean much to me, I was more afraid that the docile and pretty little girl would receive such a punishment. Even though in retrospect, I doubted that my parents would have gone to such extremes for an accident. The thought of what happened behind closed doors must have terrified Evey, for that night she snuck into my room to apologise. Climbing into my bed, she sat next to me and looked at my beaten hands. Silent tears began to run down her round cheeks. It was the first time she showed her true emotions. Even though it was not expressive, I could tell that she was in pain, for I too was a child that would only ever weep quietly and in solitude. The tears she cried were not only for my hands but for herself. For having left everything she knew behind, for being surrounded by strangers in a country so different from what she was used to … for having someone take the blame in her place. Then there was a warmth that filled my heart because I knew that I was the first person in her new home in whom she trusted to reveal her desolation to. She asked me why I did not once mention that it was her fault. With my aching hand I patted her head. It was the only thing I could imagine would console her, and upon touching them for the first time, the softness of her locks soothed me. So much that I barely felt the pain anymore. Then, I told her that as the elder of the two of us I should carry the responsibilities for anything that happened whenever she followed what I did. Through all the years that sentiment never changed. I would readily take the fall for the wrongs that we committed together. However, nothing alike the incident with the broken object ever happened again. Of course not, because she was an upright and demure girl … until I made her a fallen woman.

13
The Homage Vice pays to Virtue

Impatiently I paced around the reading room, looking at all the trinkets adorning it. It had already been thirty minutes since the parlour doors were closed and I was wondering what in the world they were talking about. After all, a rejection to a proposal was something that could be dealt with within a matter of minutes. I stood in front of the fireplace mantel, sliding my fingers down a delicate Dresden Porcelain figurine of a lady in a lavish dress. Shivering at the touch with the texture, I was instantly reminded of the sensation of Evey's skin.

From the distance, I could hear the creaking of hinges, and loud thud of a door echoed in the hallway. They must have been done talking. I went to stand at the reading room door, covertly peeking into the direction of the entrance. Thompson walked out of the parlour, with a dejected look on his face and headed toward the entrance where the butler was holding out his coat, hat, and cane. Evey, who was wearing an airy but elegant rose-coloured visiting gown, followed him. Aunt Gwen remained at a slight distance. None of them said anything as the dragging of the dress' train, and heavy steps were the only things reverberating in the silence.

"You are a friend, Mr Thompson. And therefore, I am … I am truly sorry that I cannot reciprocate your sentiments." She said, looking up to him who was just putting on his hat.

"Do not worry yourself, Miss Hollings. I understand that a lady cannot immediately accept the first proposal in her life. I know that it is only courteous to give you enough time to consider." He answered wearing his usual elegant smile.

However, there were certain pained wrinkles noticeable.

His pride had received a considerable blow. Surely, he would not give up just yet, and probably he would involve Father too. He was the type of individual to be a sore loser.

"Give my regards to Clarence junior ..." I could hear him say, shortly before he exited the building.

Emerging from my exile, I came to join Aunt Gwen and Evey. All three of us returned to sit in the parlour.

"So ... how was it? Why did it take him so long to understand a 'no'?" I asked.

"It did not show in his face, but he did not take to it well." Aunt Gwen pondered, "Would you like to tell Arthur, pet?"

"I'd rather let you, Aunt Gwen. This was indeed tiering."

"Very well. Little Evey here dove straight into it and told him that he was a wonderful gentleman and a great marriage prospect, however not for her. He stiffly asked why not, and Evey explained that he must have misunderstood her feelings, for she did not once foster any sentiments of affection for him beyond that of friendship. Gosh, you should have seen the look in his eyes, as though she repeatedly stabbed him in the heart."

"Please, Aunt Gwen." Evey implored consternated.

"Ah, yes, pardon, my dear. Well, anyway, he ran down a list of things she did, and asked if it truly did not mean anything to her ... Which she confirmed. It was all due to obligation, friendship, and gratitude for how he helped my brother. And then he said he felt like she had put a wool over his eyes with all her sweet smiles and soft laughs."

"Didn't I tell you that he's a selfish cad?"

"Oh, dear, Arthur! You would not believe how upset I was to hear him say it. Our little Evey a coquette deceiver? With her docile nature ... I told him to mind his manners, and he apologised straight away, stating that he didn't mean to say something hurtful. Then he went to play a different tune, asking if *you* had any hand in this, somehow coercing her into declining."

"He really did?" I asked, feigning surprise. How foolhardy was he to think that he had any chance to redeem himself after dragging me through the mud ... even though I admittedly had my hands on her.

"He did! His phrasing was more subtle, but I will repeat it to you the way I heard it: he asked if having an amoral element like you around was giving her funny ideas. But then, little Evey here ... for the first time in my life I saw her become angry. She asked him to refrain from slandering you in your absence if he didn't also want to have her terminate their friendship."

I looked at Evey who smiled at me awkwardly.

"Be that as it may, he retracted that statement but still voiced his concern about how ... well, to put it nicely, you seemed to take advantage of Evey's gentle nature as well. To which she replied that, of course, you two would have a close relationship because you grew up together. It did not matter that you are not related by blood. He finally relented and decided to retreat. Truly, that Thompson boy isn't as boring as his father, but being impudent isn't any better. Did he think he could nonchalantly insult the two of you in my house? Maybe at my brother's, but not here!"

But I genuinely felt ashamed because Thompson was dead on. As a successful businessman he must have had a good intuition and known when there were lies and deception to be found. She was as much of a deceiver as I was a bad influence. I did not in the least care about having gotten the better of that rat but seeing Aunt Gwen become so upset over his insinuations — which happened to be the truth — made me feel guilty. She may have had caught on to my desires for Evey, but she was too much of an honourable lady to think extreme thoughts. She was not as wild as a raging river, even though she fancied herself so. Rather, she was like a lively, gurgling, but steady stream. Let alone suspect, I doubted that she would even be able to consider it a possibility what obscene things went on the night before. In her house of all places. And I could tell from her anxious fidgeting, that Evey too felt guilty for deceiving Aunt Gwen. She eventually excused herself, stating that it would be best to get dressed for travel and depart as soon as possible, for surely … Father would receive the news sooner than us returning to the estate.

"What makes you think that?" Aunt Gwen asked surprised.

"They were exchanging telegrams all the while." I scoffed.

"You knew?!" the ladies exclaimed, gasping in unison.

"Certainly … Thompson was the one boasting about it yesterday at the opera."

"Oh, that little weasel. Not only the Thompson boy, but my brother too. To disrespect Evangeline to that extent."

"Do not concern yourself, Aunt Gwen. Please do not be upset. You will only become agitated and that's not good for your health. Arthur will help me talk to Uncle Arthur."

"Indeed, I will have no problems joining Evey in facing Father who will undoubtedly be in an unpleasant mood. I'll be there for her, so rest assured."

We prepared ourselves for the journey back down south. Aunt Gwen and Agnes joined us to Waverly Station. On the platform she gave both of us a kiss on the cheek and announced that without fail she would come in September to Forestedge. Then she encouraged us again, especially Evey, not to give in to my father and do as she saw fit. We waved her goodbye as we climbed into the train carriage. Shortly after two in the afternoon, the train departed with Edinburgh Castle disappearing from its lofty outlook, upon us entering a tunnel. For a time, we let the scenery pass us by, as we sat opposite of each other in our first-class carriage compartment. Neither of us spoke. While the magnificent remnants of Linlithgow Palace escaped from our view Evey decided to leave her seat and sit next to me. Hesitantly, her gloved fingers went to intertwine with mine.

"Why haven't you said anything yet?" she asked, blushing.

"What is it that you want me to say?" I replied while staring out of the window, painstakingly hiding my own shyness. I did not even know why I was suddenly acting aloof even though I wanted to talk to her so badly in the morning. Wordlessly, she squeezed my hand tighter.

"There is no way around it, I'm sure Uncle Arthur will want to talk to me. I will explain it to him properly, and I will make Mr Thompson understand as well ... that I'm not interested." She said with resolve.

"Will you need more encouragement?" I asked rather tactlessly while facing her.

Evey, turning evermore crimson, was silent. But then she looked straight at me with her crystal blue eyes that gleamed with a lascivious, yet sincere flicker, asking, "Will you keep encouraging me then?"

"Certainly, if that is what you want me to do."

Notwithstanding the temptation, and ignoring that we were in a public space, I kissed her tenderly.

"Say, Evey, you are aware that my health is improving and that I will eventually return to my regiment in the near future."

"Yes, of course."

"And you are aware that I am not going to ask for your hand in marriage either, aren't you?"

"Yes, I did not think that you would."

"You are surprisingly calm about this." I pointed out because I personally was restless.

"I know you well enough. Besides, you ... you said you needed me. Was that a lie?"

"No, it wasn't."

"Then, only for the time that you are still staying home it will be fine for us to be together, wouldn't it?"

"Are you fine with that? With being ..."

"... your paramour?"

Paramour. It was an illicit and hurtful ... an uncouth word that befit her in no way. As I thought about our situation, I felt genuine anger and frustration with myself for having overstepped the line once too often. At the same time, I was content. I went too far this time, but I would not step back and give her up either.

"Don't say that. Now you are the one to liken yourself to something distasteful." I reprimanded her.

"What am I to you then?"

I was unable to provide her with a proper answer and instead said, "You are what I want the most right now."

Then, I went to kiss her again, this time for a long deep kiss. As a person passed by the compartment, Evey quickly broke away and looked down to her boots. Her hand however remained tightly connected to mine.

"How do we even plan on carrying on?" I wondered thinking out loud. "If our behaviour towards each other drastically changes, people are bound to find out. Besides, the manor is always busy. There is no chance for us to ever be really alone."

I knew too well how easy it was to be found out. In fact, it was a miracle that no one saw us kiss before in the reading room. Quietly contemplating we both looked out of the window at the passing scenery. The Scottish countryside was lush with life, here and there spotted brown and white by the scattered cattle that roamed the lands.

"There is a place on the estate that no one but me frequents." I finally said.

"Really? There was such a place? Where?" she asked, pressing her petite body tightly onto my shoulder.

The eyes were sparkling with curiosity.

"Hm, let's make it a surprise. Shall we?" I answered playfully, to which she beamed with excitement.

The rest of the ride in a way resembled previous travels we had taken: we chatted lively while she held onto my hand. She complained about the opera for having missed the finale. She wondered what would be served for dinner and made trivial remarks about the landscape. Yet, it was not the same. Every now and then I would lean into her, whispering delicately and reminiscing about the previous night, which would make her squirm and blush. She was pleased, nonetheless. Evey returned my whispers with tender remarks of her own and other coy gestures. It appeared to me that our intimacy was like a charm that warded off outsiders, as nobody joined us in our compartment throughout our way back home.

Arriving later than we anticipated, we were greeted by old Francis in the lobby who let us know that Father was awaiting us separately in his study. We therefore were advised to refresh and change ourselves in our own quarters at our leisure ... which in fact meant 'straight away.' Supper would be served afterwards. Thompson really was as petty as we all thought him to be. He probably wired Father the news as soon as he stepped out of York Place. Our things were brought to our quarters by the servants. Having quickly changed, I went over to Father's study. However, upon arrival, old Francis informed me that the Master was already in talks with the Miss. How could she have been quicker than me even though we went into the direction of our respective bedchambers together? How, even though she was still tender? Instead of waiting in one of the adjacent rooms, I waited in the hallway, hoping that there would be a possibility to eavesdrop. Yet, the doors were to sturdy, or Evey's and Father's voices too low to hear anything. The ringing of a bell announced the end of their talks. Old Francis quickly twisted the handles of the double doors to fully open for the young Miss. Evey stepped out of the study still fully clad in her travel dress. She must have only tossed off her hat and washed her face. Smiling at me wearily, she went to stand next to me. Before we could exchange any words, I was instantly summoned in by Father. Upon entering I was not even asked to sit down, and out of reflex I stood straight as a die with my hands behind my back. Old Francis shut the doors behind us. Father was sitting in his chair, the hands folded on top of the desk. He looked up from behind his spectacles, which he only ever wore for reading purposes. Again, there was an awkward silence pertaining the room as I waited to be addressed.

"Welcome back, Arthur. How is Gwendolyn?" he finally deigned to ask.

Being silent for a few moments, I looked at his face, and tried to figure out what he was feeling. His expression was stern, but I could tell there was disappointment too.

"She is well, sir." I answered plainly.

It was not like he genuinely wanted to hear about her health from me.

"Now, boy, I'm sure that you are perfectly aware of why I summoned you here?"

"It can only be because of Evey rejecting Thompson's marriage proposal."

"Yes, indeed. That's the reason, but why do you think I called for you specifically?"

I wasn't sure why he was pussyfooting around it, but I was certain he was aiming to draw some sort of confession out of me. If he had something, he wanted to accuse me of, he should just have said it straight away. I would not play along and instead was so irked by his ways that I became petulant.

"I can only guess that Thompson laments the fact that, in spite of the *unexpected time* we spent together, we were unable to deepen our friendship."

"As expected of you, being impudent as always," he snapped at me, "Thompson junior informed me about how unpleasant you have been towards him and that you were in a way involved in Evey's decision. You—"

"I see that he didn't spare any expenses on the telegrams." I scoffed.

"Don't you dare speak unless you are asked to!"

"..."

"I can imagine in what ways Thompson and you have clashed: he's

174

industrious, steadfast, and reputable. Those are qualities which you have been lacking all your life. It is no wonder that you would be irked by him as you were yet again shown your own deficiencies."

"Sir, I doubt that you know what kind of a person Thompson is."

"That's irrelevant, for I do know what kind of a person *you* are ... and I told you not to interrupt me!"

"..."

"However, that you would go as far as to dissuade Evey, only over the fact that there was personal animosity towards her prospective partner is appalling."

"Is that what you truly believe, Father? That I have so much influence over her? That she lacks the will to decide on her own future?"

He sighed and gave up on reprimanding me for talking out of line.

"You are dear to her as a brother. She has always been looking up to you, even though your relationship has been strained ever since you've returned. I know that very well. She never was anything else but an obedient child, and a rational one too. I am certain that if you hadn't fed her some wild fanciful ideas, she would have agreed to the engagement, because Thompson is the perfect choice for her. He can offer her status and security. She will be well taken care of."

"That's how it truly is: you are upset that along with me, Evey will not have any duties imposed on herself. It's not about her future or security, you are vexed by her disobedience."

"I consider this statement to be your admitting that you have spurred her on. Why else would she reject him?"

"Father, she *doesn't even like* the man." I retorted irate.

"There! That is what I am referring to: *pipedreams of romance.* Love can grow out of duty. Surely, she could have come to like him. Thompson is an amiable fellow."

"You're a hypocrite for imposing your sense of duty onto others but having married for love yourself!" I haughtily reiterated Aunt Gwen's words without dragging her into it.

175

"How dare you disrespect your father like this? If only Harold were here … he was the only one with the ability to talk some sense into you."

"If Harold was here, you wouldn't need to peddle Evey to your business associates."

His mouth was agape. His complexion became pale. Father started up, slamming one hand onto the desk, and pointing the other towards the study door.

"Out! Out of the study with you! Now!" he shouted without looking at me, his head drooped.

I turned on my heel and stormed out of the room. Old Francis had quickly opened the double doors before I reached them. Our roles were reversed, Evey was standing in the hallway in my spot. The only difference was that she likely heard every word of our argument. I swiftly walked into the direction of the main landing, passing through the corridor. Suddenly, there was a strong tugging, and I was pulled into the music room. The doors were shut behind me. In my clouded state of anger, I hadn't noticed that Evey was in quick pursuit of me. She hastily glanced around to see if we were truly alone and then slung her arms around my waist, firmly pressing her lower body onto mine. I looked down at her stunned. She was standing on tiptoes and swiftly kissed me. The touch of her warm lips was revitalising. I did not let her pull away when she wanted to, having grabbed her by the shoulders to support her stance. Our lips remained connected until my agitated breathing had slowed down to match her calmed one. Then I withdrew from her.

"Have your nerves settled?" she asked, smiling at me.

"It certainly helped … Although, we really can't do this here."

She did not reply but continued gazing at me with her lovely mouth curled up.

"What did you tell him then?" I asked.

"The same things I told Mr Thompson: that my sentiments towards him were never more than that of friendship, and that I never considered him to be a prospective partner."

I nodded silently, as I did not want to further dwell on the whole courtship matter.

"It's not true what Uncle Arthur said. Please don't take it to heart, yes?"

"What are you referring to?"

"You are steadfast."

"It's nice that you think that way. I'm however neither reputable nor industrious."

"Those aren't important qualities."

With her arms still around me she rested her head onto my chest. I draped mine around her small back and we remained like that for some time. Once my mind had fully calmed down, I realised how ridiculous the whole argument with my father was. We were both hypocrites. I was arguing for Evey to marry out of love, yet there I was with my hands on her, spoiling her for other decent marriage prospects. But just like any other woman she had agency over whom she would take as her lover, and she had made her choice.

For the following week an atmosphere of contention dominated the halls of Forestedge. The household of course had heard about the Miss having rejected the proposal of the fine Gentleman, the master's choice, who had visited in May. While what was said between Evey and my father had stayed discretely behind closed doors, the way I had argued with him made it's rounds through all levels of employees. It was made even worse, for Father had taken ill after our argument.

Yes, it was the young Master again. It's always him who is sowing discord. Why is the Miss so fond of him? Can you believe it? Treating the Master that way, despite his brittle health? How vile ...

Doctor Armitage had assured me that even though our differences may have agitated Father, the actual cause for his weakened state was that he had been working too much again. Evey checked continuously on Father and kept him company whenever he requested her to. I was certain that he was attempting to persuade her to accept Thompson's proposal, as dripping water hollows out a stone. While I went about my usual everyday activities, mostly escaping the subliminal revulsion of the servants, I did not have much opportunity to spend time with her beyond mealtimes and the mornings for listening in when she played the piano. One particular morning, I entered as she was already playing a piece. It did not sound like those that she used to play, and sheets were laid out. I walked over to stand at the piano and had a look. The composer's name stated was Satie.

"Where did that come from?"

"Would you believe it? It arrived yesterday. Violet sent it to me."

"How thoughtful ... from France?"

"No, she returned just the day after we left. She failed to let me know her return schedule in her preceding letter. How very scatter-brained of her... but typical."

"Good on Thompson. His sister was there to pick up the pieces of his broken heart."

"Don't be malicious, Arthur!"

"Did she write something about that though?"

"Hm ... yes ... well. It was the main topic of her hurried letter: she wrote how shocked she was to hear of my rejecting her brother's proposal, and that she thought it was unbelievable. She said, she was so positive about me being infatuated with Mr Thompson that she encouraged him more than once, urging him that he must pursue me with more conviction. Furthermore, she wrote that she was happily looking forward to the prospect of us becoming sisters, legally. The sheet music was a gift she wanted me to have, not to influence me but to remind me that we do remain friends. Then she implored me to reconsider ..."

I could vividly imagine how many written pages that curt summary was actually long. Then, I chuckled at the irony of Thompson having spoken so ill of his sister and still having followed her advice concerning his own romantic ventures.

"Did she write anything about me being involved?" I inquired, as I was curious.

Evey did not answer instantly and went into a silent deliberation.

"I don't think I want to repeat what she wrote about you." She finally replied.

"Then don't."

"By what were you provoked to the extent of feeling the need to upset her?"

"I did not like her attitude, that much should have been obvious to you. You yourself said that she would not be to my liking."

She nodded in affirmation.

"And what was it that you did to upset her?"

"It was nothing, really. I didn't touch her indecently if that is what she claimed."

"She made no mention about what you did herself."

"Good, then we can leave it at that."

That morning Father re-joined us for breakfast as he had regained his health. Pretending that nothing had happened, he reverted to treating me the same way he did before we set off to Edinburgh. Even though she did not mention it to me, Evey must have somehow assuaged his anger during all the time that she was spending with him. The fragile equilibrium of the household had returned to its former state, as the day passed peacefully.

Continuing with my habit of sleeping in the smoking room, I was awoken in the dead of the night by a pinching sensation in my cheek. It was Evey who was leaning over the back of the chaise longue to peer at me mischievously. Startled, I sat up. She came around to sit next to me, having set the paraffin lamp on the gueridon table at the top end.

"What are you doing here?" I asked, instantly awake.

"I couldn't sleep," she answered and flopped sideways to lean her head against my shoulder. Her hand went to stroke my thigh with assertion, while she noted shyly, "It's been a week since we returned, but we were unable to spend any time alone ..."

"Aren't you still hurting?"

"No, it stopped being painful some time ago." She replied.

Even in the dim light I could see the tips of her ears brighten. I leaned in to make out her obscured features, her lips were curved up to a coy smile. Slinging her arms around my neck she confidently placed her parted mouth onto mine, hungrily pushing her tongue through, flicking, and teasing me. I was without guard at her improvement but would not admit defeat either. Reciprocating, I put my hands around her waist, holding her tightly. Yet again, we were caught up in a tangle. A passionate back and forth until I made our lips part by turning my face away.

"I told you that we can't. Not here." I reprimanded her.

"Why not? It's so late at night and everyone is asleep ..." she asked.

The scarce light of the lamp made her strong expression of yearning visible.

"It's too quiet, one could hear a pin drop ... people would become suspicious about suddenly hearing noises."

However, she did not listen and instead drew me close again. We kissed anew, and with one hand resting on my cheek and the other on my neck she took hold of me. Her touch was gentle, yet firm, as she would not allow for me to pull away again. In-between, she softly murmured my name to entice me ... successfully. Words would not reach her, therefore I resolved to show her. In waves we connected through passionate kisses. She let out small, excited sighs and moans as I massaged her bust, twisting the most sensitive part. My other hand went to stroke over her quivering belly, gliding towards the sweet spot between her legs. Slowly, I rubbed and caressed it through the fabric of her nightdress. There was moisture seeping through the thin chemise. She impatiently gathered up the hem of her dress above the waist, urging me to slip in my fingers. Thrusting in, Evey's sweet moans grew louder.

"Hush, now. Be quiet!" I demanded, lightly biting her neck.

However, she easily lost control, the body and her senses were still quickly overwhelmed by my experienced touch. I steadily continued to move my hand, until she finally let out an exulted cry. Her whole body tensed up momentarily, the small hands gripping hard onto the sides of my smoking jacket, strong enough for me to feel the sensation through its thick velvet. Then she shivered in relief. Afterwards, she looked at me with glazed, yet gratified eyes, and gave me a light kiss as a reward. Embracing her, we lay stretched out on the tight chaise longue.

"I told you to hold in your voice ..." I whispered in her ear.

She simply nodded in response and, like a tamed beast, rubbed her face against mine.

"I really do hope that nobody heard you." I said, while feeling slightly anxious about us being found this way. Then I promised her, "You must be patient ... soon ... soon we can go somewhere else."

"Yes ... " She answered meekly.

Kissing her one last time, I sent her away to her own bedchamber. Having come back to her senses she rose and straightened her nightgown. She turned away from me out of embarrassment over the dampened area on her dress. Bidding me a good night, she picked up the lamp and retreated from the smoking room. I fell back onto the chaise relieved that she had gone away, leaving me in the darkness. My own tension slowly dissolved but a certain feeling of shame remained. Although I couldn't see it in the gloom, I could feel the judgement of the dreadful eyes that had observed us from the frame opposite of me.

14
Gnosis

In the morning of the next day, I came to sit with Evey in the music room, where she was again practising the piece from the sheets Miss Violet had gifted her. The tune mostly jingled around the minor music scale, and in its meandering movements evoked an atmosphere of oriental quality. To me it appeared depressing and somewhat disharmonious.

"What do you think?" she asked, twisting her upper body to look at me, who sat in one of the armchairs.

"It sounds like a sad and mysterious tune. Not relaxing at all."

"It's funny that you would say that. The title is mysterious too: *Gnossienne.*"

"What does it mean?" I asked. My French wasn't particularly good.

"Violet wrote that it was somehow related to gnosis. However, I don't think it means anything at all. It's meant to be *chic*, I think."

"A pretentious gift from someone with pretentious tastes … do you even enjoy playing it?"

"Hm … not really. I find it hard to play. I like things with more structure."

"Why do you practice it then?"

"Maybe one day Violet will come to visit me and may want to hear it. I wouldn't want to disappoint her." She answered, as she continued to practise a certain section repeatedly.

I walked over and sat down next to her on the piano bench, patting her head amicably.

"What a goody two-shoes our little Evey is."

"Oh! Be quiet." She huffed and pouted.

With my hand still resting on her head, I leant in to talk to her in a low voice.

"I know that you are not that strait-laced, which is why we will be going for a walk after breakfast. I promised to take you to my den one day."

She nodded demurely, and playfully twiddled the fabric of my trousers between her fingers.

"I'll be looking forward to it, then." She replied.

After breakfast we both dressed to leave for a walk. She wore almost the same attire as she did when we ascended Calton Hill, the main difference being that her hair was in simple and unfashionable braids, fastened up. It was Father who stopped us at the lobby doors, young Francis right behind him. As always, the valet glanced at me dismissively.

"Are you heading out together for a walk?" Father inquired.

His pleased expression made me uncomfortable.

"You seem to be on better terms ever since you have returned from Gwendolyn's place."

The jovial smile felt stifling. It was as though he was doing his utmost to pretend that there never was an argument and that Thompson's proposal was not still an issue.

"It is as you say, sir." I answered curtly.

"Even after having lived here for so long, I never explored the forest around the estate grounds. I was intrigued by Arthur's account on how lovely the scenery is supposed to be." Evey interjected with an excuse ready.

"Master Arthur has the tendency to physically exhaust others. You appeared tender after your return from Edinburgh, Miss Evangeline. Therefore, please mind your own pace." Young Francis pointed out not even looking at me. If only the nosy bastard knew what he was saying.

Father nodded in agreement, and urged her, "Indeed. Make sure that you do not exhaust yourself, Evey."

She reacted with a sweet but at the same time wary smile, and then chirruped, "Of course I will, Uncle."

Finally, she gave him a quick peck on the cheek, which he received happily.

"If only I could join you for your walk. Do be mindful, boy!" he then demanded from me.

"Sir." I replied affirmingly.

"We will be off then. Shall we?" she said to me.

With a nod we headed out.

"Quite the bare faced lie." I said after a while of walking.

We had just entered the forest.

"Did I say something that was not true?" Evey asked innocently.

She skipped over a root and linked into my arm. We walked like that for a while, enjoying the scenery and each other's company. The leather of our boots was moistened as we crossed through the moss-covered forest floor. Even though it was only August, colourful foliage had already fallen from the multitude of beeches and sycamores, while birds chirped from the varieties of high-grown conifers that were spread throughout. We finally arrived at a modest clearing on which an old ash tree had spread its roots. It had grown broad and knobby, but a part of the tree was dead already. Barely outside the reach of its thick canopy, there was an old stone hut. Moss crept up the lithic edifice, making the hut merge with its surroundings. A newly fitted wooden door and shutters on the windows made it a safe place from changing weather conditions. The area around it was open and firewood had been stacked beside the chopping block next to the entrance.

"Oh, how lovely!" she exclaimed, her face shining with excitement, "Or should I say ominous? Do you reckon a witch, or a wolf will await us within?" she asked, smiling at me teasingly.

I pressed her tightly onto me surprising her with a kiss.

"A wolf, certainly." I answered with a grin.

It satisfied me to see her flustered. Still holding on to her hand I bid her come in. The cramped cold space was scarcely occupied, only a table with a single chair, a campaign bed and a furnace filling it. The other smaller objects in it were tools, brushes, and binoculars. Cobwebs glistened in the corners as dim rays entered to the crooked, glassless windows.

"It is a lot tidier than I expected. It is even furnished." She noted. Her ears turned red at the sudden realisation that this was our destination.

"Oh, so this is where you stay most days?"

"Yes," I answered, "Or did you think I was hiding in a cave? I am not that primitive …"

Her laugh eased the pressure we both felt due to being completely alone.

"It's not a very comfortable, nor a decent place to spend time at."

"I don't mind, as long as I can spend time with you." She said smiling at me, and then asked, "I was wondering where you were. Do you also sleep here in the daytime?"

"At times, I do."

"And what else do you do?"

"I'm keeping myself busy with menial tasks like chopping firewood, clearing the area around the stone hut or the inside, watching birds or game pass by. Things like that."

"You are industrious after all."

"I wonder. It's nothing of consequence. I just … due to the service I've grown used to being outside and doing physical labours. Sitting in the manor makes me restless. And you know that I'm not particularly fond of reading or other intellectual activities."

The air within was cold and humid due to the density of the woods. Having prepared logs in advance I lit a fire in the furnace to warm up the room. She sat down on the wooden campaign bed, which was already too tight for me alone. I asked her to hand me the blankets next to her which she did. Then she shyly observed me spread them out on the floor in front of the furnace.

"It used to be a hermitage of sorts. Must have been fashionable when the manor was built." I told her, "Ever since my return, I have been refurbishing it. It had become considerably run down."

"You put so much effort in this place. Even though the manor is extraordinarily spacious, you choose to be here?"

"It has more people in it than it has rooms. It's like a hive." I said, for it was true that the place only existed to provide the livelihood of those that worked there.

"So, does that mean no one knows about this place?"

"No. I'm sure everyone knows, but no one cares. Which is why I am here. Just upon my return I had the gamekeeper help me bring things here … I could not bring them alone. He never comes here either. He knows that I don't like people near this place."

"Why didn't I know then?"

"We stopped using it shortly after you arrived, and besides you never explored the whole estate."

"We?" she repeated, surprised.

"Harold and me. This used to be our hide out. As children we often played here, even though Mother did not like it and thought it to be inappropriate for sons of such a prestigious family. Father, however, found it to be good for us boys. The summer that you came to the estate, that was the last time we spent time together in here. Harold was already fifteen, so he may have thought it too childish. Look," I pointed to a faded etching in the wall, "He tried writing his name but gave up at the letter 'R' because the stone was too tough."

My own name was clearly visible beneath it. All six letters. Whenever I was in trouble I hid here, therefore there had been enough time for me to complete it. It was always Harold who came after me to give me a good brotherly scolding, telling me that I mustn't run away from my problems.

That I should face my mistakes with dignity.

"Our tempers and demeanours were as contrasting as night and day. He must not have cared much for this place for it to have almost fallen apart. I however, always found this to be my refuge." I said thinking out loud, my fingers tracing the craggy lines.

With the dawn of adolescence, it became harder for Harold and me to understand each other's way of thinking. A melancholy shroud laid itself upon the confined space.

"You miss him very much, don't you?" Evey asked.

"Of course, I do. Forestedge lost all its joy and purpose with him. My return is no consolation for his loss." I answered, going over to sit next to her on the bedside.

I always wished to be more like him. In my childhood, I also wanted to be upright and admirable, someone my parents could present with pride to other people. But I was always easily frustrated and gave up as soon as I felt that I could not measure up to Harold and the things he was doing so well. Thus, my frustration turned into anger, ending with me doing the opposite of what I set out to do. Nonetheless, I had nothing but love and respect for my brother. For his memory. And yet, here I was planning to do shameless things to his bride-to-be.

"Don't say that. Do not doubt that your father is happy for your return!" she proclaimed with an expression that bid me reconsider my words.

"I am happy that you returned. The most happy!" she said, softly placing her lips onto mine.

I inhaled her sweet breath as she opened her mouth to invite more action. Then I began undressing myself and her, who timidly hid her eyes behind the palms, frightened by all that the light of the day exposed.

"Evey, we went further than this." I said taking her hands into mine.

Her eyes still shut and more embarrassed than before, I gently brushed with my lips against her fine neckline, my hands caressing the soft, shapely flesh that was only concealed by a thin layer of sheer fabric.

Evey's trembling fingers glided along my bare skin. Upon contact with the scar tissue on my left flank, she gently pushed me away and opened her eyes. The sight fixed on the crumpled and damaged surface that ran from back to front; it was the first time for her to behold it. Having to look at it every day made me oblivious to the fact that it was an unpleasant sight, for it had not healed nicely.

"It still looks so very painful." An awed whisper reached my ear as her lips touched to kiss my cheek.

"It is not." I lied.

Her arms around my chest, the face tightly pressed to my frantically beating heart, I could hear her tender words of compassion, "My poor Arthur, you fought and suffered in solitude. So far away from home. But you did your best and returned to me."

I wanted to return, because I had a vision of her doing the same, of her keeping her head up to not sink in despair.

Like an obedient child she followed me as I took her hand to make her sit on the blankets set out on the floor. Readily she raised her arms for me to strip off the chemise. A golden torrent rained upon her chest, the hair covering the naked upper body like a cloak. The white skin was as pure and perfect as a pearl, the hitherto concealed rose-coloured lips reminded me of fresh petals blooming in spring. Her crystal blue irises were fixed onto me, as she timidly asked, "What do you usually say when you see the naked body of your lover?"

I would usually say nothing of significance, as I let my primal instinct take over. Meaningless compliments to soothe the mind of those ashamed of their deeds, providing a reason to go along with my will. However, my true feelings in the moment I saw her could not be put into words. Confusion and resolution. Excitement and anxiety. Guilt and content. As these emotions whirled within my chest, like a tempest that simultaneously let me reach out and tear away from her, I wordlessly pushed her onto the blankets the weight of me entrapping her. The delicate limbs shivered in excitement. The fingers were intwined, folding the hands over her chest. She gazed up to me, doe-eyed, the shyness had yet to disappear. I first kissed her forehead, her temple, silken streaks touching my lips while I slowly traced the features to meet the parted mouth. Then, I carefully broke the barrier placing her hands next to her head. The softly heaving mounds were in full view of daylight, which caused her again to become flustered. She averted her gaze. The pink tips hardened, at the touch of my tongue. Her breathing became more erratic. The flushed profile was so endearing. I slipped my fingers in between her thighs, watching her reaction. She softly moaned as I stirred the walls of her sanctuary and felt the dews of anticipation. As I placed myself inside her, the slender hips wrapped around me, and she put her hands on my chest, running her fingers through the hair. Evey groaned when I began to move.

"Is it unpleasant?" I asked, wary.

Shaking her head in denial she stretched out her hand to stroke my face. After Kissing that lovely palm, our fingers interlinked, and I began moving anew. Slowly, but surely, she caught up to my motion and matched my rhythm. As this happened, our eyes finally met. I beheld the look I had often seen in other women. The usually serene blue eyes were gleaming with sensual avarice: demanding more kisses, more caresses … more force.

A greed that was boundless and could not be satisfied, urging me to give my all. I readily offered it to her alone: my wit, my senses, my heart. The arms thrown around my neck, I became her possession – not to be shared. I too, pressed her ever closer to myself while she bit into my shoulder, as though I was her prey. With a growing voice she repeatedly called out to me. Unable to bear it any longer she contracted with delight. Evey. My Evangeline. She was my woe and my bliss. My paradise … and I made her reach hers.

I awoke, my face resting on her bare bosom. The embers in the furnace were dying out. It must have been past midday already. Not lifting my head, I asked her how long she was awake, that was if she had even slept.

"I dozed off for some time, but mostly watched you. You slept peacefully." Evey remarked while gently stroking my hair back.

I felt rested and yet ill at ease.

"If we stay any longer, they will send out people to look for us." I said, rising from the blanket. I picked my clothes up from the pile on the campaign bed, "Or rather, they will look for you."

"Why do you think so?" she wondered as she threw over her chemise. The crimson marks I left were well hidden beneath the white fabric. Her skin bruised easily, "I am with you after all." She said.

"Is not that the reason to worry?"

She smiled but could not laugh because she knew that it was the households' shared sentiment. Evidently, they were not wrong either. After I had helped her into her clothes, she sat with me on the campaign bed. I ran my fingers through her soft hair and braided it carefully.

"You are surprisingly good at this." She noted.

"I had lots of practice; you see …" I answered, having already finished one braid.

"Is that why you specifically asked me to wear my hair like that?"

"Yes … we wouldn't want you to return all dishevelled, would we?"

She nodded bashfully. I fastened the hair back up again with all the pins I was able to gather. Looking onto the exposed nape, I could not resist and kissed her there. It surprised her at first. However, she then seemed to enjoy it as she titled her head slightly to allow for me to touch more bare skin. Resisting the urge to undo all my work, I rose from the bed and told her, "There we go. We're ready to head back."

Eventually, we returned and there was no commotion. Instead, Father had waited to have luncheon with us. Before long we sat down to eat together, and he inquired about our morning and what we had seen. Evey described the mundane scenery of the woods with vivid detail and finally concluded with an unconcerned laugh, "Arthur took me to his den."

I froze up instantly, the knife I was using stuck mid-motion in the tender meat on the plate. Bewildered, I stared at the red and watery juices which were flowing out, spilling onto the porcelain. Father had an equally confused look on his face, but upon contemplating on her words must have understood what she meant.

"Ah, you mean that old stone hut he used to frequent as child. Is that where you tend to spend your time, boy?" he asked.

"Sir, it is." I replied.

"Did you know, Uncle Arthur? He has been refurbishing it all by himself. The military does make men self-sufficient. It is quite charming." Evey explained, then smiling at me.

I could not help but blankly stare back at her, not knowing why she would mention … no, elaborate in detail on our whereabouts.

She continued, "Arthur lit a fire in the furnace. The sound of the crackling embers blending with those of the lively woods was very soothing. It would have been even nicer if we had refreshments."

Content with Evey's high spirited demeanour Father insisted with his usual benign smile that we should bring some along next time.

"Of course, that is if it pleases you, boy. I know that you cherish your solitary time."

"Evey is pleasant company." I answered without thinking.

"Lovely!" she exclaimed, carrying on with her lunch as this seemingly trivial matter was settled.

It was frightening how callous she could be. Evey truly had become a woman.

Afterwards I caught her alone and quickly pulled her into the music room.

"What were you thinking?!" I demanded in a low voice, careful as to make sure that we were not overheard.

"No one will wonder anymore where we are if we go out and stay longer."

"No one will? Are you sure about that? After all, I—"

"Yes, yes. I know the household suspects *you* of doing all sort of things. But nobody would ever suspect *me* of anything"

"You certainly come up with excuses easily." I scolded her.

"Plans, you mean." She retorted, with a pure smile. No malice, not even a hint of mischief. As opposed to me, she did not seem to feel any remorse for fooling those around us. Rather, Evey exuded airs of complacency.

"Seeing your befuddled face was quite endearing." She chirped, stroking my cheek.

This kind of flirtatious teasing was so new and attractive, I was wiled in. My body moved on its own, being tugged along by her allure, kissing her first softly, then passionately. From that day on there were no boundaries anymore. No dread of consequences, nor regard for the future. My sight was narrowed down by insatiable desire. Days and weeks merged into an indistinguishable blur, only regaining clarity whenever I was able to be with her, whenever we touched, whenever we became one. I did not pause to wonder why an up to then virtuous girl like Evangeline would submit to pleasure and the ways it distorts oneself. All I cared for was seizing that slender body, making it shiver in ecstasy. Her afterglow was my beatific vision. The loneliness that was sometimes flickering in her eyes was dispersed, and I saw myself reflected. The me that struggled to find a place in this estate had a home within her, in our secret that transformed my hiding place into a sanctuary.

15
Vestiges

We made sure that no one would suspect us. To our fortune the summer of the year 1899 was a very dry one, giving us the excuse that we needed to enjoy the good weather and nature's bounty, being away from the manor as much as possible. Habitually, I went for my walks alone, only leaving for walks together once or twice a week ... rarely more often than that. Still, it made every passing hour feel like an eternity. The little time we spent together in the manor was allocated towards meals and trivial activities, such as games, me sitting in the music room and listening to her piano practice, or her talking to me about books and poetry in the reading room. She never came to surprise me in the smoking room anymore.

I did become more conscious about my conduct. To ensure that nobody was let on to the change of relationship between Evey and myself. Inside the manor I made sure to show her the affection of a doting brother, but outside of it I showered her with the passion of a lover. And yet, Evey often succumbed to capriciousness. The tamest instance was her brushing up against me as though it was an accident when we entered a room, all the while affectionately stroking my hand. Whereas on other occasions she boldly went to sit on my lap, kissing me lightly when she seemed sure that nobody would come. It appeared to me as though she was taking joy in making me anxious.

The distinction between familial love and desire was clear to me, but for her the lines seemed to blur with each passing day. It became the most apparent when we went for one of our walks. The woods were dyed in the colour of the ending summer. Passing through the usual path we walked arm in arm.

"Did you receive a letter from Thompson again?" I asked, having seen old Francis pass an envelope with his handwriting on in the morning

"He is persistent. He asked me to reconsider. I am sure he is writing Uncle Arthur as well." She said, while whimsically kicking small heaps of foliage in front of her.

"He should just accept his defeat." I noted.

Then I gently placed my hand onto hers which was holding onto my arm.

"To be fair, he does not know that there is someone else." She replied and gave me a quick peck on the cheek.

After a brief silence I suggested with a chuckle, "You could still marry him once I'm gone."

Evey stopped abruptly, making me halt as well. I asked her if there was something amiss, but she simply stared down. Leaning in to look at her, I saw that the brows were tightly knit, the face flushed with fury.

"Don't ever say something horrid like that to me again! Ever!" she demanded in a low consternated voice.

"I wasn't serious. I was joking." I said smiling, trying to ease her anger.

However, I could see that she was labouring to hold back tears.

"I don't find this a laughing matter!" she replied and finally began to carefully wipe her eyes with her gloved hands.

"I'm … I—. Forgive me. I did not mean it. I … in fact, I hate it! The idea that you should marry him." I reassured her. Thinking about it honestly, I even hated the thought that she should marry anyone.

"Then … why can't I marry you? Why don't you want to marry me?"

It certainly wasn't an unexpected question. At some point, I was sure, she would pose it. However, I was still shaken to hear it. I really did not want to get into the subject and asked her, with trepidation, "Why is it always about marriage with you women? For one there is the fact that I'm not inclined to due to my career, it is even discouraged. For the other don't you think there should be more of a basis than ..."

"Than what?"

"Than sexual passion." I said, and she wore a hurt expression.

"Even I know that my only strong suit is my physique. I'm not fooling myself into thinking that there is more to me. Besides, you know that I am not easy to be with and you wouldn't want to spend your life with me." I further explained.

It was the undeniable truth.

"Aren't you making excuses? You are always so self-deprecating. It hurts to hear you talk that way. And isn't it for me to decide if I want to spend my life with you, after all I—" she heatedly protested.

But before she could finish the sentence, I pulled her close and kissed her. I knew what she was about to tell me and did not wish to hear it, because I knew it was not true. It was a mere childish fancy. She was just as foolish as I was when I gained my first experiences with the opposite sex. I wanted to spare both of us from having words uttered that she would regret saying and I would regret hearing. I wouldn't be able to carry their weight.

"I'm sincerely sorry for making such an awful joke. Let me make you forget what I said." I whispered in her ear, while her arms wrapped around my neck ever tighter, refusing to part from me.

The distressing emotions stirred up by this event were quickly overshadowed by another one that was worse in nature. It was early September. As Father and me sat at breakfast old Francis informed us that Miss Evangeline was feeling under the weather and would not be able to join us. Of course, we were quite aware what that meant because she was feeling under the weather cyclically, form month to month. Despite that, I wanted to see Evey at least and made my way up to her bedchamber. Knocking lightly and informing her that it was me, she sent me away. I ignored her plea and entered anyway. Lying in her canopy bed, with braided hair and still in her nightgown, she turned her head towards the door.

"You mustn't be in a lady's quarters when she's in a vulnerable state." She said, pouting.

"I only wanted to see how you are feeling." I noted and scanned the room.

It had been several years since I last entered her bedchamber. In fact, aside of the time I peeked in to watch her, it was the first time that I dared to come into it. The interior had changed much to look less childish. There were no more toys or dolls to be found anywhere. On her desk there were elegant writing materials and worn volumes of poetry. Even a notebook. I wondered if she was attempting to write poetry herself. At some other occasion I would have liked her to read it to me. Several watercolour paintings in delicate metal frames adorned the room. Some must have been painted by her and some by other people, as there were certain distinctions in skill visible. A vase with a bouquet of fresh flowers was placed on the low windowsill. However, the room was filled with her warm scent of lavender. I went to sit on the ottoman at the foot of her bed continuing to look at the room.

"I'm miserable, as you can see." She answered, with her head back on her pillow.

"A curse upon you females for your deceitful nature." I laughed.

"Oh, be quiet!" she hissed, and had turned her face towards me, darkened with annoyance.

"How precious! Your angry expression is very adorable, too." I laughed, yet again.

She did not answer to my teasing.

Having noticed something that seemed out of place within the framework of the rest of the interior, I got up and went over to the dressing table. Just next to a photograph of us three children of the house, there was a hand painted square porcelain box with gold paint decorations. In size it was as wide as two sheets of letter paper and had considerable depth. Sets of frolicking putti, playing with flowers and birds were the motif in the bands around the sides. The fitting and hinges appeared to be made of pure gold. However, the delicacy of the box was destroyed as it was irrevocably damaged. The lid had been smashed in before and was somehow repaired, creating cracks in the top relief, a motif of chubby little angels residing in pink hued clouds. It was offensively gaudy and looked like nothing that would suit her taste.

"What's with this garish looking thing?" I asked, letting my fingers glide over the cracks.

"That's my treasure chest. Don't open it!" she called, sitting up hurriedly.

"It looks old and worn, but I've never seen it in your room before. I would have remembered seeing something like this."

"You never saw, because I used to hide it."

"You did not want your treasures to be found? That's endearing."

"You really don't remember the box? You sometimes are a dunce. And to think I was so worried …" Evey sighed annoyed, and uncomfortably shifted around in the bed.

"There's no need to be rude." I replied, baffled at her remark.

"Do you remember? A long time ago … I had only arrived at the manor, we were playing hide and seek. I broke it."

"Ah, that's what it is? It seemed familiar." I mused, after having only recently thought of that event again, it was odd to have the missing piece of my memory in front of me.

"Why is it here?" I asked.

"I wanted to keep it, so I begged Aunt Grace not to have it thrown away."

"Because you liked the way it looked?"

"No, I kept it because I felt guilty about breaking it in the first place … you see, I intentionally threw it onto the floor, and it made me feel better to hold on to it afterwards."

I was confounded. She was always such a docile child, and she never had tantrums. Telling me that she intentionally destroyed something, was like telling me that there were fairies on the moon. It was something I could vividly imagine but never believe to be the truth. Curious, I went over to sit on her bedside.

"You did? I wouldn't have guessed … I simply thought you were clumsy. Why did you do it?"

She contemplated for a few moments, and then started what seemed to become a longer explanation than I anticipated.

"I never told you this, but Nanny and the maids noticed how you were constantly staring at me in the days after my arrival. They called you a pretty-faced devil, and they warned me that you were a malicious child that was plotting something. Therefore, I should be careful if I should ever end up alone with you." She said slowly.

"Hah, witches. All of them." I noted through grit teeth.

"And when we were playing hide and seek, you had troubles finding me the first few times … and it took longer … and longer … "

"Well, you were good at the game."

"… and I thought that maybe you went away and left because you thought that it was an amusing prank. I was completely lost and wandered around and became scared. I did not even see a servant. Then I came across this box … it looked exactly like one my mother had … and I … I felt intensely angry and upset … that my parents had died and had abandoned me, and that you too were abandoning me then and there. I was just an irrational child, so I threw it down in a fit. But once I saw it broken on the floor, I became truly terrified," she explained, then putting her hand on mine that rested on the bedside, she continued, "… especially when you turned up because I didn't think you would … I realised that I was wrong … that I wronged you … and then you also took the blame for the broken box."

"And you felt so guilty that you held on to that thing? Maybe you did not know then, but later it should have been clear to you that I was very much used to beatings, so it did not bother me." I noted. I couldn't believe that she still felt guilty about it.

"But it should have! Because … without even hearing you out, everyone had determined that you were the perpetrator even though we were both at the scene. Not once did they ask if it in truth it was me, and also … also I did not say a word in your defence. I was afraid of being thought a naughty girl … and you would just idly accept the punishment. It was so very upsetting." She said, agitated.

It almost seemed like tears were welling up in her eyes. Her vulnerable state made her more sensitive.

"What complicated feelings over an ugly box. You're so sweet and sensitive." I chided her and stroked her hair.

"I am not … not at all …" She contested, shaking her head.

"If you still feel remorse, you can make it up to me once your body is well." I suggested, and gently pushed her back into the pillow. My hands rested at each side of her head. She looked up to me, a slight blush putting colour to her pallid face. After she teased me with a coy smile, I leaned in to kiss her, tenderly caressing her pale cheeks. Immersed in the moment, I failed to hear the door open for the lady's maid to enter.

"Miss Evangeline, I brought you the— Oh my!"

Evey and I both started as we saw Eilers stand in the door with a heavy hot water bottle in her hands.

"I – I'm awfully sorry, miss! Sir!" she stuttered and bowed, to then retreat out of the room backwards.

The door was somehow shut with a bang.

Breaking out in a cold sweat, I jumped up from the bed, wanting to pursue her. But Evey clung to my arm with her whole body.

"Don't! Don't go after her just now!"

"What? Are you out of your mind, Evey? She'll have nothing better to do than to tell all the other servants."

"What will you do when you catch up to her? Intimidate her?"

"Of course! What other choice do we have? Now let go of me

before it's too late!" I said, panicking, but unable to be rough to her when she was feeling unwell.

"No, you mustn't," she continued to plead, "She … She knows! Elaine knows about us."

It was an awful confession. The impact of her words knocked me down and I settled back onto the bed again.

"Since when?" I asked, not looking at her.

"Since that time … that we first went for a walk." She admitted in a low voice.

Instantly, I felt a sort of rage I had never felt for Evey before … for any woman, in all my life. I was used to their cunning, and to being someone's dirty secret. But this was a gross betrayal. All the while I thought that it was our secret. That us being lovers was our safely kept secret. Instead, I was unwittingly the secret being kept by her and her lady's maid. It was impossible for me to find any reasonable words to say to her with the feelings of anger and hurt distorting my mind. I slowly rose from the bed while Evey was still clinging to my arm.

"I'm sorry that I did not tell you, I truly am! I didn't mean to hurt you! Elaine, she—"

"She's a failure of a lady's maid and a chaperone … or maybe she is an excellent one for keeping her lady's dirty laundry out of sight?" I barked at her, furious.

Then, actual tears started to flow from her eyes. I hated this the most about women. When they were guilty, they would use it as their last resort to sway the heart.

"Stop crying!" I demanded.

Yet she continued to cry quietly, with little sobs that made her shake while she still hung onto me. Raising her head, she looked me straight in the eyes with a combination of desperation and defiance.

"How was I supposed to hide it, Arthur? Tell me! You've been carelessly leaving your marks on my whole body! How was I to hide it from the other person that sees my bare skin every day to help me dress?!

She's not an imbecile, she's a woman too!"

I sat down again.

"You— you ... don't know what it felt like, being found out just like that. Simply, because I was not aware myself! I was so frightened I ... I did not know what to answer her when she pointed it out. I was not frightened because it meant I would be admonished or punished, or even worse become a social pariah. I told you that night at Aunt Gwen's: I did not care for any of it. No, it was because of you! You would have been banished from Forestedge. Probably even banished from all of Cumberland by Uncle's influence. The thought of never being able to see each other again, I could not bear it. But Elaine ... Elaine, said she understood, and she wouldn't tell."

I did not respond and silently listened.

"I trusted her words. I knew I could believe in them. It was a blessing that she came after you went away. In all the four years that she's worked in this house, she has always been impartial. She listened to all the things I had to say about you without passing judgment. She was always on my side ... She's been *my only friend*. The only person I could rely on when you were away, and this place turned into a nightmare." She sobbed; the tears incessantly flowed from her eyes.

"Why did you not tell me that she knew?" I finally asked.

"I know that you hate the servants, and that you trust none of them. I was afraid that you'd turn away from me the instant I told you that she knew, and that you would go back to avoiding and ignoring me as best as you could."

It would have been the more rational and sensible choice, but I doubted that I would have turned away from her even with knowing that the lady's maid knew.

"And I was also worried that you'd somehow force her into resigning and making her go away. That would have been unfair. Don't you see? She hasn't told anyone. Not in two months. Our secret is safe with her."

"Very well ... I understand," I said. Yet, a bad aftertaste remained,

"Nonetheless, I will have a talk with her."

"But promise me that you will not be harsh to Elaine. Promise that you won't frighten her."

"I promise." I said and rose from the bed.

Without another word, I exited the room leaving her to settle by herself. I did not turn around to see whether her gaze had followed me or not.

I put on my walking clothes and went out, not letting anyone know that I went, and not thinking about where to go other than away from the manor. Eventually, I ended up at the stone hut after all. Looking around the small space, the space that was supposed to be the only keeper of our secret, I became angry again. I tried to find anything to do to overcome my fury and started chopping firewood.

She was keeping a secret from me. She should have told me. She was so naive. For such a stupid reason. Wasn't I the experienced person? It was my fault. I was careless. I had lacked the foresight. Simply because I lost all reason when I was with her. And now we were in a bind. At the mercy of a third party.

I mindlessly continued to chop wood until I was exhausted and the excruciating pain in my flank forced me to stop. It had been more than a month since the pain had become that bad. Looking at the heap of logs I thought to myself how I would never stay long enough at Forestedge to use up all of them. I went back into the hut to rest. The anniversary of Omdurman had already passed, and I would still suffer from the injury. This was probably the best it would become, which meant that I would be ending my leave of absence soon … Soon enough, this hut would return to becoming a rundown ruin and whatever went on there a mere memory. Once I was away, wouldn't that have settled all issues? *Only for the time that I was still at home,* was our agreement.

I returned to the manor just in time for supper. It was only Father and me at the table, for Evey had herself excused again by old Francis. We ate our meal silently. After having refreshed myself in my chambers, I planned to talk to her again but ran into Eilers, who was just exiting from her mistress' room. What a serendipitous occurrence.

"You. I need to talk to you!" I demanded.

"Sir, I was informed by Miss Evangeline. Please follow me." She answered, curtly bowing. Stretching her hand out in the direction behind her, she led me to one of the empty guest apartments on the floor.

"We will not be disturbed in here." Eilers said as she opened it, urging me to step in first.

"After you." I insisted.

She looked at me quizzically and then went in waiting for me to close the door. I had to insist on her taking a seat first as well, as she kept motionlessly standing in the middle of the room. Oddly, she did not seem intimidated but sat with a straight back and perfectly poised, indicating that she had experienced some sort of stricter and refined education. I did not know where to start the conversation, but she did it for me.

"Sir, rest assured. I will not tell a living soul of you and Miss Evangeline." She began.

"I wonder if they are good at keeping secrets, wherever you are from." I said mockingly, and crossed my legs.

"My mother was from northern Scotland and my father was from the northern part of the Prussian Kingdom. In both countries they say Northerners are stoic and taciturn. I am not likely to talk, sir."

I did not even mean anything by my statement, but she was being surprisingly serious about it. There was sincerity to her austerity.

"… aren't you afraid of losing your position if this ever sees the light of day?" I asked.

"My loyalties lie with Miss Evangeline. She is a sensible lady that needs support. If she was to be found out, then surely she would need an ally, sir."

"And that is you? What makes you think you qualify for that?"

"Please pardon my insolence, sir, but even though I've been here for four years only, I've come to view the miss like a younger sister. We've been sharing our everyday as such, almost. But I would not know for sure, because I have no siblings. I … I too do know what it's like to be an orphan in a household without blood relatives and in foreign shores, sir."

"So, you sympathise with her for that reason?"

"Yes, sir."

"Aren't you worried for her?"

She threw me a puzzled look, but then understanding what I meant, reassured me, "Sir, I am well aware of the stories and rumours which are shared about you among the servants, but I know they are only half-truths. Nay, partial-lies."

"I've only been back for half a year; how would you even know?"

"Sir, I …" she started but then fell silent.

"You don't know, do you?"

"It's not that, sir … It's … how shall I say? I've come to know Miss Evangeline to be an upright and delicate girl who has suffered much from Mister Harold's death—"

"Yes, she suffered. They were eventually to be wed after all … what does it have to do with any of this?" I interrupted her irritated. Why was she bringing Harold up?

"Everyone would suffer from *close relations* passing away so suddenly, but having to watch her afterwards, day in and day out, being pushed to her physical and mental limits by the madam … She was only holding on because … because she had you to think about. After the madam's death too, she held on because of your letters, sir. However, it was actually … Even before Mister Harold's passing, her greatest joy was to talk about you, sir, and your exploits. Quietly dreaming of the day of your return. Of course, I would trust her account to be more reliable than that of the other servants, because she is truly close to you, sir and … she dotes on you so …"

"What are you implying?" I inquired, starting to feel uncomfortable.

"Master Arthur, surely ... surely you are aware, aren't you? Why Miss Evangeline would go to these ends just for you ... just to be with you? To throw away all moral conduct ..."

I did not answer.

"My apologies, it is not my place to address this matter. However, I know very well how Miss Evangeline ... I have been in a similar situation in the past. Therefore, I can relate. There are worse things in life than to lose a position or having to leave a place and start new somewhere else. It's a matter beyond reason, sir." She said, and thus concluded her austere explanation.

There was nothing else I wanted to hear from her. In fact, I felt like having heard too much. I rose from the armchair and instructed her, "Very well, Eilers. I'll tell Evey myself about us having talked. Be vigilant and don't let anyone get near her chamber until I'm done."

She rose as well and simply bowed to me as I exited the room. Knocking lightly at her door and telling her that it was me, Evey this time asked me to enter. A smouldering fire was burning in the small fireplace of her room, giving it a comfortable warmth. Evey sat up in her bed, the tip of her fine nose rubbed red and her eyes puffy. I went to sit at the edge, just next to her straight away.

"Silly girl. Have you been crying all day?"

Without answering, she pushed her face into my chest, and I put my arms around her.

"There, there ... I'm not cross with you ... not at all." I reassured her, gently stroking her back.

"You aren't?" She mumbled; her face still deeply buried in the fabric of my clothes.

"It's a predicament you came into due to my actions."

She nodded, rubbing her face into my shirt.

"Did you talk to Elaine?" She asked, her voice hoarse.

"I did ... If you trust her, then I shall too."

Looking up at me she smiled with relief.

"Thank you, Arthur. I'm sorry … so sorry for—"

"That's enough apologising. You seem exhausted. You should have some sleep."

She nodded and wordlessly settled back into bed, closing her eyes.

"Rest well." I said and kissed her on the forehead.

"You too, good night." She answered, still holding on to my hand.

In the dim light of the crackling fire, I watched her fade into sleep. Then I looked over to the gaudy box on her dressing table. She was right to have hidden it all those years from my sight because I was provoked to peek into it by a strong desire to know what she was treasuring … and what she did not want me to see. I still felt slightly petty and sore from the events of the day.

Once I was sure that she was fast asleep, I finally gave in to the temptation of peeking into the box and went over to it. Carefully, I unfastened the clasp and a scent of spiced incenses emanated from the opened porcelain container. A scent I had grown familiar to in India. There were two generous compartments. One was filled to the brim with small trinkets, such as ribbons and a charm bracelet that she used to wear as a child; a pair of rings that looked like they had belonged to her parents; small trouvailles such as shells and a shiny stone, and some other things which we had collected together; a small cameo brooch which I had sent her for one of her birthdays, it had suffered a crack. There was even a tin miniature figurine of Greyfriars Bobby. In the other compartment, there was an assortment of papers and cards: a photograph of her parents, and another one of her beautiful mother holding the infant Evey in her arms; familiar postcards of India and Africa; some older, yellowed letters I sent her; even a letter from Miss Violet; and finally, a photograph of me just past the age of twenty, proudly smiling in my dress uniform. The paper was worn with small blots at the base, indicating tear stains. I returned all the contents and carefully shut the lid again. And I came to think that this delicately made, yet damaged container, this precious but discarded box, in many ways resembled her heart.

To throw away all moral conduct for it ... the matter beyond reason ... of course, it was love. Not the love of a foster sister for her foster brother, but the love of a woman for a man. I had pushed it away from me finding several excuses: that she had loved my brother and I was a mere consolation over the hurt of his loss; that she was just as immoral as I, satiating base desires; and again, that she was like me, confusing two types of emotions with each other. Excuses. To someone desperately in love the words 'I need you' were equal to 'I love you.' But they weren't the same. It was a greater betrayal than what I had suffered that day, and there was no justification for me being angry anymore. I was bound to go away again, and she knew very well but still decided to take risks and go along with my whims. The more rational and sensible choice was to avoid her for the rest of my life, but I was too caught up in it all. To think that she had always only loved me ... Elation and misery incessantly pricked my heart as though a thorny vine had grown around it upon the revelation of her love.

16
Envy & Greed

With the knowledge of Evey loving me, I began to look at her actions differently. The smiles had a different shine to them, her touch appeared gentler to me, and there seemed to be a certain distress evident in the ways she teased me. When before I thought that she did it only out of mischievous joy in seeing me flustered, it instead started to look like she helplessly got back at me for not returning her love. And even though I should have stopped using her the instant I came to know, I couldn't. I wanted to indulge in her affection. Only a few days after our argument, I came to see how it gave me repose.

The heaths and dales had already turned a brownish yellow with the advancing golden autumn. However, the lingering spirit of summer was generous that year and I went out for an extended morning ride due to the sunny weather. Deciding to give my Thoroughbred a break on the way back, I left it at the stable of the village inn and walked around, making a short detour into the grocery and sundries store. Letting my eyes wander over the stacks of newspaper a bit on *10,000 troops having been sent to Natal, South Africa,* caught my eye. After I made a small purchase, I left again to return to the inn for setting back to the maor. The eponymous wisterias of the inn had long lost their bloom; their scrubby remnants crept up the half-timbered house and listlessly hung onto the pergola leading up to it. As I passed the fenceless garden of the inn, which had numerous cyclists drinking and chatting at tables, I was stopped by a loud unmistakable charge at me.

"I smell a stray, Geoffrey."

"My word, you are right! It reeks of lowly Army dog, Grant!"

Not too far from me, I saw two men standing at a tall table, stouts in their hands. They were wearing bicycle suits. One was of moderate height, the other slightly taller; but both lean. The elder one had a heavy moustache. Geoffrey and Grant Graham were Juliet's brothers. Each of them respectively one year older than Harold and me. They were of the same stock as Thompson, only more rustic, and franker. As they went to Harrow School, they had nothing to do with my brother and me ... except for my escapades with Juliet, which this was likely to be about. Even as an adolescent, I knew that the Grahams would never be openly outraged by my involvement with their sister, as pushing the issue into the public eye would have damaged their family's reputation, not mine. Especially at present, seeing that she was already married. Harold always reprimanded me, for abusing the fact that our family had more money and a higher status as means to deflect my delinquent behaviour. It let me act whichever way I wanted. He was right, and apparently, I hadn't learned. It was only a question of time for that to come back to bite me, and I felt slight remorse at having even gone to Juliet's. They sipped on their beverages, staring at me with a bovine quality to their visages. I should have moved on and ignored them, but the sight of them provoked me beyond my ken. I went over to them.

"The Graham brothers on an outing. It has been some time. Even though, Geoffrey and I had the pleasure recently," I replied, tipping my cap, and smirking at the elder, "Capable of pursuing some exercise again, I see?"

Being the more choleric of both, Grant stepped forward in a menacing movement, but Geoffrey halted him.

"Never mind that, Grant. Clarence gives cheek, but he already was slugged by me for his ways. There is hardly any capacity for learning in that empty shell of a head, it seems, or you wouldn't shamelessly gambol around the place."

"What? Was there something I should be ashamed of?" I asked, sarcastically.

"A brute like you is incapable of abstract thought. Of course, you wouldn't figure it out yourself, but there are countless things you should feel shame for." Geoffrey said with a sideway glance to his brother who was leering at me.

"Like giving your sister a good time, I suppose?"

Grant was not stopped by his older brother at this turn and stepped closer to me.

"You leave Juliet out of this!" he exclaimed, menacing, "I can guarantee you that I know better than Geoffrey how to put runts like you in their place."

This speech inevitably drew the attention of all the other people in the inn garden and we were observed. What were they expecting me to say when they were out to provoke me?

"I'd like to see you try." I replied, moving in as well.

Geoffrey put the hand on his brother's shoulder to restrain him.

"You really love to live up to your despicable reputation, don't you? A pest wherever you go. You see, we care about our siblings, unlike you who simply takes joy in being a nuisance to them. First Harold, who had to not only run after you but also kow-tow in your stead — Bless him! — and now Miss Hollings, by insulting her good prospect's family and putting the chap off altogether. How is she ever to marry, with you around? Everyone pities her for that." Geoffrey being the more eloquent brother, dealt me this blow.

So, it was about Evey and Thompson ... it had made its rounds even to them, of course in the shape of a malformed partial truth. And by the looks of it would be further perpetuated as rumour and ill-intent travelled the county on bicycles.

Seeing my consternation, Grant oafishly chimed in, "I can only agree. To have such an embarrassment of a brother, what a poor girl."

"Embarrassment indeed. And what a ridiculous fool you made of yourself. Who would be dim-witted enough to pass on going to Sandhurst and instead *take the Queen's Shilling*? Only Arthur Clarence, the younger and dumber." Geoffrey said, and the brothers guffawed.

Then he lent onto the table and pierced me with taunting eyes, "Was it worth it? Being tread on by people of the lower class? Your stupidity is not accidental, but a trade."

"Oh, I'll show you the arts of my trade. Only this time Juliet is not here to stop me and save you, Geoffrey."

They wanted a fight; they would get one. They were confident in taking me on as pair, but numbers meant nothing to me. I was ready to continue where I had last stopped with Geoffrey at Juliet's, raising my clenched fist. They were eager for it to come their way. Suddenly, a bony hand fell onto my forearm to stop me.

"Good morning, if it isn't the two young Grahams!" said Doctor Armitage, who had appeared out of nowhere.

Both dropped their smug attitudes and greeted him cordially. The doctor entangled them into a verbose conversation about their parents and congratulated the elder Graham brother on the recent birth of his second daughter. There was a certain atmosphere of disappointment in the inn garden, when it became clear that there was no action to be witnessed. People returned to their drinks and conversations, re-establishing an incoherent and carefree racket. Then, Doctor Armitage excused us, ushering me away. They saluted him and grinned gleefully after me, revelling in their apparent triumph. We went to stables where I was to pick up my steed. While we walked, the doctor explained to me that he had come to the village for lunch with his successor at the surgery.

"This was a very close call, young Clarence." He said, mopping his face with a handkerchief and lifting his bowler.

"Thank you, Doctor, but I could have dealt with that situation on my own." I replied with resentment.

"You were at each other's throats, young Clarence, and this was a public scene. With charges for battery and assault you would be unlikely to return to service any time soon, or at all!" he reproached me, justly. I felt silly for not having that much foresight but was still fuming with anger.

He sighed, "This wasn't what I meant when I said you should return to your old ways …"

"They provoked me first." I retorted pettily.

Doctor Armitage raised his brows, baffled.

"Come now, you are no child anymore!" he said, "You should have shown a more dignified bearing. Especially as proud cavalryman. And, yes, I did hear what they threw at you. You are judge of those things, not them. Nonetheless, you all are gentlemen … one should think. Hotheads, the lot of you! In my days this would have been settled—"

"… with a duel and one of us dead?"

Doctor Armitage laughed, the wrinkles of his face all lifted in amusement, "Giving me cheek too, eh? Now, you do have some wit about you, young Clarence. Go home and forget what happened. I'm not keen on treating your bruises again anytime soon."

Rather unwillingly, I saluted the doctor as he watched me quit the place. I hated to retreat like a coward.

The ride back home had not calmed me down, it upset me more. The general way for me to vent my anger was to become physically active. As Doctor Armitage had thwarted me from giving the Grahams their dues, I was anxious to hold Evey. She happened to come my way as I entered the lobby, clothed in one of her simplest tea gowns. Good.

Evey greeted me happily, "Arthur, you just missed lunch! Would you like something to eat?"

"No. Do you have any plans?" I asked her, while scanning the lobby. Nobody was in sight. Nobody would see how chafed and restless I was. I walked over to stand close to her.

"Not at present. Do you care for a game of cards in the drawing room?"

The end of a long emerald sash was dangling from her waist. I took into my hand.

Scrutinising her while desire was tearing at me, I said, "I'd rather go for a walk. The weather is fair."

"N-now?" she stammered, bewildered.

Her cheeks were aflush crimson.

"This instant. Will you come?"

"I— let me get changed. I'll change. Right away." She bumbled and turned towards the main landing.

I went to sit in the drawing room by myself, impatiently tapping my foot and angrily thinking about the Graham brothers. Evey came to pick me up after about twenty minutes, in her usual attire — which was crumpled — and wearing her hair in a simple plait. It appeared to me that she had changed all by herself without the lady's maid. Wordlessly we walked out of the manor, her trailing behind me into the forest. As soon as we entered, I held her by the hand and increased my pace, while she did her best to keep up to it. Sooner than usual we arrived at the clearing. The air in the hermitage was crisp and cold. I spread the blankets out without lighting the fire and flung off my clothing. Hastily, I helped her to do the same. Then I took her, sharp, intense and without restraint; ravenously pushing into her until she could take it no more and she let out pleasured cries. Having exhausted myself my left flank stung, as I lay still, covering Evey's small backs with my own body. Our faces resting side by side on the blanket, mine half buried in her hair. Hot little clouds filled the space as we panted to catch our breaths. The bodily fatigue had slowed down my agitated blood. At last, she turned around to look at me.

"Are you upset?"

"I am."

There was no point to hiding it.

"Still? With me?" she asked, troubled.

"No! No … not at all. Not with you." I reassured and kissed her.

As I could feel the coldness of the floor pushing through to my face, I rose and covered her with the second blanket. Then I lit the fire in the furnace.

"Why are you upset?"

I did not answer. Why I was so furious, I could not quite understand myself. Doctor Armitage was right in advising me to let it go. I thought to have outgrown becoming peeved. Especially over the daft gabbing by pale-faced caitiffs like the Grahams. Having been ridiculed and tested over and over in the service had hardened me. At least I had believed so.

"Please, tell me! What made you so cross?"

"It's ... On the ride back I took a break in the village and had a bit of a tussle ... if Doctor Armitage hadn't been there, it would have without a doubt ended in a brawl."

"And instead, you took it out on me?"

"Was it unpleasant?" I turned around worried, only to see her giggle.

"Oh, no, no." She protested, lying sideways her gaze lifted towards me. Adjusting the blanket over her shoulder for it to outline the sloping curves of her body, she added with a dreamy whisper, "On the contrary, it was lovely."

I grinned at her with moronic satisfaction. My calm had returned.

"Who was it that you argued with?"

"The Graham brothers. Geoffrey and Grant. The cotton mill family. I am not sure if you know them. Both light blondes, but one with a moustache ... Grant is a rambunctious half-pint, and Geoffrey is a windbag."

She chuckled at the descriptions, "Ah yes, I danced with Mr Grant Graham at the Fawcetts' ball. Mr Geoffrey, I don't quite remember right now. Why did you argue?"

I turned back to stare into the fire that was licking away at logs, poking them quietly. Truthfully, I did not want to tell her, but I thought it wrong to hide it, "I was seeing their sister, Mrs Juliet Kendall a little while back, and they are still sore about it. It was an opportunity for them to insult me."

"A little while back?" she repeated astonished, "When?"

"July. Before my birthday."

"Oh ... But you aren't now, are you?"

"No, of course not. I have you." I replied instantly.

Then I returned to lie with her under the blanket and put my arms around her. As she stroked my cheek her countenance was flashing with a complacent little smile.

"And what did they say?"

"They went on mocking me about the Army, about having been a nuisance to Harold ... and being one to you. They heard about the failed proposal of Thompson's, telling me how everyone pitied you for having me stand in your way. Drivel like that."

"But it's just drivel, as you say."

"I know, I know ... I never could stand the Graham brothers, and Harold didn't care much for them either. They are a different type from us altogether."

The stroking motion stopped as she noted shyly, "Ah ... I think I do remember Mr Geoffrey Graham. He was pallbearer at Harold's funeral along with Mr Thompson."

"He was? Those two weren't even friends!" I exclaimed, surprised and angry. The thought of it dismayed me. Having Thompson do it as fellow Etonian and 'friend' of the family, at least made more sense.

"I didn't know," she apologised insecurely, "There were many gentlemen who offered to do him that service. Harold was that prominent. The choice was somehow left to me because Uncle Arthur and Aunt Grace were overwhelmed at that time. Even Aunt Gwen couldn't help me ... with Sir Ian recently deceased."

I instantly felt regret for expressing my ire towards her. It was not her fault. How was she to know who Harold's friends were? She was a mere child. Evangeline was left by the adults with a duty I should have fulfilled, had I been there. But all my life I ran away from all kinds of duties. I brushed aside her hand and rolled around to face the other way. It struck me then, that what angered me the most alongside the Grahams' words and attitude, were my own childish sentiments. I looked over to the half-finished etching of Harold's name on the wall which was the portent for a life cut short; and beneath it my own: strong and bold. The bitter feeling that had seized me upon seeing such a commonplace scene — a pair of brothers having a good time on the weekend and having each other's back — it was envy. I was envious of something I couldn't have anymore. Something that I had in the past but cast aside. The envy made me irrational, placing me in a stranglehold for the past two hours. I was utterly standing beside myself because of it. I should have walked away from the confrontation without anyone's interference, instead I made a fool of myself in public.

"They are right, I am dumb … useless and embarrassing."

"Arthur, no …"

"But it's true. I never stop to think. Not now, not then. I ran off like an idiot, with the idea that I was showing everyone how stupid they were, telling myself that it would serve them right for admonishing me. Yet, all I did was upset everyone dear to me with my self-important and dramatic disappearance. Taking matters into my own hands, I deluded myself into thinking that once I returned, I would have grand stories to tell, and that would make everyone be sorry for underestimating me. When Harold and you … when you came to Brighton to stop me I, in truth, did know that you were hurt by my actions. But I ignored it. It was too late anyway. Had I gone to Sandhurst … had I joined a domestic regiment … I could have spent more time with Harold." The confession gushed out of me as I blanky stared at the wall. There were so many things I wanted to tell my brother and thank him for. There were things I never apologised for.

"Arthur … you would not have been happy in following your parents' plan. Surely you'd had rebelled more."

"Yes, I'm foolish like that, aren't I? I was extraordinarily naive, not even understanding what kind of situation I was getting myself into. And what good did my rebelling do me? In the end, I simply wasn't there when I was needed. I couldn't do anything for Mother, for Father, and for you. I wasn't even there to carry my own brother to his grave." I said, as I hid my face in my palms.

At these words Evey grabbed me by the shoulders to pin me down with conviction. Her long golden hair brushed over my face, lying loosely scattered around me as she beheld me from above.

"Arthur, please stop this! You mustn't hate yourself. It is true that it was not shrewd of you to run away, but for everything else you mustn't blame yourself."

"Evey, I should have been here … when he died."

"You mustn't hurt over something that was beyond your control. It will drive you into despair and eat up your mind!" she insisted compassionately.

However, remorse and guilt already had been disintegrating my spirit for the past three years. The regret I felt had emboldened me on the battlefield, and I unexpectedly returned alive to a home that wasn't a home at all anymore; with half the family missing, with myself so changed and wanting something that was never meant to be mine.

"I can never make amends."

"Forgive yourself and try to do well by those who are still here with you. You are here now, and that's what truly matters."

"How can I ever?"

"You already are doing well by me." She smiled, and her eyes were overflowing with the warmth of her love for me.

Then she bent down, raining kisses on my face and neck, while gently curling the hair of my chest. I let myself be spoilt by her: by her loving kisses, and loving embrace. Her hands wandered down to comb through my other hair, tenderly caressing my loins; and her other lips rubbed with a dulcet moistness against my leg. Again, I held her fast: the girl … the woman that excitedly awaited my touch … mine alone. She opened to receive me in reverence, offering up her softness and warmth, which let me forget. The sincerity of her love for me, I became greedy for it and the way she looked at me when I held her, as though I was her whole world. Upon looking back at her, I wondered if she knew that I was aware of her unrequited feelings. But if she was, she didn't show it. Incapable of reciprocating them, I attended to her desires, and in the act became more vigorous and careless. Having her love let me think that it could all be forgiven: having mistreated so many people in the past, having killed, having survived when others died, having returned to a place that I had grown estranged and unwanted to ... only because *she* was there waiting for me.

As we prepared to head back, I watched her plait her hair while I had my hands in my breeches' pockets. Feeling something that I had forgotten over the run-in with the Graham brothers, I pulled out a small paper parcel. I unfolded it revealing a long, French blue satin ribbon. On impulse I bought it at the store, as I thought about how I did not see here wear hair decorations like that as often anymore.

"For me?" Evey asked surprised.

"I'm not the one wearing ribbons."

She took it out of my hand and tied it to the end of the plaited hair. Then she rose to embrace me, lifting her face to grace me with an elated smile.

"That's very sweet of you! You used to always bring me a new one whenever you returned from boarding school. I'm being spoiled again."

"Harold as well, kept telling me that I spoil you ... but it's only a cheap ribbon. You have more exquisite finery than that these days."

"But none that you chose. Does it suit me?"

"You look pretty. It matches your eyes."

She kissed me.

"Do you like this colour?"

"Yes. It reminds me of ..." I said slowly, "It's the same colour as the facing of my dress uniform."

It was a subconscious choice.

"I see ... the regiment is always on your mind, isn't it?" she noted, with a hint of sadness.

"It appears so." I replied, disconcerted about not having realised the gravity of my choice before.

Leisurely, we walked back to the manor. Her holding my arm, and me talking some more about my regiment, for I had become more comfortable to talk about it. We did not break away from each other even as we were on the lawn towards the backside patio, where we ran into Doctor Armitage. He had only returned from his visit to the village and strolled back from the stables.

"Young Clarence, Miss Hollings. A good afternoon to you!" he greeted us.

We both reciprocated politely and continued our relaxed walk towards the patio as a trio. As attentive of a gentleman as ever, he noticed the ribbon decorating her hair, and she proudly explained how it was a gift from my morning outing. With the discretion paramount for his profession, he made no mention of the scene he had saved me from, unaware that I had told her about it anyway.

"That is more like it! Don't you agree, young Clarence?"

"What do you mean, Doctor?" I asked, puzzled.

He had a merry little twinkle in his eyes as he intently looked at Evey's arm linked into mine.

"You and Miss Hollings at least seem to have returned to the old ways."

Evey blushed but did not separate from me, inquiring bashfully, "Does it seem so?"

"Oh yes, Miss Hollings. At first, I was worried about the rift between the two of you … the whole household was in wonder, really. However, this is a pleasant sight: your sibling-relationship mended!" he explained, and turned to me, "I hope you don't mind me saying this, young Clarence, but the doting side that a rapscallion like yourself exhibits whenever you are with Miss Hollings makes you more agreeable. It always gave a bit of softness to your edges."

"Evey is my weakness, for better or for worse." I confirmed and locked eyes with her.

She smiled at me, sweetly whispering 'Oh, Arthur' under her breath.

"She draws out the best in you!" was Doctor Armitage's observation, and Evey chuckled softly.

But my view on this was ambiguous. She was good for me, I knew. She gave my troubled heart peace, and I would become calmer. All the same, I exploited her love and satisfied myself with her intimacy. Lovelessly bedding my foster sister; ravaging her like a savage animal … was that the definition of drawing out the best in me?

I was still a useless fool that did nothing for her but give her sensual pleasure. And within, I could feel the desire growing stronger to give her happiness. Yet, how was I to do it? Was that even something I could offer? As we had finally reached the rear-side entrance, I broke away from Evey to open the door for her and Doctor Armitage. While I stood by to let them enter, my focus was on the regimental colours affixed to her hair, flying in the wind as she passed me.

17
Philia

Near the end of the month, just as she had announced, Aunt Gwen came to visit Forestedge for Harold's death anniversary. She arrived earlier than anticipated, and incidentally, Evey and I returned from our walk out in the forest. Upon hearing that old Francis greeted us, Aunt Gwen did not even stay seated in the drawing room but stormed out to the lobby to meet us. As per usual, she attacked us with her embraces and kisses.

"Dear me, it's only been two months. But look at how the two of you have changed yet again. I must say Evey, you are glowing!" she exclaimed and held her by both hands.

"I … uh— Thank you." Evey answered, casting down her eyes in what appeared to be modesty but was in truth shame.

"And Arthur, you also look more handsome with that perpetual frown on your face gone."

"You look well too, Aunt Gwen." I replied, and subconsciously went to rub the spot between my eyebrows.

"I see, you are both in high spirits! Who wouldn't be after taking *a nice long walk* around the forest?" she warbled cheerfully, her gaze still fixed on me while I smiled wryly.

"You know, I used to enjoy that too when I still stayed here," Aunt Gwen reminisced and smiled at Evey, "I used to take Harold and Arthur out on them as well when they were wee bairnes. However, you never struck me as a person that would enjoy walks in the woods around here, pet."

"Uhm … Arthur made me appreciate them." She stammered and cast me a helpless look.

"Is that so? Good on you Arthur, teaching Evey about the *pleasures of physical activity!*" she exclaimed, and I tried not to choke from suppressing embarrassed and inappropriate laughter.

It was probably in my mind, but her comments always appeared too aware of our situation.

"Well, it definitely keeps the body in good health." She further added.

"Gwendolyn! At least let the children refresh themselves!" Father called, as he came up from behind her, rapping his cane.

Seeing Aunt Gwen and him next to each other made it more apparent how much he was physically changed. He was only nine years older than her but with her youthful looks and his brittle one, it appeared to be an age gap more than twice that much.

"I can't help it, Bear. It's because you keep them all to yourself."

Even old Francis could not suppress his smile at being exposed to Aunt Gwen's cheerful energies. Before we could take a break in our chambers, young Francis had returned to let us know that tea was prepared in the drawing room. Thus, we gathered to greet Aunt Gwen properly who was dominating the atmosphere of the room with her vivaciousness, despite her visit being of solemn nature. It was quite evident how my father was barely able to handle her. Aunt Gwen recounted our stay at her place to him in detail. She had neither forgiven nor forgotten about Father scheming with Evey's suitor, and nonchalantly congratulated her on having got rid of the Thompson boy. Then, to all our surprises, she asked why there weren't any plans yet for Evey and me to be wed.

"Gwendolyn, are you mad? What kind of ridiculous question is this?" Father huffed.

He was slamming his fist against his chest, having had a too huge swig of tea.

"It was merely asked in jest, Bear. There is no need for an impertinent reaction!"

"Impertinent? You are the one being impertinent. Besides, I know your 'jests.' Always this sordid! To imply that the two of them would be in anyway inclined towards each other is not amusing at all. They are like siblings – no different than you and me." Father said.

Evey and I exchanged unsettled glances.

"But they aren't siblings. It's always the same story with you, you think that you can command all your female relations to do what you want! However, Evey here, she is not even an actual Cl—"

"Pardon, Aunt Gwen," Evey anxiously interrupted her, "I … I don't feel comfortable with this topic."

"There, you have it. Gwendolyn, you are being impertinent towards the poor child."

"I do apologise, pet. However, wouldn't Arthur also like to add something to the conversation?" she demanded looking at me.

"Aunt Gwen, Evey is my dear little sister. I told you that before." I insisted, hoping that I did not sound nervous or betrayed us in any other way.

She cast me a sceptical, and maybe disdainful, sideway glance.

"Very well, I apologise for having said something that upset the three of you." She conceded.

Father shook his head and reprimanded her, "In your forty-three years in this world, and even after having been married, you still haven't stopped to chatter like some silly adolescent girl."

"Oh, shush! Just accept my apology, Bear, and stop chiding me."

Thus, the topic was not touched upon again and Evey and I sighed in relief.

We did not stay for very long in the drawing room afterwards. Having had morning tea that late, we decided to all refresh ourselves to meet for an afternoon walk in the gardens. However, it began to rain as we regrouped in the lobby. Instead, to pass the time, Aunt Gwen, Evey and I went to the sitting room to play card games, deciding to start with a game of *Old Maid*.

Once I had all the cards served, Aunt Gwen sighed dramatically, "What a shame! I really did want to play Whist."

"Father is a busy man. Especially now that he must take things slow. Work seems to double."

"Oh, no … he's simply a very sore loser. And he's always been really bad at card games."

"Isn't it better then? He won't become upset and is able to have a good rest later this evening." Evey said sympathetically.

Aunt Gwen rolled her eyes and sighed again.

"If only Rosalind was here. I thought that this time she would actually come. You haven't seen her recently either, have you?" she inquired addressing me, while sorting through her cards.

"I've only seen her once, in March when I arrived in London. To my letter asking her to come she replied with an excuse, saying that she did not want to upset Father with her presence. Surely, he has long forgiven her … I think. He took me back after all. While she did love Harold, not coming is a mere justification for not having to be near Uncle Richard's grave." I answered, taking up mine.

"Who could blame her?" Aunt Gwen noted.

"Good Riddance." I said, setting down some cards.

"Indeed."

"Is that really something that should be said about the departed?" Evey asked, taken aback while the cards were still laid out in front of her.

Aunt Gwen and I looked at another and remembered that no one in the family has ever talked about him beyond one sentence. He was long dead. Therefore, Evey wouldn't have known. No one did deliberate on his person. Even all the pictures that had Uncle Richard on them were allocated into some obscured corner where no one would tread.

"Oh, Evey-pet. You should count it as a blessing that you never met him. He was a horrid brother, tyrannical husband, and an abysmal father. I told you that there are Clarence's that are like raging rivers, but Richard ... he was a flash flood. Short-lived, but destructive in its wake." Aunt Gwen said shaking her head.

"Is that so?" Evey inquired.

"I say, he was a dirty and rotten ... a bona fide scoundrel. Not in the way our Arthur here is called scoundrel. Pardon any offense, dear—"

"None taken."

"No, no, Richard inherited all the ruthlessness from our father, without even the tiniest speck of his benevolence. He made poor Rosalind and her mother suffer."

"He even put the fear of the Lord in me. He was a violent man." I said remembering his vicious aura.

The only time I remembered seeing him was when I was five years old, shortly before his death. He had come to the estate with Rosalind. She was all bones. A macabre figure that looked poor and miserable in her rugged, grimy frock. Nothing like the radiant beauty she had grown into. I did not even know that she was my cousin. As I innocently peeked in on them in the drawing room and addressed the other child, Uncle Richard came over and wantonly slapped me. Without holding back. I never dared to imagine what Rosalind had to suffer through in her life.

"I don't understand why my brother allowed for him to be interred on the family grave site. Being in a pauper's grave would have been right for him. Probably Bear felt responsible because Richard was the third son after all and had not many prospects in life ... but that was only an excuse for Richard to not amount to anything. After Marigold's death, Bear had always refused Richard money ... even though he was right to do it. He would have never used it for Rosalind. The Lord only knows what indecent things he would have used that money for, instead." she explained, and then shuddered, "Well, let's not dwell on the past. I fear that we will invoke his spirit and he will start haunting these halls, if we continue to utter his name."

Evey quietly nodded and looked at her cards. Talking about Uncle Richard reminded me that I really was not the worst Clarence that was ever born. At least I was able to lead a steady life, and while I had my vices, I was at straightforward about them. In recent times there even was an inclination towards bettering myself. Rosalind never once talked about Uncle Richard, but when I stayed with her before my posting, I came to know how much he must have damaged her. She was suffering from somnambulism, reliving some of her worst moments in life. He really was the dregs of the Clarence family. Uncle Richard would have been rotting alone at any cemetery, completely forgotten, had father not granted him the grace of sharing the space with those that did matter to us.

"Arthur … Arthur isn't much like Uncle Arthur … whom does he resemble then, Aunt Gwen?" Evey suddenly asked while Aunt Gwen held cards towards her.

"Oh, him? He … hm … I mean his appearance he certainly inherited from Grace's side. The character … yes, you do have a lot in common with your grandfather, dear." Aunt Gwen said, looking at me top to toe.

"It's the first time my hearing that I'm ruthless. Amoral, yes. But ruthless …" I noted.

"Oh, don't be silly, dear. That's not what I meant. Papa was resilient and defiant … he would not have ascended into his position if he wasn't. Hm … he was always challenging towards the male relations and loving towards the female ones. Yes, I think that's what you inherited from him … he had the most charming smile, too. Just like you do." She said, winking at me.

Evey, as well, glanced over to me after the explanation and I put on that charming smile alluded to. She reciprocated with a sweet one, but then shyly hid her lower face behind her cards, conscious of our blatant love making being observed.

I never thought much about who I resembled in the family, but rather whom I did not. Harold was so much like Father. He was his spitting image not only visually, but in character too.

"Did Father and Grandfather George get along well?" I wondered aloud, picking a card from Evey's hand.

"I'm sorry, dear, I can't really tell. By the time I would have been able to form my own opinion on it, your grandfather had already passed on. I only know that your father truly respected ours for various reasons."

"I see." I answered plainly and pondered on what made him respect someone who I was supposedly similar to. I knew that he was impressed by Grandfather George's magnanimity, but that was all I knew.

"You should ask your father sometime, dear."

I nodded, but I would not do it. Not once in my life had I interacted with my own father the way I did with Aunt Gwen. All in all, it was pointless to think about even attempting it then.

The next day the weather was fair again, a pleasant day for visiting the cemetery. After heading over from the music room, Evey and I were the first to enter for breakfast, and unexpectedly Father was not seated yet. Once Aunt Gwen entered and we all sat down, old Francis announced to us that the master was feeling unwell and would not join us for the day.

"Say that again, John?"

Old Francis looked at Aunt Gwen nervously and then repeated, "Mister Arthur is unw—"

She jumped up from her seat and rushed past old Francis, who clambered after her calling, "Wait! Miss Gwe— I mean, Lady Murray!"

"What do you reckon that was about?" I asked Evey, who was looking after them with a worried expression.

"I don't really … I can't think of a reason. If Uncle is unwell, then it's sad but there is nothing we can do …" she said pensively.

"Do you think …" I began, contemplating on possibilities, "Do you think he does not want to go to Harold's grave today?"

"I wonder … I mean, it's always been hard for him to visit Aunt Grace's and Harold's graves. Still, he would always join me for their

227

birthdays and anniversaries … Maybe you should go after Aunt Gwen? You seem to be able to stop her. More than Francis … and if Uncle Arthur is truly unwell, it wouldn't be good for him to have her disturb him. Aunt Gwen seemed agitated too, it's not good for her health either." Evey urged me, anxiously.

"You are right." I agreed and got up again.

But once I exited the breakfast, they were nowhere to be seen. Aunt Gwen could really bounce off like a leopard, if she wanted to, and I rushed towards Father's quarters just to be stopped near his door by old Francis.

"Please, wait here Master Arthur." He said, his face damp with sweat.

However, I brushed him off and he helplessly shuffled after me. As I reached the door of the chamber, I could hear an argument.

"Have you no heart, Arthur?!" Aunt Gwen shouted.

"Be quiet, Gwendolyn!" Father said, his voice loud as well.

"I know how Harold is irreplaceable to you, but Arthur too … he was his brother. You should mourn together … as a family."

"I can't … I can't be there with him … in front of their graves."

"To be so cruel! Arthur is your son, too. Why do you always … always mistreat him so?"

"You would not know what it feels like, Gwendolyn. You have not raised children of your own."

There were no more words exchanged and I could hear the loud clacking of Aunt Gwen's boots. She flung open the door of Father's quarter almost running into me and started as she saw me stand there. Nervously, she looked back inside, then threw an angry look at old Francis who was behind me as he shied away.

"Arthur, dear, you were out here?" she noted, carefully closing the door.

"Yes … I wanted to make sure that Father is well … is he?"

"Oh, it's merely that … the sudden changes in weather must have worn him down. Let him rest for today, yes?"

"Certainly … we should have breakfast and then head out … before the weather changes again."

"Yes, absolutely. You are right."

As she decided to ignore the possibility of my having heard the conversation, I too decided to not dwell on what information I had come to know.

And so, we were in the carriage towards the village cemetery. Aunt Gwen wore a dress of muted plaid, and a brown morning hat decorated with grouse feathers and a Claddagh brooch. It was overall a rare sight to see her so modest. However, Evey had put on what appeared to be one of the mourning dresses she had worn in the past: dark purple, fitted with layers of black crepe and lace over the skirt, bodice, and sleeves. To accompany the dress, she wore a simple cap of jet, silk, and beaded details, which was held in place by a long black satin ribbon tied at her chin. On her collar, there was fastened a gold and black framed memento mori brooch. Behind a round sheet of glass flaxen locks were finely crafted into an endless knot. It was the first time of me seeing her in one of the dresses she had to perpetually wear for two years, and I felt a strong discomfort.

"Dear me, pet, you still have not thrown out the dresses?" Aunt Gwen asked.

"It's the only one I still kept."

"That you were forced to go through the whole period for poor Harold. Even Sir Ian did not want me to and told me on his deathbed I could be free after a year. It's commendable that you did but you really did not need to. It's not like you were his actual fiancée, let alone wife. There is no need to wear it now anymore, either."

"It would not feel appropriate to me, wearing anything else in front of his grave." She said, looking out of the carriage window.

We arrived at the cemetery, which was packed due to the sun being out. People were greeting us, many of them gathering for picnics or anniversaries, like us. Some of them recognised Evey, and of course knew the departed scion and mistress of the Forestedge estate. Along with those that we had brought, we were handed shares of flowers to put down at Mother's and Harold's graves. In March I had come alone. It was unendurable for me to stay longer than ten minutes at the cemetery, as I greeted them both, left flowers and returned to the estate again. It was different to be in a group. I felt more strength and resolve to face my departed family, having Aunt Gwen and Evey with me.

We passed the headstones of those siblings of mine that had not lived more than mere days at best, and Evey left for each of them a flower. She was compassionate towards them as always when we visited that place in the past. Then we moved on. The servants who went ahead of us had set up folding chairs in front of their graves and we went to sit down. There they were, just next to each other: a weeping angel of life like size, guarding Mother's grave, and for my brother a half-pillar covered with a shroud, varieties of sculpted flowers creeping up its base. Beneath them there was the inscription:

To the Memory of
Harold George Clarence
Beloved Son and Brother
Who Died September 21st 1896
Aged 24

Both headstones were modest for a family of our standing, some might have said. They were not as pompous as the mausoleum in which Grandfather and Grandmother rested, but they were far off from being as sorry as the weather-beaten slab of stone under which Uncle Richard was lying. Because Father avoided it all back then, the responsibility for choosing the headstones for both had fallen to Evey, and she made sensible choices. However, I wondered why she did not include epitaphs, especially seeing that she valued poetry that much. I asked her about it.

"I really … I had no mind to think of any."

"Understandable." Aunt Gwen said pensively looking at the graves.

"I'd rather read poetry to them whenever I am here. I brought some today." Evey said, and she took a volume that was laid out on the side.

It appeared familiar to me.

She read the poem.

"I feel like I've heard it before." I mused.

"It's the one from the anthology Violet gave me. The one I read to you in … that I read to you before."

"Oh, I see … what was it about?" I asked, as I was only vaguely able to make sense of it.

"Not being able to move on," Aunt Gwen interjected. Of course, she would have understood it right away, "How dreary, little Evey. Isn't there something more cheerful in there?"

"Unfortunately, not …" she replied, "They are all quite melancholic."

Suddenly tears welled up in her eyes. I instinctively rose from my chair and walked over to her when she started to cry. Without thinking where we were and who was watching, I knelt next to her and we embraced. While stroking Evey's hair, I lifted her face with my gloved hands. Giving her the consolation of a warm touch, I kissed her forehead. She wept quietly, sobs making her body quiver.

"Why would you read something like that if it makes you cry?"

"It's not for … it was … It makes me cry for you." She replied in between sobs.

"It does?"

But before I could pursue this thought of hers, Aunt Gwen made us aware of her presence by clearing her throat. I got up again and remained standing, only leaving my hand on Evey's shoulder to console her. Once she settled, I returned to my seat and we shared our memories of Harold and Mother, passing the afternoon in serenity. When we arrived back at Forestedge, it had already become late afternoon. Elaine greeted Evey, and they headed straight to her chamber in order to cast off the awful mourning dress. Before I could go to mine, Aunt Gwen stopped me by holding on to my arm. It was very unusual, but she wore a serious, almost grave expression.

"Is something the matter?" I inquired, wary.

"Dear, it's about what happened at the cemetery."

I was befuddled, unsure what she wanted to urgently tell me.

"It wasn't a happy occasion, but seeing the two of you so close together ... so tender and loving to each other ... I felt that it was a warming scene."

"Aunt Gwen, that—" I began; however, she would not let me speak.

"I know, Arthur, you said that she was as dear as a sister to you. But I told you that you are both adults now ... and if ... if things between the two of you change — and I know that is something that can quickly happen — then you should not be afraid to act in fear of what your father may think. I know that beneath all the layers of mild-mannered joviality, there is an obstinate side to my older brother ... and that he is hard to persuade into changing his opinion on certain things ... well, whatever happens ... in case of you and Evey changing your ways, then don't hesitate to come to me for help this time, yes? You don't need to go all the way down south to Rosalind. I am next to you." She said and smiled at me earnestly.

"I ... I will keep it in mind. Thank you, Aunt Gwen."

Even in the evening, Father did not join us for supper. As it was a very emotional day, we all decided to retire early into our respective quarters. That night I went to sleep in my own bedchamber. I hardly ever entered it other than for changing clothes, grooming myself, and at very rare occasions for sleep. All the objects inside the room were merely remnants from my adolescent days, and I held no particular emotions toward them anymore. Even though I left the house abruptly five years prior, everything was kept in order and cleaned regularly. I was genuinely surprised to have found it that way upon my return, because I was sure that my parents would have thrown out or sold everything that ever belonged to me, but one of them must have stopped the other from doing so. Or perchance it was Harold that stopped either of them. I wouldn't have known and Evey did not either, because I had asked her. The curtains were not drawn shut, as the night was clear and the view onto waning moon calmed me. The softness of the bed would never be comfortable to me again. A quiet clicking, a squeaking and then shutting of the chamber door announced Evey's entrance. Like numerous times before I went away, she snuck into my room and went to sit on the bed next to me.

"I was sure that you would be in the smoking room, but for once you are actually in your bedchamber." She said in a low voice.

"If Aunt Gwen found out that I was loitering around, and sleeping in the smoking room, she would scold me and never give me the end of it."

"You really fear her, don't you?" she laughed softly.

"I respect her. There is a difference between those two things." I noted.

She gathered back my blanket and quickly slipped under it, nesting herself into my arm.

"Only for a little while, let me stay here, yes?" she asked for permission, even though she knew I would not put up any protest. "However, don't do anything lewd! You said yourself: not in the manor."

"That thought never crossed my mind." I answered, and truly meant it.

I had spent much time in many different beds. In fact, so much, that I came to think that sexual intercourse was the only thing a soft bed was good for. But of course, I never had any other person sleep in my bed with me other than Evey. When she was small, she would have me read something to her. When she became older, she would start to read things to me. When I appeared distressed, which I hardly showed, she knew and would come console me. And even that time when I consorted with the maid and was beaten badly, she came not knowing why I received such harsh punishment. Once she had fallen asleep, I carried her back to her chamber right next to mine. The many hours we had spent together in my bed, in fact those were our tender secret. Nobody ever knew, neither our family nor any servant. The sanctity of this space and secret, I did not wish to tarnish. I did not think of doing anything to her while she was lying in my arm, thinking nothing other than how much solace it was to have her there after a distressing day.

"Don't fall asleep here ..." I chided her yet pressed her tighter onto me.

"I won't. I promise." She answered sounding sleepy already, "Do you think Aunt Gwen became suspicious?"

"She's been having funny ideas about us for some time now." I confessed.

"But she does not seem against it."

"Well ... she does not know what we're doing. I doubt that she would condone it."

"Is it that condemnable? I'm sure that Rosalind would—"

"Shush ... don't bring her up just now."

Evey giggled faintly.

"Say, Arthur?"

"What is it?"

"Do you think ... if Harold was still alive ... do you think we would have still become like this? I wonder what he would have thought ..."

"There's no point in asking that question. He isn't with us anymore." I answered curtly, and she accepted that I did not want to dwell on the topic any longer. She simply shifted to be more comfortable, and I lay there, staring up to the ceiling.

But in truth, I wanted to contemplate on it quietly ... on my own, as I had avoided asking myself that question before. *If Harold had lived, what would the world have looked like?* I would have still been severely injured. I would have still desperately clung on to life in Sudan, not because Evey was living through hard times and I wanted to return to her side. No ... Harold living, would have meant my mother never suffering and dying, my father never taking ill, and Evey having had a cheerful adolescence. A bridal gown instead of a mourning dress. Maybe I would instead have wanted to live on to see her in her wedding dress? Yes, a wonderful thought. To have seen her as bride. The prospect of celebrating a day that would have been the start of a happy and prosperous future, and me ... I would have returned around the same time as I did then, to recuperate at home ... and to celebrate with them. If Harold had watched on in that fatal moment of reunion, that moment when she threw herself at me in relief that I returned alive, her beauty would have still fuelled my desire; her enticing scent would have still filled my lungs, and her warmth would have still enveloped my heart. Just as they did in that very moment when I held her in my bed. However, would she have followed duty and married Harold even though she was infatuated with me? But I still wanted to see her as a bride to the House of Clarence, because I ... I would have still been deeply—

That night I saw him again after so many years. I saw him in my dreams, for the first time since his death. He was the same age as the last time we were together: Harold still fresh-faced, and I formed and forged from the five years apart from home and family. We wandered the grounds of the estate as we used to in our childhood. Once we had reached the stone hermitage, he paused and asked me thrice if I loved him. I said yes, I loved him, but I would not aspire any longer to be like him because I was content with the choices I made and the person they made me. And yes, that I loved him, and that I would be unable to replace him in the hearts of those around us, but that I would instead imprint my own existence onto them. Finally, I said yes, I did love him, but that I took something that was meant to be his, yet I would never give it away, as it brought me happiness. Patting my shoulder like he always did when I confessed something to him, he smiled and forgave me for my decisions, for my shortcomings and my wishes. Before he left, as always he would point out something to me that I was oblivious of, even though it was common sense: that happiness was something only the living could strive for, and that to obtain it I needed to take responsibility but also be ready to surrender myself to—

Awaking again, I still held Evey in my arms. Her lovely sleeping features scarcely illuminated by the soft rays of the moon. Despite her promises she was unable to stay awake. For a few more moments I held her close, taking in all her warmth and then woke her with a kiss. Drowsily she looked at me, while I told her she should hurry back to her room before it was to become too early in the morning. Early enough that the servants would roam the hallways. She did as I asked and left my bedchamber. However, shameful, or painful it seemed at times; it was more happiness than I ever wagered for. Having her by my side and enjoying the moment, memories of long forgotten prayers came to mind, while I was wishing for things to never end. But just as I lay alone again, uncomfortably in that soft bed, in an obsolete chamber, I knew that I did not belong in that place. There was a strong pull from outside as I had become a stranger to the estate, and yet it should have been clear to me that as a Clarence, misfortune was still inbound. The revelation to the world what a shameful sinner I was would come one day.

18
The Reward for a Dog

Pushful, the Younger has made his way down to South Africa as war correspondent, they say,' was a line in the letter from my former sergeant, referring to Lieutenant Winston Churchill who so valiantly had joined us in our exploit at Omdurman. I could only be in awe at how a man a year older than myself was zealously throwing himself into action, eager to leave his mark on the world. Apparently, the Victoria Cross gained in Sudan was not enough recognition for him. The Boers had declared war on Great Britain a week earlier, and I wondered to myself: if I had the health of Lieutenant Churchill, would I have soon found myself in the field uniform on horseback in foreign lands again? However, while I had dedication towards my regiment and loyalty towards her Majesty and the Empire, I had neither industriousness nor ambition to match his. I personally would have been satisfied with simply returning to my position.

With the final third of the year, my condition had significantly improved. I could ride out for long durations, sometimes even being away from the manor for a whole day. Evey, of course did not like my being away for that long, especially because she could not join me. I apologised to her over and over, promising to make it up to her some other time, to go on outings and giving her all the attention that she wanted from me … and all she did was ask me to take her out for walks more often. I did, frequently and fervently. But what me disappearing for almost whole days meant, was that the day drew near on which I would disappear wholly. However, a change different from what I had predicted would come and mark a fateful day. It was an unusual warm late October morning as I returned from my ride out. I ran into Doctor Armitage in the lobby.

"Young Clarence, could I have a brief word with you?" he asked.

Surprised at this request I went with him to the drawing room.

"It pleases me to see that you have been frequently riding out. I take your injury does not bother you that much anymore?" he inquired, as he sat down.

"It has become manageable." I answered.

"Your spirits seem to have been lifted as well. Being with family does that to a weary mind." He further mused.

Again, I agreed.

"I take, you consider returning to your regiment soon?" Doctor Armitage suggested.

"That is what my recovery means, Doctor." I answered curtly.

"Are there any certain plans then?"

"I have correspondent with the command, and it was decided that I should be checked by military physician soon to see if I was fit to return. Ideally it would be before the end of the year."

"So, you will be going back to India or Africa?"

"No, the regiment will be situated in Dublin from November."

"Well, that is a bit of a relief. That's not too far away." He sighed.

"Pardon, Doctor, but I don't quite understand the nature of this conversation." I stated.

Naturally I was unsettled about all these questions.

"Hum ... how do I say this? Your going-away ... That does explain Miss Hollings' condition." The doctor said.

He had a sombre look on his face.

"Evey?" I asked in surprise as I had feared it was in some way related to Father.

He explained to me how Father had requested for the doctor to look at Evey because she appeared to him fatigued and downtrodden as of recently. She insisted on being fine. But I too had noticed it: she did not eat properly, and she would be listless. Even when we were alone, she would easily become tired and fall asleep.

"She must be very anxious about your pending departure. I suggest that you talk to her. Miss Hollings is the type of lady that hides her true feelings. However, it does not do her any good to act like this if it takes a toll on her body. She has been through too much already."

"Yes, you are right." I replied, conscious to conceal the alarm in my voice.

After Doctor Armitage returned to his quarters, I rushed to look for Evey. How could I have been so blind? No, it was not that. I turned a blind eye towards an evident change. The indicators were all there. The soft tinkling notes of the piano reached my ears. As I went over to the music room, I carefully opened the door. A melody familiar yet unknown filled the air. With quiet footsteps I went over to sit next to her on the piano bench. She played a gentle song. The melody concurrently repeating itself, each reiteration tenderly flowing into the preceding, rising and sinking over and over. It evoked the memory of prayer. Then the tune seized. Briefly glancing at the title, I made out the title 'Ellen's Third Song.'

"Ah, Arthur," she began, "I haven't played this in such a long time but suddenly, I felt that I had to. What did you think?"

"I ... it's ... you are skilled enough to play anything well, Evey." I blundered, glancing at her profile.

As neither of us spoke, the silence was unnerving. However, as she began to play a different, familiar tune from memory, I felt even worse. This time it was a more melancholic piece.

Finally, I began, "I met Doctor Armitage in the lobby, and we had a chat in the drawing room."

"Is that so?" she asked, eyes closed and focused on playing.

"He urged me to talk to you as you seemed unwell."

She silently nodded, signalling that I should continue to speak.

"He said your worry over my departure may make you ill." I repeated plainly. Stupidly. My frenzied thoughts were contrasted by the tranquillity of the piano tune as I desperately looked for the right words to say. Yet, I knew I was not tactful enough to come up with any. There was no delicate way to ask it. A blunt question spilt out.

"How long have you been aware?"

Instantly she stopped, opening her eyes that rested on the sheet music momentarily. The hands glid down from the piano keys to gently fold over her womb.

"Barely more than two weeks."

This time I could not feel any anger or upset at her for not having told me. This time it was remorse, for the sum of all my wicked actions had manifested itself in her body. I had not only succeeded in dragging her down to my level, I did even worse. Not one innocent life, but I cursed two to come into shame. It was the result of my carelessness. And she had kept it from me because she was overwhelmed. It was just as Celia said, mocking me about my misdeeds. I never spared a thought. I had my fill and that was it. Dramatic scenes flooded my mind: trembling fingers ripping at the hem of my coat, begging me to look their way; shouting, raving, losing the last shred of dignity; holding their own life hostage or threatening to ruin mine. Empty and fulfilled promises. I laughed. I shrugged them off. Why should I even care knowing that I would be some other place in the vast world anyway? This time it was all different. Any prospect of me going away then filled me with anguish. My remorseful apologies echoed through the music room.

"I'm sorry. I ... I'm the one who should have known when to stop ... I shouldn't ... It was wrong of me to indulge in mindless passions. You were only going along with me and ..."

Placing her hand on my thigh as to soothe me, she bid me stop.

"Do not be sorry. I am just as responsible as you are … and a new life is a blessing." She declared with earnestness, to then ask, "So is it as the doctor says? Will you be leaving soon?"

"Yes, it's very likely. Probably, I'll be gone before the end of the year." I stated. I did not want to lie to her.

Her posture and countenance did not waver or reveal any emotion, except for the fingers that firmly held onto the rough fabric of my breeches. She too was drowning in despair, and I was her lifeline.

"I will not go anywhere. I promised you. I promised that every wrong we committed together … That I would take responsibility for it. I will take care of this … of you."

Solemnly promising her this, I pressed Evey tightly onto me, yet I knew there was no perfectly peaceful solution to this issue. She leaned into me and suppressed distressed tears. This was the worst it would get, I thought. Yet, it was not a totally hopeless situation. There was always one option to straighten things out.

"Marriage is the only solution." I said matter-of-factly, after both of us had calmed down.

"Marriage," she repeated, "Is that really it? Is that what *you* want?"

"Of course," I said, feeling uncomfortable, "I meant it when I said I would take responsibility."

My discomfort must have been clearly visible on my face, as her expression turned sombre.

"You … why do you dislike the idea of marrying me so much?" she asked dejectedly.

Remembering our previous discussion on this matter I carefully thought about what to tell her. Why was it so obvious to me but not to her?

"Evey, I am not going to inherit this estate. I do not wish to either. I am a soldier of her Majesty's cavalry and don't hold any significant rank. You will have to move with me when I re-join my regiment. You will be ripped from your home, your friends … from Father. You will have a less comfortable life compared to what you are used to. Eventually, I may be sent into action again and you will be all alone. I cannot offer you anything." I finally explained.

"Why do you think these are all things that mattered to me?"

"It may not seem important to you as a lady, Evey, but a man takes pride in caring for his woman ..."

"But look at Rosalind, she is fine with her inheritance and her lover."

"Oh, don't be silly and bring Rosalind into this. She is not the marrying type ... but you certainly are. I know that."

"If it was comfort and wealth that I wanted from marriage then I would have accepted Mr Thompson." She retorted and got back at me for mentioning that hated name before.

"Then what is it that you seek in a marriage? Marrying to avoid a child being born outside of wedlock can barely be it." I demanded, haughty.

"Lo—" she started, and then cast her gaze down. Her ears turned red. "Loyalty, of course."

It was an unexpected answer.

"And you think a womanising scoundrel like me can offer you that?" I then laughed, teasing her.

"Don't say something so distasteful." She chided me; her cheeks puffed with a pout. Smiling gently she added, "You were always loyal to me, even when you were suffering and close to death, you did not forget to write me. Not even once."

I kissed her tenderly on the forehead.

"Do you think Uncle Arthur will be very upset?"

"He will not be pleased, that is for sure." I answered, not being able to anticipate his reaction to this whole affair. I already declined the succession of the estate, so he may as well have cut me completely out of his will. Every other type of punishment was beyond my imagination.

"Arthur, why does everyone think it would have been fine for me to marry Harold? You were brothers. Why was he more justified than you?" she asked.

"Obviously, because he was your perfect match." I said and thought about the duality of our positions within the family. At best, my role was to contrast his person, highlighting his virtues with my own vices. "He was perfect in every way ... and I am not."

In the past I was never able to envision myself as either a husband or a father. For a man that was using women for his own gratification, I was laughably sensitive. There were myriads of loveless marriages, but I never thought there was a point to a marriage unless there also was love to be found alongside duty. For I saw how my parents loved each other and were able to bear with me for that reason, because I was the result of love. I was certain that this was unattainable for me. How in my life would I ever be able to love another person that much? How was I supposed to love something that was like myself? However, in the situation that we were in then, all these doubts needed to be put past me. I could not abandon Evey. Thinking about it thoroughly I knew that at least, I would be able to love a child that was hers. It was a happy prospect, to hold something that was born from her.

We settled on me talking alone to Father, as I did not want to put her through the humiliation without having a firm grasp of how he would react to her. However, in the following days I did nothing. Every mealtime, every time we would start a trivial conversation, I was paralysed. The fear and guilt I felt would not let me find the right opportunity to request a conversation with Father alone. Evey was growing increasingly uneasy, as her symptoms became more apparent. Her unusual daily nausea and fatigue concerned Father deeply, and she had a hard time preventing him from having Doctor Armitage check on her again. Despite this, she did not push for me to talk to Father, waiting faithfully. To clear our heads and to talk things over where no one could hear, we went for a walk one afternoon. While we marched through the dying scenery of the forest, I tightly held onto her hand, ensuring that she would not trip and fall. Subconsciously, I had grown more alert about her every move. While we were in the hermitage, I stirred the embers of the furnace whilst she sat on the campaign bed.

"It's still warm for October, I think it will be too hot in our attire if you put in more logs." Evey berated me, but I was more concerned about her body cooling out.

"It's almost November already. The cold makes my injury sting." I said as excuse to appease her.

"Did you receive a message about how to proceed with returning to service?"

"Not yet." I replied and thought about how I should inform them that I would be bringing her along once I passed the medical examination. There were numerous things to take care of after that: registering our marriage, arranging for a place to stay … I hadn't even thought about where we should be wed.

"We should have the ceremony fairly soon, or else you will not fit into a fashionable gown anymore."

"Is that your major concern? A fashionable gown? It's not that important, is it?" She asked surprised, and muttered, "I'm not sure if I even should wear white … I don't really care about all that."

"But … I would like to see you in a pretty gown." I said while my face felt hot, not because of the fire in front of me, "I would like the boys from the regiment to see what a beautiful bride I got myself. I'd be their envy."

Even over the crackling embers, I could hear her suppress a laugh behind me.

"Am I to be put on show? By the person who always hated to be made a spectacle of the most?" she inquired in a teasing tone.

Then I walked over and sat down on the bedside, lifting her onto my lap, affirming, "I've come to appreciate that there are things one wants to present to the world, such as a lovely wife."

Then we kissed.

For a while we lost ourselves in planning and imagining what it would be like: I had checked my pass-book and my savings would have been enough for modest rings but not for a grand celebration. Maybe I would have needed to ask Rosalind for money, and Evey laughed at this, chiding me that I should just open a credit account with her. A small ceremony with family and close friends only, here at the estate then. A honeymoon? Maybe in Bath, if by then she still was able to travel? Perfect for cold winters. Should we try to find a house or a flat? It would be hard to sustain us with my wages alone. But she said that there was always her family's inheritance. I never knew how much it was. Without a doubt, it would be a life less luxurious as we had to check our expenses. I did not mind and neither did she, it seemed. I had no idea what living in Dublin was like. It could not be worse than out and about in India or Africa. Life in a big city, that would have been something new for both of us. Then she asked me about names I'd like for the child.

"How about Edmund?" I suggested.

"You really enjoyed *The Count of Monte Cristo*, didn't you?" she laughed at me yet again for not putting more thought into a name, because we only had finished reading it recently.

"It's a good book, and a fine name ..." I replied flustered. It was a decent name for a boy, and I did really enjoy the story. What other criteria should there have been for a name than naming it after something I liked? I then mused, "I wonder if I would be able to deal with a son at all. Especially if he was like me."

"If he'd be like you, then surely he will follow my every word."

"Oh? Aren't you audacious?"

Evey giggled, and whispered amused, "Edmund Clarence ... like Edmund Spenser."

"Is that funny?" I asked puzzled.

"Oh, not really ..." she said and smiled, an evidently patronizing smile, "We would share the same initials. E.C."

"That's true. Mrs Evangeline Clarence. It sounds nice." I agreed, but for some reason I felt sadness when saying it out loud.

Evey looked up to me as she must have noticed and asked, "Is it really acceptable for you ... to marry me?"

"I'm not going back on my word. I'll take care of you. I know that … in the past I … I was always careless." I said slowly but seeing her uneasy expression I tried to sound more resolute, "Nobody in this estate expects anything of me, but I have changed. You can rely on me. It's my duty to take care of you."

"Duty — I dislike that word. It sounds like a burden."

I did not respond immediately. Of course, it was a sense of duty I felt, but there was more to it too. The right words would simply not form in my mouth nor in my mind.

"Am I a burden to you?" she asked, leaning her head onto my shoulder.

To comfort her I placed my hand on her stomach, which made her tense up at first. But then she relaxed into me. I confirmed to her that she wasn't.

"I honestly want to take care of you. Both of you. I cherish you, Evey. I always have and always will." I reassured, firmly pressing my hands onto her.

But 'cherish' was not the right word either. It was something beyond that. Certainly, it had to be something more than that, for I held my future wife and mother of my child in my arms.

"Are you sure that we shouldn't talk to Uncle Arthur together?" she asked.

"No, I don't think it's a good idea. He will … surely, he will be angry with me, and I don't want you to see that. How furious he can become."

"Are you afraid?"

"I am … yes, I am. I can't imagine it. What he will say. I have never done anything *this* despicable before." I replied.

In the past, I may have tarnished the reputation of some ladies, but at least I was cautious enough to not impregnate any. Not to my knowledge. Instead, I had succeeded in doing both to my foster sister.

"Disobeying and running off were minor offences compared to this, as well." I added, turning to face away from her to hide my distressed countenance. However, she placed both hands on my cheeks and forced me to look at her.

"Arthur! It's not an offence. Us being together ... it's nothing to be ashamed of. We will share our lives with each other from here onwards. You are trying to avoid for us to live a life in shame. Please remember that!" she urged me, and it was her who was trying to reassure me.

Yes, I was trying to do the right thing. Those words offered me a little solace but the trouble over what reaction my actions would stir up, continuously unsettled my nerves. That it could end in violence and a scandal, I did not foresee. It was the option I did not want to weigh, at all costs.

A week had quickly passed, and I finally resolved that I would take matters into my hands that day. As I returned from my morning ride, the groom was ominously quiet while taking the horse away. I entered the lobby to be met by Elaine who seemed to have waited for me. She looked pale, and her eyes were puffed.

"S– Sir—" she began, stammering.

"Sir!" I heard someone call behind me.

Turning around I saw it to be young Francis, his tone was more tense and hostile than usual.

"Sir, the Master awaits you in his study. He urgently wants to speak to you." He announced.

His eyes too had a more intense coldness than usual. Elaine flinched as Francis looked at her. She hurriedly bowed and went away. I did not further ponder on this occurrence, as I was eager to talk to Father myself and asked Francis to lead the way. However, as I followed the valet along the corridor, there was a sense of foreboding. There were servants scurrying around, which was unusual as they all used to be good at their task of staying unseen. They all seemed to be taken aback upon my passing them by. As we reached the study doors, I asked Francis if something was amiss with Father, referring to the gloomy atmosphere. He ignored me.

In a forceful motion, he quickly twisted the handles of the study doors to open them and announced that I had come. Father bid me enter. I saw him standing in front of his desk with his back to me, leaning onto his cane.

Only upon passing him, young Francis deigned to answer my question from before, "Everyone is concerned, because Miss Evangeline has fallen down the stairs this morning while you were out riding, sir."

Without a moment's notice, and before comprehending his statement, I felt a harsh blow to the side of my head. I stumbled forward and barely caught myself, one knee on the ground and the other bent. Genuflecting. I turned to look up at Father who still had his cane raised. Even when punishing me for my missteps he never had more than disappointment in his eyes. But in that moment embers of white rage were glowing within them, the face distorted in a hateful grimace. Crimson stains blossomed onto the brown fabric of my breeches, instantly merging with it. A stream of blood trickled down from where I was struck. A bloodlust had revived Father, and with more force than I thought for him possible he struck me again. This time at the place of my injury. I let out an anguished groan and looked over to young Francis. Silently, he stood next to the desk, anticipation making his body waver lightly. I did not need to guess what this was about, and yet he explained: Evey had fallen from a flight of stairs shortly after I rode out. Young Francis was present and instantly had someone get the doctor while he attended to the young miss. Doctor Armitage came rushing and found her to have an internal bleeding. She resisted inspection but had to give in to the doctor who was increasingly alarmed by the amount of blood. It was not the shock of the fall that made her bleed, it was the bleeding that started first and made her waver … made her fall … and she knew what it was that caused it. It could not be hidden anymore. Desperate and in pain, it was me she was asking for … crying for.

"Speak! Did you know she was with child?" Father demanded in a low menacing growl.

"Yes ... I knew." I answered, not averting my eyes.

My apparent insubordination spurred on his rage. He was about to strike me again but then unexpectedly paused and leant onto the desk. Francis understood the cue and eagerly took the cane from Father.

"You act like a dog; thus, you shall be treated like one."

And so, I was struck a third time. This blow was aimed at my uninjured side, however it was exceedingly more painful, for the valet had more vigour than his decrepit master.

After I regained my breath an inquiry began, and every time he thought I lied I should be struck:

When did the whole affair start? – Before she rejected Thompson. – Was I the reason for her rejecting his proposal? – No, I wasn't. – Strike. For he did not believe it. – If I wasn't the reason surely, I had something to do with it. – Possibly. – Strike. For the impudent answer. – Where did it happen? – I refused to answer. – Strike. – Was it when I took her for walks? – I simply nodded. – How long had I known that she was pregnant? – About a week. – Was it due to intimidation? – What? – Strike. – Had I forced myself on her? – No.

At this reply I was struck with an even harder blow than all the strikes before and the question was repeated.

"I did not." I answered, painfully.

Strike.

Yet again: did I force her?

"I never did. I knew I never did because she longed for my touch. *She yearned for me.* You can beat me within an inch of my life and the answer would not change." I panted, indignantly glaring alternately at young Francis and Father.

There was clear disgust in both their faces upon hearing my insolent statement. This display of aggravating defiance was what caused me trouble more than once in my life. However, Father knew that it was a marker of truth even when he refused to face reality. If I had been culpable, I would silently have taken the beating. He saw it over and over, and he was coldly observing it again as both, judge and jury. All the while young Francis was beating me with a zealous obedience that appeared to me almost ecstatic. Raising his hand, Father made him pause.

"Then let me at least ask this: why did you put your filthy fingers … why did it have to be her?"

As this question echoed within me, a great chasm opened its maws separating me from my father. In the maelstrom of misfortune that had befallen this house, to him I was yet another vulture that preyed on its happiness, ripping at the carcass of better times. Since my return, I was never thought to be part of the concept of a happy home. Not once. He could not think positively about his devious son being infatuated with his angelic foster daughter. To him, there was no value in our blood connection anymore. The superficial well wishes for my future were simple mechanisms that should ensure my exclusion from the place. The thought that the one remaining person he loved dearly was seized by the person he hated made him livid. Yes, I was hated, and my whole body ached because of it. He would not stand for what I've done. Even though, after having seen us grow up together, after witnessing how I always treasured her above anything else, he could not come to deduce the one sound answer that explained my committing the sacrilege of touching Evangeline.

"I love her. I love Evey." I replied breathless.

The fact that it was hard for me to say those words, to even admit them in my thoughts, it was all rooted in the knowledge that I had been forsaken. Forsaken by everyone. She was the beautiful angel that a miscreant like me could not help but desecrate. This explanation was easier to extrapolate than the simple answer that I loved and sought her for the same reasons every other honest man would: her warmth and goodness. Even I had deluded myself into this type of reasoning. The pure irony of it was comic. I again confused two emotions with each other:

whenever my heart hurt out of guilt for desiring her, it in truth was the pain of falling deeper and deeper in love. I was just too broken to understand it. All this time, I did not only want her body I wanted her heart, too. For in truth, I always held her close to mine. Even when I was at the threshold to death, she was all I thought about. Had I died back then; she would have been my last thought.

"Do not speak to me of love! Is that what a miserable cur like you does when he loves someone? Make her your plaything?"

And a new blow was enforced. He was right, this was not the socially acceptable way to express love. Yet, was I in the wrong to claim affection in the only fashion I ever properly received it?

There was no next strike. Things had escalated so rapidly that Father and Francis had forgot to lock the door. They forgot the crowd that would gather outside too, or maybe they thought it right to let them witness my punishment. However, unexpectedly Evey had fought her way to the study. Elaine must have informed her about my return. In her condition, she marched against a stream of servants that protested but could not halt the young lady of the house. Instead, they followed.

"Stop her from entering!" Father barked at young Francis.

At the word, the valet dropped the cane and rushed to the door.

"Don't you dare touch me!" I could hear Evey's reverberating snarl, which resembled that of a wild animal's.

The whole room fell silent at this unprecedented response. I was still bent forward, my eyes fixed onto Fathers' finely polished shoes and the cane next to them. Instantly, she had flung herself at me, her quivering arms around my neck.

"Oh Arthur, my poor Arthur." She whispered almost inaudibly, and then with a clearly louder voice demanded Father stop.

"How can you be this unreasonable? After what he has done to you?" he asked stupefied, unable to comprehend her actions.

"Unreasonable?!" she repeated harshly, "You are having your own son beaten, Uncle. That is unreasonable. You are horrid! You are inhuman!"

251

Again, everyone was aghast with Evey's behaviour. Not once before had anyone seen her defiant, no, rebellious. The docile miss was furious. Old Francis was painstakingly trying to disperse the crowd outside the study doors, that lingered and looked on like pack of rabid dogs.

"Look what you have done, Arthur!" Father shouted, his voice full hurt and desperation, "Look what you have done! I knew you were influencing her … You returned and spoiled her. Spoiled everything. I wish you had never—"

"You mustn't say it, Uncle! You mustn't, hah …" Evey huffed with laboured breath.

" … never returned." It was I who completed the sentence, first looking up at the grief-stricken and haggard face of my father, and then turning to Evey.

She was as white as her gown and shivered all over. It was hitherto not audible in her voice, but hot trails of tears were etched into her pale cheeks, revealing that she must have been crying all the way.

From the moment of my return, no … even before then I knew that nobody was particularly glad for having me around. There was a truth lingering in the back of my head. A truth which I did not want to hear spoken out loud but was aware of. The truth that was permeating the halls of Forestedge and making it such a cold place was simply this: there was no forgiveness for the sin of surviving while my brother had to die. Had Harold lived instead of me, peace would have been with each and every soul inhabiting this cursed soil.

"Miss Evangeline, you must rest!" young Francis implored as he had pulled her away from me.

A scornful look pierced me, adding insult to injury.

Hysterical, she thrashed and struggled, exerting every last bit of strength that she could summon.

"No!" she shrieked, "Unhand me!"

Resembling a child throwing a tantrum, no one recognised the usually so refined Evangeline. And I was to blame for this transformation.

Eventually, she was able to free one arm, lightly slapping Francis in the process. He froze on the spot.

"All of you! You do nothing but hate Arthur. Yet what did he do to deserve it?!" she panted.

I was anything but a saint that much should have been apparent to her, but with fresh tears escaping her blood-shot eyes she suddenly insisted, "It was me! I did it! It was all my idea!"

"Evey, you have gone mad." Father uttered, brittle. Pitiful.

I was dumbfounded at her words, as well.

"I ... I ... it was me who seduced him!" she stammered.

All the servants peering in were shocked. Not a single person would believe this statement.

"Evey—" I began, but she cut me off.

"It's true. It was all by my design. From the moment that you returned. *I knew that you wanted me ... you wanted me so much. And I ... I as well, I wanted you.* Yet, you would never have acted on your own accord," she said, and added calmer, without a hint of shame, "I made you act."

The sheer mortification made Father's legs give in. Both Francis' rushed to aid their master as he staggered.

"Please, Uncle Arthur. Unless you want me to elaborate on every single action, I made Arthur take, please let him go. This instant!" Evey threatened, rather than pleaded.

Without waiting for his consent, she returned to my side and held out her hand, requesting that I escort her back to her bedchamber. I rose and straightened myself. The surrealism of the situation extinguished every thought, numbing my whole body, and I mechanically offered her my arm. She took it. We emerged from the study. I was unable, and she was unwilling to look back at Father. What a gruesome picture we must have painted, the ghostly white lady, and the bloody and beaten beast that defiled her. The servants still gathered in the hallway shrunk away in awe, creating a passage for us. Looks of disgust, disbelief and hatred heavily rained upon us like hailstorm. In the past I already experienced very similar moments, but Evey ... I shot her a sideway glance to see how she was fairing. Even in her wearied state she had returned to being the immaculate and graceful lady that she was known to be.

19
Flowers of Anger and Misery

At the foot of the main landing, we were met by Elaine and Doctor Armitage. Faithful Elaine, her eyes were swollen as she whimpered, "Miss Evangeline!" She must have run to inform the doctor after Evey hurried to the study.

"Heavens! Young Clarence! I cannot accept this. What in the blazes were they thinking? And Miss Hollings, you mustn't leave the bed in your state!" he exclaimed.

Doctor Armitage and the maid came forward to take Evey from my arm. Her breathing became more laboured, and she was in visible pain, her hand clutching her womb. As the three of them went up the stairs, the previously muted aching overcame me. The throbbing pain made me pause. The doctor let go of Evey who was safely held by Elaine. He hurried down the steps.

Assuring me, he placed his hand on my shoulder to ask, "Young Clarence, can you walk? Hurry along so that I can tend to you as well."

Sincere concern was evident in his voice.

Our group returned to Evey's room, and she was placed into her bed for rest I collapsed onto the stool of her vanity table, hand on my injured side. At the doctor's urging the maid rushed out, a pilgrim in a precarious frontier, to retrieve water and other necessities. Somehow, she managed to return swifter than expected and Doctor Armitage was able to inspect me thoroughly, dressing my wounds. All the while Evey anxiously observed.

"This is absolutely outrageous, to beat a convalescent man ... not only that, his own son," Doctor Armitage huffed, his brows folded in anger, "Bad bruises and lacerations, a cracked rib, a gash that will leave a scar, but the most concerning thing is the possible concussion ... and you did not even fight back, young Clarence. It's only due to your strong physique that the injuries are not worse. I've known your father and your family for a long time, but this is intolerable. I will have this persecuted."

"No, please don't, Doctor. It would only create more damage. I survived worse ... and I did deserve it." I said, coughing painfully.

"You say such things! You did nothing wrong!" Evey burst out, still resting.

Her complexion had improved slightly.

"If I did nothing wrong, then you would not be suffering in bed right now."

"I am the one to blame. You did what I wanted you to do, thus I am the one who wanted wrong things. However, I refuse to believe they are wrong."

"Evey, not in front of the Doctor and Elaine!" I snapped, in order to end the discussion.

Without a doubt the whole household must have been ablaze with a wildfire of gossip. It was the type of theatrics one would usually have to pay for to enjoy. While the doctor and the lady's maid were evidently in favour of us, I still did not wish to have an argument in front of more servants. I did not want her to humiliate herself anymore.

"If I may," Doctor Armitage interjected, "In my profession one comes across stories like yours a number of times: young people that are at the mercy of their passion. Especially you are known to entertain this vice, young Clarence. But Miss Hollings is right regarding the fact that this was a disproportionately savage attack. If she had not interfered surely, they could have beaten you to death. What spurred their anger so, I don't know," and then added with the concern of an elder, "Were you planning on running off, sir?"

I jolted at this question and jerked my head up from my hands to glare at him. What impudence. So, this was the rumour going around: *young Master Arthur will re-join his regiment and leave behind the dishonoured Miss.*

"Pardon?" I uttered irritated.

"This morning Miss Hollings confided in me that *you* were very well aware of her circumstances. However, you have not taken any action, one can only conclude that—"

I jumped up from the stool, ignoring the sharp pangs in my sides. Truly, I wanted to grab the doctor by his collar, yet restrained myself whilst Evey was looking on.

"Is this any of your business, Doctor? How dare you meddle?"

"Young Clarence, I as well have been watching over Miss Hollings since her childhood and was concerned. What were you going to do? I can only be in awe over your inaction."

It was undeniable. I acted like a coward. I stalled and did not take responsibility from the moment I had become aware. If I had gone to Father the very same day and laid out to him how I wanted to be united with Evey in marriage, would the results have been the same? Would there have been less pain and humiliation, for all of us? After what had transpired that morning, I knew that what I in fact was running away from was the truth about my place and value within this family. I was protecting only myself.

"Doctor Armitage, this is something for me and Arthur to discuss. If neither of us require your attention anymore, would you kindly leave?" Evey ordered with stern determination.

Her shift in character was ever surprising to me and the doctor, who was baffled.

"Of course, Miss Hollings," he answered and bowed curtly, "Should you need me, then please let Miss Eilers know straight away. She will come and fetch me from my quarters."

With this, him and Elaine exited, while the maid had a clearly wary expression on her face. She must have been frightened by the thought of all the household swarming her like flies for any foul shred of information they could rip from her. As for the doctor, I was certain that he was headed to wherever Father was, concerned over how this may have been a hit to his constitution. However, I was too bruised myself to ponder on his condition.

"I wasn't contemplating on abandoning you, not for one second." I said. Doctor Armitage's question stung like a thorn in my side that needed quick extraction. I needed to reassure her.

"I know that. You would never abandon me," she replied solemnly, "Although, I wish we could just have eloped."

"Eloped? That thought never crossed my mind." I blurted out in wonder.

An almost childlike laugh rang through the room, unbefitting to the dire situation we were in. Evey sat up.

"Of course, you did not. You already ran away once and saw what it did. Doing it again, it would have broken Uncle Arthur's heart. More so than what has happened today. That is the last thing you wanted. You were thinking about how you could resolve the situation without causing him too much hurt and prevent me from losing face or comfort. You are exceedingly loyal and full of filial piety. More than I am." She said with her most graceful smile.

My heart ached as she announced to me her unwavering faith in me.

Motioning to her empty bedside she implored, "You need rest as well. Won't you lie here with me?"

I did as she bid me and slowly crawled next to her. In spite of my still wearing the sullied attire, I relaxed onto the soft silken sheets. For once, it felt good to lie in a cushy bed.

"Let us sleep and talk some more afterwards." She said feebly.

I agreed and took her hand into mine, kissing its back. She squeezed in response. For a while we simply lay side by side. The events of the morning had the semblance of a sordid play that I wouldn't have wanted to attend. What a rotten day. There was no time to think about anything, until that moment.

"Arthur, I am so sorry." She whispered drowsily.

"Sorry, what for?" I turned my head to look at her.

"It would have been your child, too."

A silver stream of silent tears sprung from her closed eyelids as she faded into sleep. While listening to her peaceful breathing, I turned my gaze towards the canopy of the bed. The white sheer fabric and intense rays of the rising midday sun let my sight flicker. A stinging sensation made me rub my eyes. As to not wake Evey, I wept quietly.

I awoke to the dying light of dusk. Alarmed, I noticed that Evey was not next to me, and I sat up to look around the room. She was sitting on the windowsill staring at the rose and orange tinted sky, her hands neatly folded on her lap. The small fireplace was lit and warmed the space, but as she sat so close by the window, her breath fogged up its panes. With a relieved groan I fell back onto the pillows.

"Oh, you are awake!" she hurriedly came over to sit next to me.

"Don't rush," I said, for even though she did not grimace, I saw how she was putting her hands to her stomach, "How long have you been awake?"

"I am not certain, I lost track of time while watching the scenery." She mused with a nonchalance that so starkly contrasted the overall gloomy atmosphere.

"Did anyone come?" I inquired, still drowsy.

"Yes, Elaine brought a fresh change of clothes for you," she answered pointing to a pile of garments on the ottoman just at the foot of the bed, "Doctor Armitage, as well, came to have a look at you, asking whether I observed any symptoms of concussion … checking if you were actually conscious."

"I see." Was all I could say, still dizzy from the combined pain of my injuries and thoughts.

Attempting to rise and reach over to the clothing, I stopped barely sitting up. Throbbing pangs made me keel over and I instinctively clutched my sides. Evey clambered next to me.

"Oh, look at you. Let me help you." She said, carefully stroking my back.

Then she began to undress me, top first. The bruises had changed their colours over the day, aggressively shining in different hues: purple, green, black, red.

"So cruel ..." Evey muttered, wary to touch any of them. Indignant tears trickled onto my bare skin. As we could hardly manage to change my top garments, I settled back onto the pillow in a loose shirt and left my blood spluttered breeches on. Closing my eyes, I lingered in the moment of stillness, thinking of Father and at the same time trying not to.

"Why did you say something so outrageous?" I asked, my lids still shut.

"What do you mean?" she replied, having stopped sobbing.

"What you told Father ... That it was all your idea ... Why did you say something like that?"

"It's true. It was my idea and I made you act the way you did. Not once did you do anything without provocation, did you? I always pursued you where I could." She laid out with sobriety.

I could by no means follow her convoluted thoughts ... after all was I not the one who could not look away, pursued her, and then acted without provocation? That was untrue. She provoked me several times. When did it start? When I watched her lovely figure shiver with pleasure in the dead of the night. That was by chance. It was not. She said so herself the next day, that she waited to hear when I would head to my bedchamber. Every night. Was she putting up a pretence or did it truly happen? And when she entered the reading room whilst I was sleeping there? She purposefully threw the book onto the ground. Knowing how clever she was, she put enough thought into a title that would rile me up.

Not backing away, provoking me even more. She was steadily driving me mad, knowing ways to manipulate me … haunting me in the smoking room in her nightclothes ever so often. Especially when I was vulnerable. More than once attempting to get me someplace alone and playing the coquette: Carlisle, the ball, trying to ride out with me … but only succeeding in Edinburgh. And while she had no complete control over the other actors, she still perfectly knew how to pull their strings and exploit them: using virtue and docility that would leave Father unsuspecting, in fact, oblivious to what she would be capable of in my presence. Using Miss Violet and Celia to probe my reaction towards other women. Using sweet smiles and soft laughs that weren't directed at Thompson but at me. However, I was to see them in his presence, so that jealousy would flare in my heart. Finally, she pushed me over the edge at Aunt Gwen's place, when it looked to her as though I would give up. It was hilarious to think, that she was that bold due to her certainty of us never being caught that night. After all, Aunt Gwen was confined in a deep sleep due to her medicinal cigarette.

What a childish farce befittingly plotted by a woman. Of all the sly creatures I had known, she was the worst because she used her image of innocence that I held dearly in my heart as a game piece for her scheme. If for a moment I had stopped to think with my loins and instead with my head, I could have seen through it straight away.

"I am a primitive simpleton." I said and could not help but laugh dejectedly.

"Please, do not hate me!" she implored, firmly grabbing my hand.

"I don't," I answered, "I love you."

Evey rushed to kiss me. This gentle moment, I did not wish for it to end and yet our lips parted.

"I too, I love you!" she declared. I opened my eyes to behold her relieved smile, "I always did, from very long ago."

Yet, I knew already. And looking at her like that, there was still an untainted purity in her smile. She was not a mere schemer but acted out of desperate love for me. Would things have turned out differently if we had just admitted it to each other from the start?

"You would have never accepted it yourself if we had not broken rules," she noted, as though she had read my mind, "I was on a quest to catch you. I never fully grasped what was meant when everyone said that 'young Master was a promiscuous scoundrel,' because to me you were always a kind brother. More than that. But that day at your friends' place, I saw it with my own eyes, the meaning of those words. I noticed right away that you did not like Mrs Irvine, and still … you decided to engage with her, so primitively and without affection. It was a revelation. You were a creature of passion, easily extinguishing every light of reason, readily tearing away at the moral world. Watching the two of you, it showed to me that which I lacked in your eyes to make you act. It revealed it to myself as I grew disturbed, jealous, and excited. I had to deeply excite your senses first before I could get to your heart. Availability and attainability were the things missing. Thus, I appealed to your instincts."

It was true, it was the only way to get through to someone as hard-boiled and amoral as myself. There were also too many things weighing me down: my past, my self-esteem, and my position in this house. I would have never believed a word she said without having experienced her affection with my senses.

"But then … if you were trying to seduce me, why did you refuse me in the smoking room at first? You had me where you wanted me."

"I … I was intimidated … of course I would be, wouldn't I? Because I knew nothing … and also, seeing the family portrait then … it frightened me."

It was relatable. I too was constantly put to shame and torturing myself by looking at the accursed painting.

"Arthur? We said that we would talk, but could you only listen for now? I was wanting to tell you this for a while, but it is a lengthy story." She asked, lying back down onto the bed, turning her face towards the canopy.

She started to fidget with her hands.

"Yes, of course. We have all the time in the world." I responded, still lying motionless on the sheets.

Surely no one would come to Evey's room. Not with me still inside. The whole household must have evaded its door as though it had a seal on it which, upon being broken, would unleash the greatest malice over the world. At the same time, they must have been dying to know what was going on in here.

Finally, she began, "I always thought that we are alike."

I could not understand what she meant by that.

"Whenever I am asked about my parents, I tell people that I do not remember them well. Yet, I do. I remember them vividly. They were beautiful people. Respected by everyone, and beyond anything, superficial and self-centred. Even a young child like me was aware of their shallowness. Or maybe it was because young children are sensitive? They did not love each other beyond the prestige either party had to offer, and it was the same for me. They only approved of me when they could parade me around for my looks and accomplishments. Of course, I was a small child so I would lash out in anger when I did not get their attention. But I quickly learnt that pleasing them would instead give me all the things I wanted. Unwittingly, pretending and pleasing had become my penchants and by the time I came here it was always my aim to be a 'good girl.'"

I was not surprised that even as a small girl she had that level of sophisticated thought.

"How is that in any way similar to me?" I inquired, seeing that I only ever was on people's bad side.

She continued, "I was welcomed here warmly and given time to settle. I was taken in as family but always remained an outsider and had years to observe everyone. To me the ongoings in this house were like a play, and you were made out to be its villain. With time I was able to notice that Uncle and Aunt were kind-hearted people whose magnanimity extended to everyone ... everyone but you. In that respect, they were just as shallow and superficial as my own parents. They had no faith in you and no patience. They could not understand you and punished you, therefore. You were clumsy and wild but never malicious. Even when you tried to please them, they would not look your way because you were constantly walking in Harold's shadow. When I became part of the household, they even took more attention away from you. However, instead of being angry or jealous, you would be kind to me. You would love me. I like to think that you were in love with me even then."

"That's possible." I said and smiled faintly.

"And you know, you and I were equally unloved for who we actually were. That made us allies, with the difference that I already knew how to make life easy for myself whereas you desperately lashed out."

Allies. The only ally in this house. It was true, that she was the only person to ever believe in me genuinely. The only person that made me truly cling to my life.

"I know why you upset Violet ... she told you how she pitied me and my situation, didn't she?"

"She ... yes." I was surprised by her sudden mention of Miss Violet.

"At first, I too was offended by her statement, but honestly thinking about it ... she was right. It was convenient for your parents, wasn't it? Raising an unrelated child as their own to be the perfect trophy for the scion of the estate. The longer I contemplated on it, the more insidious it appeared to me, but I only understood it later. I was so used to meeting everyone's expectation. I lacked the imagination for acting out of line. And ... I was frightened of being cast aside."

"Does that mean you just pretended to put up with everyone around you? You made yourself look perfect ... going to that end to be appreciated?" I inquired. Those were thoughts and actions infinitely beyond my understanding.

"No, not consciously I wasn't. I truly did love everyone: you, Aunt Grace and Uncle Arthur. Harold as well! You can love people and still see their faults. And—" she paused, deliberating on the right words, "I did not even realise that I was being pretentious, until that day."

It was clear what day she meant. She hesitated and would not continue for a while until I spoke up.

"Harold's death ..." I pointed out.

Evey nodded.

"Harold, he always treated me respectfully. Loved me, but never beyond the love of a brother. He was fine with our engagement plans stating that it was 'for duty's sake,' but I was troubled by them. During my childhood it was just a vague and shapeless future set up by the kind people that took me in and cared for me like their own. Once you were away to India, I realised that it was something I truly did not want. I only knew then that I wanted to be with you. I was distraught and could not understand why nobody was worried for you ... so far away. In a place where I lost my own parents. No one saw the error in it because you were an inconvenience to them. The whole household continued their life comfortably and complacently, except for me. That was the first time I was truly upset with every single person in the manor. However, I was only thirteen then and would never have had the courage to voice my objections about all these things. Instead, I prayed for a miracle."

Tears welled up in her eyes as she paused yet again. I raised my arm to brush away strands of hair that had fallen over her face, as she turned to look at me.

"When I saw him lying lifeless on the lawn, I could not believe it. Dead in an instant and gone from this world. The man I was supposed to marry once I was of age. Yet, for a second, I thought that this surely was providence. I then felt sick and horrified, fainting at the realisation that this was my miracle. Good Harold, Aunt and Uncle ... I repaid their kindness with such a disgusting thought."

She let out a heartrending sob. That was why she lamented his loss so in her letters ... the reason for mourning him so long and intensely. She blamed herself.

"It was a tragedy beyond anyone's control, and yet I still felt responsible for it. I grew restless, unable to sleep over the guilt for the second of happiness that I felt at being released from duty. Therefore, when Aunt Grace became unwell, I decided to give her my all. I found it very trying … my negative emotions quickly multiplied. Once, I had the impudence to ask Uncle Arthur if Harold's passing meant that I would marry you. He looked at me compassionately, ensuring me that I need not fear and that it was out of the question. And then I realised that they were always denying you everything. They did not even consider that you could hold genuine love for me. You were made to look at me as a brother only. They had imprinted that way of thinking onto you, and the way I felt about you that would not matter either, because you were deemed unfit to receive a carefully reared prize. Your flaw being that you weren't Harold. Seeds of anger implanted themselves in my heart that day and just sprouted as more time passed by.

"Especially with me having to watch Aunt Grace. It was all so exhausting. Uncle Arthur, he initially tried his best after the funeral. He tried to reason with her … but she was so full of anger and pain, she said things that … I wish I had never heard them; she was out of her mind with grief, and I think … yes, Uncle Arthur, he was afraid that he would lose his sanity and his heart, too. He did today … finally.

"Uncle then escaped into his study and left it all to me. Continuously there would be things for me to do as Aunt Grace's substitute, all the while I was trying to help her recover. I desperately tried to make her eat something, and she would just push it away … or, once she was annoyed by my insistence, throw it at me. I had to hold her down whenever she had her fits … and the servants just looked on, afraid to touch the Madam without a word from the Master. My body would always be covered in bruises. Occasionally, Doctor Armitage came to administer drugs to her, so that I may get rest as well. However, the drugs became increasingly dangerous for Aunt Grace with her body in such an emaciated state. All I could do then was to play the piano hour after hour because that would calm her enough to make her sleep. The doctor advised us to have her sent away, but Uncle refused. I refused. I could not let her rot and perish in an asylum. I owed it Harold to take care of her, pushing myself with the hope that one day she would come to terms with his passing. But every waking moment, she would perpetually mourn him, mourn my lost future, mourn the dismal future of the estate. Each day ... every day, raving like a mad woman. I could not understand her, that mother who had lost her first born and lost herself over it. She did not spare a single thought for the other son ... she remorselessly cast you aside. And there was no certainty in your return either. How could she feel nothing at that thought? You were still alive and I ... I would not forget about you.

"Once, I had decided to remind her that you existed, trying to read to her what you wrote me ... and ... she just ripped the letter from my hands, tore it up and slapped me ... warning me to not mention you ever again, shouting that you had left the house and made your choices. I detested her so. In that moment, I abhorred her. However, before wickedness could get the better of me, she passed away, and again I felt culpable. I cried myself to sleep every night. There was no repose, and I still ... I too did not even have the time to mourn Harold properly. I loved him the same way you did. He was a benevolent brother to me. I still wanted to honour his memory and think of him. I couldn't. I couldn't because another time of fear came when Uncle fell ill. Another part of the family that needed me to hold on. However, it was unlike with Aunt Grace ... he was less of a burden. He even apologised and told me how he felt remorse for the way he had left me alone in the whole ordeal of her decline. He promised that he would make it up to me by finding someone to take care of me and offer me a good future. He felt so guilty about everything ... even about the way he had parted with you. He longed to see you. He sincerely did. And me? I had already become tired, and numb to the sorrow in the house, simply nodding at everything he had to say, trying to soothe him. Because it made life easier. Because I did not care what we spoke about anymore. I went through the motions of the mundane routines of life without any thoughts whatsoever. Just like all the walls of this place were clad in black, my mind as well had been dyed by the colour of mourning.

"But then I received the message that you were severely wounded and clinging to dear life. The shock woke me from my apathy. The thought of losing you was unbearable. Not you, too. I went to Harold's and Aunt's graves begging them to not take you away from me, and I was heard. You wrote me … like you promised, you never forgot. I regained hope with every message that you sent, no matter how short they were. I resolved that if you returned home, I would stop at nothing to make sure that we would be together. Even if it meant stepping on protocols and decency. I would readily stop being a good girl if it meant that you would be with me. One by one, I cast them away: my shyness, my modesty, my consideration, and my chastity. Upon this path, I too, broke the fetters of the perfect lady into which I was carefully bound over many years. I was ready to do anything for you. I would not anymore be afraid to become hated by anyone … anyone except for you."

The things only ever alluded to in her letters, it felt painful to hear them described in minute detail. Her mind had become twisted by the responsibilities, solitude, and strain that crushed her small frame in my absence. It was not that she had neglected herself, but that she abandoned her former self. My own shame and guilt dissipated over the course of her narration. While I had her placed on a pedestal, the sentiments I carried for her always appeared to me indecent, even sinful. However, in the moment that she bore to me her human heart with its ugliness, its cracks and edges — sinister yet beautiful — I loved her even more.

Remaining silent for a while, fully taking in her account, I wondered to myself what the right thing to say would be. Not awaiting any answer or comment, Evey carefully placed her head onto my chest while I slung my arm around her slender waist, bodies pressed against each other. Her warmth was soothing.

Finally, I asked her, "And if I had not returned?"

"Then I would have died too."

Darkness set upon us like a thick blanket. It was a moonless night. Could our happiness really flower from this putrid heap of misery? With this question in mind I went back to sleep.

EPILOGUE
Gossip and Biscuits

Ever since Master Louis was born the handsome gentleman would frequent the Garden Mansion. It was always a pleasure to welcome him, as he was such a treat to look at and he would have a charming smile for every female in the house, even though they were only servants. As the weather was not at all fair that day, the Madam had instructed to serve the tea in the parlour, instead of on the patio. She liked to be outside more than inside because it meant the baby's cries were confined within the mansion. Along with the Master, she awaited the Guest indoors. After greeting the pair, the Guest darted over to the nurse who was cradling Master Louis in her arms.

"Look at him, becoming chubbier by the day. What a roly-poly little man!" the handsome Guest exclaimed while squeezing the cheeks of the baby.

Its big blue eyes stared up at the familiar face, still unable to properly discern the features. The Madam pursed her lips.

"Mr Thornton, I would prefer that you not do that every time to *our little Louis!*" she demanded.

And as though he was aware of the hostility in his mother's voice, the young Master began to cry. Instantly, the Madam ordered the nurse to take him away, and the baby was transported to the nursery. Its miserable wailing was still audible through the shut door.

"Wonderful lungs, that boy. Just like his mother." The Guest laughed and the Master laughed along with him.

They all went over to sit at the table where high tea had been prepared.

"How was Edinburgh then?" the Madam inquired, impatient and irritated.

"Oh, wonderful. It was the perfect weather for a wedding. Very blessed." He answered.

"Do show us the picture, I am dying to see it." The Master urged.

"Here's the happy couple. Look at the proud groom, and his exquisite bride." The Guest replied, produced a piece of paper from the breast pocket of his sack coat and set it onto the table.

The maid peeked at it when she poured tea into the Madam's cup. It was the photograph of a stunningly handsome gentleman in a military uniform … an officer, it seemed. Holding onto his arm there was a sublime lady in a lavish, yet elegant wedding gown. If marital bliss could be advertised with a picture, that could have been it. Instantly, the Maid remembered the pair, as they had come to the Garden Mansion sometime in the last year. Or had it been already a whole year? All the servants were in awe at such an unearthly beautiful couple. However, back then there were talks about them being related to each other. Cousins perhaps? Someone must have known. At least the maid knew that the man was the heir to the biggest estate in the area. Well, not exactly. He was the second son of the Clarence family. Everybody knew about him and his bad character: a man as devious as he was handsome, that brought grief to his unfortunate father. Then, she remembered that there used to be a young lady at that manor, too. The ward of the Clarences. Yes, a virtuous beauty. Was it really her?

"It's a shame we could not come along. I would have wanted to see it with my own eyes. But this! Look at Arthur and his daft grin." The Master said and shook his head.

"He was absurdly happy. Very out of character. I almost liked him more when he was melancholic," the Guest mused, but then added with pride, "Nonetheless, it was refreshing to see him like that. A very private but lovely wedding, it was."

The Madam glared at the picture, so intensely that it evoked fear and anxiety in the Maid. She had seen that look often, especially when the Madam was in different circumstances. Whenever she was upset, she would have that vicious flicker in her eyes that signalled an outburst at which she started hurling objects at servants or the Master.

"Charming. Now put that cursed image away. It makes me nauseous." The Madam demanded coldly.

The Guest did as the Madam bid him and returned the picture into the safety of his breast pocket.

"Who would have guessed? Clarence married. He of all people." The Guest mused, taking a sip of tea from his cup.

"Dear, I must say, your bet was spot on. To think he would be that savage." The Master said and put a biscuit in his mouth.

"Savage, indeed. There were rumours of him and a maid, but to put hands on his own foster sister. I underestimated him." The Guest noted.

It sounded more like admiration than criticism.

For a moment the Madam was quiet. She rapped with her fingers on the table, which made the china rattle faintly, and then said, "Savagery has nothing to do with it, Arthur is simply a *sensitive fool*. That is all."

"Sensitive? Him?" the Guest blurted out, letting the cup in his fingers droop to spill slightly.

Then the usual ominous smile adorned the Madam's face. That which made her mouth curl up, but the eyes look cold and dead. Again, the Maid that was attending to the Master's teacup felt anxious.

"Of course. You didn't really think that he was the driving force behind it, do you? It was apparent from the time he showed up here with Miss Hollin ... Mrs Clarence. I saw it in their eyes. There was a romantic undercurrent in their relationship, and *she was the one* steering them through it." The Madam explained to the two men who seemed baffled.

"I would have never guessed! She looked so innocent ..." the Guest said, having picked up a biscuit that he turned around in his hand.

The Madam let out a triumphant 'Hah!' and crossed her arms complacently. Her venomous green eyes shining with malice.

"Innocent? She was duplicitous, I could tell!" she proclaimed.

"No man can beat a woman's intuition, it seems." The Master commended her, smiling at his wife with admiration.

"Although, I knew he was good for another scandal." The Guest insisted, and laughed heartily.

Taking her cup and saucer in the hand, the Madam took a generous sip of tea, "Mind you, Mr Thornton. This is probably the last one …" She then said.

"If you say so, Dear, then it must be true," the Master mused and asked the Guest, "What are you going to do with the picture?"

"Clarence asked me to deliver it safe and sound to Clarence senior, as he would not accept any letters of the relations involved." The Guest stated plainly.

And the Maid started to wonder if he would be going to Forestedge Manor right after having dropped by here. It was merely a few miles away.

"So, he is still angry?" the Master inquired.

"He couldn't be that angry. After all, I heard the maids gossip a few months back that he was bribing people here and there to keep the scandal at minimum." The Madam explained and glared at the Maid, who was standing attentively in the corner.

It honestly was not her that had joined in the gossip. She did not even like gossiping because her strict Catholic parents had warned her of sinning by slandering. One was easily tempted to talk ill of one's neighbour when working in an upper-class household. But it could not be avoided in one household such as that of the Irvines. Clara was the one who spread the word as she was friends with a maid at Forestedge. That friend boasted about how something spectacular having happened at the manor, but that it couldn't be divulged, for the master of that estate had given all the employees generous recompense. The only hint was that the cause was the unscrupulous young master again. He had done something unimaginable … so running off with old Clarence's ward was it? Was that really something that had to be held so tightly under covers? While eloping was not something honourable, it was a common thing.

"It must be a reflex from Arthur's younger days." The Master said with a brief laugh.

"Clarence senior was really good at paying up. Irvine, I told you before, I got a fright when I visited Clarence in Edinburgh shortly after he quit his old man's place. He looked the worse for wear. Not even in our school days had I ever seen him that beaten up … and he was in so many physical altercations, Mrs Irvine." The Guest affirmed and turned to the Madam.

She had an uncharacteristic expression of disquiet on her face as she tried to picture what he was describing to them.

"He used to emerge as victor most of the times." The Master noted, stroking his moustache.

"That he did. But not that time, it seems … and when I was in Edinburgh then, Mrs Clarence was also unwell. Eventually, Clarence would not tell me what exactly happened. Makes one wonder what in the world might have transpired." The Guest pondered and all three fell into a silent contemplation, consuming their tea and biscuits.

Faintly, Master Louis who had been quiet for the duration of the conversation was heard wailing again. The Madam lifted her eyes towards the ceiling of the parlour and impatiently rapped her fingers on the table again, waiting for the nurse to quiet down the baby. After some minutes, peace returned.

"Whatever it was, surely, once they have their first child, his father will have a change of heart." She said languidly.

"I wonder how long that will take them? Knowing Clarence and his prowess, probably not that long." The Guest noted with a wry smile, while the Maid lowered her head, blushing at this inappropriate statement.

"Speaking of which … where are they heading off to for their honeymoon?" The Master inquired.

"To Paris." The Guest answered.

"Paris in the springtime! How dreadfully romantic ... so predictable for a sensitive fool." The Madam sighed and rolled her eyes dismissively.

THE END

Author's Note

Even though this work aims to be a pastiche of fin de siècle literature along with some early 20th century works, the reader may excuse the at times juvenile humour and tone as it reflects the main character's (and my own) immaturity. I was conscious to include all the exciting settings and clichés one would expect to come across in a late Victorian romance. *Forestedge* being a modern romance novel for light reading, at many points endeavours to service the reader, concluding on a happy note.

There is a conscious anachronism with regard to Baudelaire's poem in chapter five. The quote originates from *Baudelaire: The Flowers of Evil* (Cyril Scott, London: Elkin Mathews, 1909). I considered it to be the most fitting translation in the framework of the chapter.

A topic that certainly alienates and appalls some readers is the casual manner in which Arthur junior refers to the beatings he received. I would like to ask the reader to take into account the time period in which the novel is set, and consider that corporal punishment for out of line behaviour has only been abolished as recently as the 2000s, in Scotland. Beatings in the majority of the novel are to be understood in the sense of corporal punishment similar to that dealt out at schools or other institutions (such as the military). In defense of Arthur senior, the punishment was never dealt out with a sense of malice or satisfaction but rather in acts of helplesness and desperation. Where goodwill, patience and understanding did not help, corporal punishment had to do. His extreme frustration with Arthur junior also comes from Harold having been easy and pleasent. Only in the final beating which is the ultimate humilation ritual — for Arthur junior is not only severely beaten, but also beaten by the servant he dislikes the most — strong emotions are part of it. The beatings do play a central role in the plot when (ironically) sense is beaten into Arthur junior and he has a moment of epiphany concerning his emotional state.

Helplessness, loss of control, and the reaction to those are major themes of this novel (among others). It is exemplified by Arthur senior reacting rashly with violence and intense anger. Unfortunately, the one trait which him and his son have in common. Even so, Arthur junior holds himself in check for the majority of the novel.

For Evey, the reaction to loss of control is to go above and beyond what is expected of her. This is in line with her character, for she feels in control when she is in good standing with others and receives affection for it. This is also the reason why she goes along with Arthur junior's whims and aims to please him as best as she could imagine. The very moment she senses that she will completely lose hold over him is when she gives control to him, and thus reverses the situation. Her views and reactions to things are very biased, as she is a late teenager with a brain scrambled by hormones and a recent depression. Any statement of hers on interpersonal relationships has to be read with that in mind. She's nonetheless envisioned as a character perceptive, and more mature than than the protagonist.

Upon finishing the final third of Arthur's journey towards emotional maturity — albeit with an outrageously dramatic climax — I hope, there was a sense of fulfilment. As this novel was also an exercise in genre subversion, I do wish that the reader wholeheartedly sided with the villainous, womanising second son; finally, rejoicing in his happiness. This would make the novel a successful undertaking.

Revised Edition Notes

Even though this project had been long in the making, it eventually came out with a multitude of errors. Excited and tired, I rushed the final steps. Upon picking the novel up again I realised that there were a number of issues that needed mending. Along with the change of the margins for more appealing visual design, there were pargraph and spelling issues that crept in while transferring the text into Scribus. While the contents of the whole novel did not change, I did tweak the dialogue to include expressions that improved the overall reading flow.

I hope to have caught all issues now, as I don't wish for this work to be a perpetually in progress. I hope that the first edition purchasers accept my apology for having acquired an unfinished product, and like to thank them again for their support.

About the Author

Thomas Stinner currently lives in Perth, Australia. Being a nomad with no base, Scotland is the home of his heart. A graduate of the Universities of Glasgow and Strathclyde, and an English teacher, his passion for literature overflows from his profession into print. His ardour for history, cultural habits of bygone days, and the great outdoors, as well as a soft spot for romance, take shape in his first novel *Forestedge: A Fin de Siècle Romance*.